COMFORTS FOR THE TROOPS

COMFORTS FOR THE TROOPS

A NOVEL INSPIRED BY WOMEN WORKERS AT
CADBURY IN WORLD WAR ONE

FIONA JOSEPH

FOXWELL PRESS

BIRMINGHAM, UK

First editions published in April 2015 by Foxwell Press.
Paperback ISBN 978-0-9570934-5-4
Also available as eBook for Amazon Kindle and Kobo readers.

Cover design by Stuart Bache.

FOR MAVIS TAYLOR

ALSO BY FIONA JOSEPH

BEATRICE

THE CADBURY HEIRESS WHO GAVE AWAY HER FORTUNE

CHAPTER 1

13 JULY 1914

A mass of onlookers had gathered on the pavement to stare up at the clouds of smoke ravaging the bright blue sky. Jessie elbowed her way to the front of the crowd and the heat wrapped her like a shawl. The whole building – the work rooms as well as the warehouse – was roofed with flames, and her stomach turned over at the sight. Men and women stumbled out of the side exit, coughing into handkerchiefs or their jackets sleeves. She searched their faces but couldn't see him – where was he? More people came out, some carrying bolts of fabric and wheels of piping cord. 'Have you seen my husband?' Jessie shouted. 'Bill. William Paignton. In the workshop.' Her calls went unheard over the noise of the approaching fire engine, so she went as far forward as she dared until her cheeks and forehead began to sting. Fragments of ash rained down. She narrowed her eyes, determined to press ahead, but strong arms pulled her back.

Earlier that morning Jessie Paignton was shopping on Stirchley High Street. She joined the end of the queue for Marshall's, the butcher, not quite fitting under the shade of the awning but nevertheless content to feel the sun warm her back while she waited. In her mind, she totted up the morning's achievements: washing pegged on the line, the front step scrubbed, and all her shopping done except for a bit of beef to get before heading home. Meat pie was Bill's favourite treat on a Monday evening.

The queue shuffled forward a few inches. She thought of

1

yesterday's picnic and smiled. That day had started with such promise and they'd set off to Kings Heath Park and got caught out by a downpour that had drenched them both.

'Be our anniversary in a few weeks,' Bill had said, as they ate soggy sandwiches and pickles, leaning with their backs against a tree. 'Reckon you could stand another five years with me, Jessie?'

'No,' she'd replied. 'But I might manage a lifetime.' Every year he made her a gift of furniture to celebrate their marriage. For their wedding itself it was two armchairs that still sat either side of the fireplace in their sitting room, then a three-legged footstool, followed by a fireguard and a bedside chair. Last year it had been a blanket box with a quilted lid. He always worked in great secrecy and she knew if she asked him what this year's present would be he'd only tap his nose and say, *Aha, you'll just have to wait and see.*

In the shop she listened to the other women chatting. Mr Marshall glanced at the newspaper folded over on the countertop. 'Well, ladies,' he said, 'at least all that bother in Europe has blown over.'

Jessie noticed the woman in front, who pointed to two men standing out in the road looking anxious. 'What's happening out there?'

'A fire's started in one of the factories, Kings Heath way.' Mr Marshall said, wiping his hands on his apron.

Jessie hadn't been paying attention, until she heard the mention of Tressler's.

'Excuse me, what did you say about a fire?' she said, interrupting.

'A big one by the looks of it,' the butcher answered. 'Down on York Road. They say the whole place could go right up–'

The bag of carrots dropped from her hand and scattered over the sawdust floor. She turned and ran out onto the street, knocking over a bicycle and scraping her shin but oblivious to the pain. Without stopping she flew down the road and into Fordhouse Lane, calculating that she hadn't time to go home first, simultaneously checking her pocket for coins. At the end of the road she spotted a number 11 bus about to go past. With a supreme effort she made it and collapsed into the seat, shaking.

The clippie tried to talk with her but she stared ahead, wringing her hands, willing the bus to go faster. In the pit of her stomach was a slab of ice and she found herself shivering in spite of the sun's warmth. The bus stopped outside All Saints Church and she jumped off and began to run again.

By the time she reached Tressler's she was drenched in perspiration and her lungs felt raw. She looked around in panic at the bystanders gawping and people evacuating the building, bringing stock out with them and laying it on the opposite side of the road. A young girl cradled a dead cat in her arms and wept into its fur.

Someone shouted, 'This is hopeless. Someone send for the Moseley Road detachment.'

Two men, with scarves around their faces, rolled huge vats. 'Get out of the way!' the first one shouted. Jessie allowed herself a spark of hope. If they were taking out the stock and supplies, she reasoned, surely that meant everyone was already safely out of the building. 'Don't touch it, it's hot,' he said to a passer-by about to help him roll the vat upright.

'Why won't they tell us anything?' a woman said. The women were hugging each other, while the fire continued to rage.

Then she saw Bill's friend Hugh talking to one of the men in suits. Thank God. She ran over. She interrupted them, shouting 'Is Bill all right? Is he ... alive?' Hugh looked at the man in the suit and the slab of ice grew weightier in Jessie's stomach. She sank to her knees, no more fight left in her.

Leonora Lime had missed the rain shower that morning by

arriving at the Bournville Works for five-thirty and was seated at her machine before the rest of the workers had arrived. Now at ten-thirty, just before the bull went for break, she felt in her pocket for her pass and stood up. The forewoman, Miss Barratt, nodded as Leonora waved the pass at her. She left Q block and crossed over to the main building, glancing up at the sky and praying, *Please let the rain hold off. Just for this morning.*

She went along the corridor and trotted down the steps into the dressing room. The odour of wet wool and leather, although not unpleasant, made her nose twitch. She looked around in dismay at the rain-spattered coats that drooped on numbered hangers and soggy hats rammed carelessly onto hooks. Outdoor shoes were still drying off inside the metal cages. It must have been quite a downpour.

Leonora tried to control most things in life but she had to accept the weather and all its vagaries were beyond even her command. She smoothed the front of her cream pinafore – clean on that morning – and brushed down her sleeves, sharply tugging each cuff so it lay against her wrist bone. She removed her cap and patted her hair in front of the mirror, twisting her head to check the bun was firmly in place. An image of herself dressed in a green blouse, worn only by the works' forewomen, came into her mind; quickly she shook the thought away.

Satisfied with her appearance, she left the dressing room and went out via the lodge entrance, stopping first to turn over her time check from yellow to red. She walked lightly so as not to disturb Jim, the lodge-keeper, in his office. He was bent over *The Daily Mirror*, lapping up the latest news in Europe like a cat over a saucer of milk, when Leonora crept past. There was no time today to listen to his melodramatic narration of the news.

The sun was bright now and she shielded her eyes as she darted along Bournville Lane and down to the Men's Recreation Ground with its vast lawn and half-timbered pavilion.

The delegates of the International Garden City and Town-

Planning Council were due to arrive at eleven-thirty. The memo from the directors' office had explained that representatives from all over the world were meeting in London for their conference: people from as far away as The United States, Canada, even Australia, and closer to home, France, Spain, Sweden, Belgium and Germany. Fifteen countries altogether, with over three hundred delegates! A special party of around twenty members would be travelling up from Euston train station for a meeting this morning at the Birmingham Council House, followed by a tour of the Bournville Works, the pioneering 'factory in a garden' as the newspapers liked to call it. George Cadbury senior, no less, had asked her, Leonora Lime, if she would be kind enough to lead the party on a tour of the Girls' Recreation Ground, which was the area developed by the Cadburys for the female workers' benefit, situated on the opposite side of Bournville Lane.

When Leonora first heard the request, she had blushed with pride and then immediately fretted. She wondered if any of the visitors spoke English, and what would she do if they all used their native tongue? She had learned a little French at school, and had taken German adult classes when they were introduced at the factory. But that had been many years ago and now she regretted not having kept up her language studies.

To the left of the men's pavilion ran the oak footbridge that went across Bournville Lane and down to the girls' grounds. She went across the bridge and down the steps onto the vast lawns surrounded by flower beds and trees, trying to see it through fresh eyes. Unlike the men's grounds, which were perfectly flat and intended for games of cricket and football and bowls, the girls' grounds consisted of gentle mounds, with straight gravel paths for walking along and the occasional bench. The centrepiece was a rectangular sunken lily pond, which the gardener had evidently cleaned; the water's surface was smooth without a single ripple. The whole area had a hushed, private feel to it.

Believing herself to be entirely alone she sat down on an octagonal tree bench and sighed. Everything was perfectly ready for the delegates, right down to the purple clematis, the exact colour of the Cadbury Dairy Milk wrapper, spreading across the flower bed at her feet.

And then she saw him.

Up ahead on the mound stood a thin boy, young Samuel Eastwood, the gardener's assistant, dragging on a cigarette.

Leonora shot to her feet and screamed at him. 'What on earth are you doing? Put that out this instant!'

He sauntered over to her, the cigarette end dangling from his mouth. He was a scrawny thing, with a cough that rattled inside his concave chest that called to mind a stone in a tin can. Then she remembered – he had form. Six months previously he'd been caught red-handed climbing out of the girls' wages office with a handful of coins stuffed in his shoe.

'You were lucky to get a second chance,' she said, thinking how lenient her employers were in taking him on.

'Lucky it weren't you in charge then, missus. You'd have have me put away.'

He gazed out across the grass and through the trees. The boy was good-looking in a sullen way. Disrespect oozed out of him, from the way he refused to meet her eye to his hands shoved in his pockets. She reached out to tidy his hair and he ducked, like a boxer, out of her way. He balanced the cigarette stub between finger and thumb and made as if to flick it into the lily pond and then walked away, laughing to himself.

The rumble of a charabanc sounded in the distance. The delegation was arriving. Leonora's heart banged inside her chest, as she breathed deeply and stepped forward.

'It's all right, Jessie,' Hugh said slowly. 'Bill's been taken to the General hospital. Mr Tressler will take you there in his motor car.' He looked at the man, who nodded.

'Is he alive?' Jessie said.

'Come on, let's go.' Yet another journey to endure, but this one passed in a blur.

He was lying on a bed with his eyes closed and a nurse was bathing his face. For a terrible moment Jessie thought he was gone. She was too late. She ran across the ward to him and put her head on his chest. She felt the beat of his heart, and then the rise and fall of his body. She gasped, 'Thank God!' She grabbed the nurse's hand, seeking confirmation that she wasn't dreaming. The woman nodded and smiled. Jessie said, 'Thank you, thank you.'

Bill's eyelids flickered and then opened. He looked at her with crimson eyes and tried to speak.

'Shh, don't say anything,' she said.

Later, the doctor tried to explain things to her, about his injured leg, and the smoke damage to his lungs; he warned her not to expect her husband to recover swiftly. Her eyes stayed locked on Bill and she barely grasped the doctor's words. He was alive, and that was the only thing that mattered.

The delegates struggled out of the first motorcar. White-haired Mr George Cadbury, with streaks of brown in his neat beard, looked dapper in a charcoal suit. The other men wore a variety of styles of dress. Only one woman accompanied the party – a dour-looking figure, who sniffed the air and declared in a French accent, '*Le chocolat!* Why, it's true what they say. You can smell the aroma.'

Leonora had been instructed to walk with the German delegate and the two of them would be at the head of the tour. Mr George approached her, with a short man in tow.

'Good morning, Miss Lime. This is Herr Otto. A leading light in the Garden City movement in Germany,' he said. 'Herr

Otto, may I introduce you to Miss Lime, one of our longest-serving employees?'

'How do you do?' he said in perfect English, with a bow.

What was the German for Pleased to meet you? Her mind went blank. She uttered the one phrase that came into her head, apt, perfect for the moment, a remnant from her German class. *'Es ist typisches englisches Wetter.'*

Herr Otto looked up at the sky, and chuckled deeply. *'Sehr gut.'* Mr George caught her eye and mouthed, 'Well done!'

Leonora took him along the pathways, occasionally glancing behind her to see if the other delegates were keeping up. Herr Otto was a pleasant, even charming, gentleman and he quizzed her about how she liked living in Bournville.

'It's the finest place on earth to live,' she replied.

'I rather think Mr Cadbury has hit the nail on the head in building nice homes for his work people.'

Afterwards, in the men's pavilion Leonora stood at the back of the room, while the catering department served tea and sandwiches. The chatter amongst the delegates was lively and when Mr George stood up to begin his speech, the hubbub showed no sign of dying down. First, he raised his hand to call for silence but had to tap his spoon against the teacup.

'Gentleman, gentleman. And ladies, too. It is a delight and a privilege to have fifteen nationalities, yes fifteen, here this day.

'It has been twenty years,' he continued, 'since my late dear brother, Richard, and I devised the scheme for a model village here in Bournville. Little did we realise that all over the world others were of the same mind. You were also dreaming of city schemes to bring sunshine and fresh air into the lives of ordinary people, realising that no city home is complete without its own back garden.'

Leonora was warmed and stirred by George Cadbury's words. She would like to be someone who made a difference to other people's lives. She looked around the room to see how others were receiving his message. Herr Otto had a wry smile on his lips; the Austrian delegate was whispering to the man next to him; the French woman yawned. Leonora drummed her fingers on her upper arm. *They weren't even listening!*

Mr George was concluding now: 'In Europe the tension increases daily but let me say one thing to you.' He surveyed the room until his gaze settled on Herr Otto. 'Whatever may happen, you and I can never be at war.'

Applause broke out and Leonora held her arms to her side to prevent herself joining in. She glanced out of the window to see Samuel Eastwood lurking. He met her eye and waved. Without acknowledging him, she turned back to the meeting in time to hear Mr George expressing his hope that they had all found the Bournville experiment to be an inspirational model.

He wished the town planning party well for the next stop on their journey, and he shook Herr Otto's hand with extra vigour, Leonora noticed. After a night in Birmingham they would be travelling onwards by train to Mr Lever's Port Sunlight, south of the River Mersey.

CHAPTER 2

Leonora looked down at the lines of her section in Q block. Heads bowed over, diligently working their card-cutting machines. Two of the juniors loaded the brightly-coloured card onto a trolley to be wheeled to the box-making section next door. She squinted and checked the machine operators again. Someone was missing from their seat. She stood up and glided down the aisle. Young girls looked up from beneath their white caps in fear, suddenly self-conscious at being scrutinised by a senior woman. Leonora nodded, as if to say: *Carry on please. No need for drama.* She approached the empty bench. All the workers were checked in this morning and no-one was allowed to be away from their work area without permission.

'Where's Mary Morris?' Chatter broke out. Leonora clapped her hands. 'Be quiet.' If the girl had gone on a walkabout, that would be another mark in her record book, she thought, and the next stage would be the disciplinary committee.

Mary slipped back into her seat, evidently not seeing Leonora behind her.

'Phew, that was lucky,' she said to her friend, Evelyn. Leonora saw Evelyn's eyes widen in an attempt to warn Mary of her presence but the girl carried on, blithely.

'All this record book business. I preferred it before when you had a fine and were done with it.' Evelyn giggled with nerves.

Mary continued, 'The old cow's got a file on me as long as my arm.'

Leonora heard every word. Without speaking she went back to her machine and a cold, hard resolution settled in her mind. It wasn't about the name-calling, she told herself. She didn't expect to win any popularity contest. What mattered was that Mary Morris had demonstrated time and again that she was not fit to work at Cadbury. It was time, Leonora decided, to have her thrown out and to let someone more worthy have her job. Surely the Cadbury directors deserved only the best staff, she reasoned.

In the girls' dining room at break-time she sought out Eliza Barratt, who, as well as being head forewoman, also served as chair of the Disciplinary Committee. With her chest held high, Leonora marched over to the top table where the forewomen sat, and placed her cup of cocoa down near to Eliza's plate.

'I'd like to recommend Mary Morris be dismissed.'

'And a good morning to you too, Miss Lime,' Eliza said, cutting an apple into pieces. After a pause, she said, 'What's the problem?' Her mild tone managed to imply Leonora was making a fuss.

'The *problem*,' Leonora said, 'is her sloppy attitude, and her utter contempt for the regulations.' She took the notebook out of her overall pocket and began to read. 'On 21 August she was reprimanded for singing at her bench; the following week she was late checking in. This morning she left the work room without permission and when she returned she said... well, I wouldn't like to repeat–'

'Oh Leonora, you know I don't have the authority to sack people just like that. It's a decision for the directors.' She crunched on one of the apple slices and looked thoughtful. 'Mary Morris? Name rings a bell. Won a prize from the Suggestions Committee last year, didn't she? Bright girl – home life tricky by all accounts – but she's got bags of potential.'

Leonora's fingers tightened around her cup. That had been galling, too. Just because the girl had proposed using offcuts of card more efficiently, the committee had given her a cash reward. Mary seemed to think she had a licence to behave exactly as she pleased. Leonora's gaze slid to the sage green sleeves of Eliza's blouse and when she looked up Eliza was staring at her. Then Eliza quickly glanced behind before leaning in, her cheeks glowing.

'Between you and me – and this is strictly *entre nous* – the directors called me and the other senior forewomen in for a meeting yesterday. With this war starting we'll need to be recruiting more people, not getting rid of the ones we've got. Mr George and Mr Edward said there's going to be a few changes around here and we'll all have to do our best to get used to it.' With that she picked up her tray and glided off, leaving Leonora open-mouthed and her cocoa suddenly bitter in her mouth.

Eliza turned and said over her shoulder, 'Just a word of advice. I find a drop of honey is far more effective than a pint of vinegar. Why not have Mary in for a chat – see if you can get her back on the right path?'

And do your job for you? No, thank you!

Leonora stared at the woman until she got lost in the crowd of girls preparing to leave the dining room. A drop of honey! That summed up Eliza Barratt's attitude, she thought. If a senior forewoman didn't have the brains to see Mary Morris was taking the company for a ride, so be it. Leonora was satisfied she had done the best she could.

That evening, like most Wednesdays, she got ready for her lecture at Ruskin Hall. Her earlier conversation with Eliza Barratt still rankled, especially the way her legitimate concerns had been brushed aside. No one took seriously, that was the problem. She'd been in the running for the forewoman's job for months but promotion had somehow eluded her. When she'd been asked to lead the tour in July she'd felt progress was on the horizon. And now that blasted Eliza had been promoted again even though she was ten years younger. She was certain Eliza had done it by currying favour with Mr Edward Cadbury – helping him with his latest book.

Her own attributes were many. She remembered how Mr George had spoken of her as his "longest-serving employee". She knew the Works' regulations off by heart. Test me, she wanted to say to him. Ask me anything you like about the rules and I'll give you the answer. Time allowed for breaks, procedures for illness, fire drills, protocols for visiting guests – she knew it all. She had the ability to speak to anyone – from the highest down to the most humble. She had rehearsed what she would say in her interview many times. *Although a forewoman is a senior figure I think of myself as a friend to the girls, someone to turn to in time of need.* But her plan wasn't working.

Her dear mother would have soothed her by saying, *Never mind, my darling, it's their loss. You must trust in the good lord. Be patient in times of tribulation and constant in prayer.* But indignation still burned inside her.

The lecture that evening was on the outbreak of war and its significance. She could not comprehend the fact that the country was now at war. How could Herr Otto and George Cadbury suddenly be on opposing sides? She felt safer knowing they were against the war on principle. She trusted in them to bring back reason and sanity.

Meanwhile, going back to her favourite topic of her promotion, she reflected that there was nothing to stop her acting the part of forewoman, even if she wasn't rewarded with the status. She would do so freely and willingly until fairness prevailed.

Jessie wrung out the flannel. The water was still warm but starting to cool.

'Just your back now.'

She rolled Bill onto his side, taking extra care with his

bandaged leg, and lifted up his vest as high as it would go. She moved the soapy flannel gently over his back, the towel underneath catching any droplets of water. The knobs of his spine stood out like a starving donkey's. As she touched his shrinking flesh, its disappearing muscle, she felt a reconnection with him for a brief moment. She reassured herself he'd get better. *He had to.*

As if he'd read her thoughts, Bill said, 'Are we managing okay, Jessie? For money.' His voice still rasped from the smoke damage, his chest wheezed like a pair of old bellows.

'Of course we are, my love. And everyone in the street's mucking in to help. Mrs Tops brought you fresh sheets for your bed.'

Their neighbour, a good-looking, practical woman in her mid-thirties, had pressed the bunch of sheets into her arms and said, 'Don't let him lie in one position for too long. It's not good for the body. And get him to push his feet against the footboard; it'll keep his muscles built up.' It was easier said than done.

Mrs Tops had continued, 'You coming up the fair this Saturday? I'm taking the boys. Frank's away on drill practice until Sunday.' Her husband was a volunteer in the Territorial Force and often trained at weekends.

'Not this time,' Jessie had replied.

Mrs Tops had peered at her. 'You look done in. Get someone to sit with Bill for a couple of hours. Do you good to have a bit of fun.'

'Oh, I couldn't leave him. If Bill can't go then I don't want to.'

The truth is there's no money for the fair.

Jessie had gone to Aston Road fairground ever since she was a little girl. Her favourite ride ever was the merry go-round. Her father would sit on a golden horse, haul her up and place her in front of him. She could remember the excitement as they galloped round, her eyes opening and shutting, her father's arm around her waist holding her safe, the lilt of organ music, the remains of brandy snap glued to her back teeth. She'd said to Bill once, *We'll bring our children here too one day. Keep up the family tradition.*

She'd thanked Mrs Tops for the sheets and hurried indoors.

'There, all done,' she said, pulling Bill's vest back down. His deep breaths told her he'd slipped back into sleep. Even though it felt cruel she was determined to get him into the chair today and sitting up for a while. Changing the sheets was a convenient excuse.

'Bill,' she said, shaking him gently. 'You can't stay curled up in bed.'

'But it hurts. I'm sorry. I feel so useless.' A spasm took hold of him mid-sentence and the last words came out in a strangled sound. She bit her lip, waiting until the pain had passed.

'I know it's sore. But we need to get you upright.' She slid her palm beneath his shoulder.

'Put your arm around here,' she said, tapping her shoulder. He did so and she hauled him upright. A twinge of pain shot through her own back. Ignoring it, she pressed her palm to his cheek. His face was cold, his teeth chattering. The books Hugh had brought him remained untouched on the bedside table.

Still supporting him she swung his legs down to the floor, but he drooped and fell sideways, almost crushing her with his weight. He let out a groan, the howl of a wounded animal.

'All right. We'll leave it until tomorrow. It's all right, my darling. Really, it's all right.' She spoke softly into his ear and stroked his rough hair before she eased him back down. The hair-washing would have to wait until next time, she thought.

She carried the basin away. Pressure built behind her eyes and nose so she concentrated on the flannel ballooning on the scummy surface of the water, trying not to spill it or to trip and fall downstairs.

She sat in her armchair and stared at the floor. Those bloody Tresslers, she said to herself. Bill was one of their best upholsterers and she'd not heard a peep from them since the fire. His friend Hugh, a union man, had convinced her they'd be due a pay-out of some sort. 'Something to tide you over until Bill can go back,' he'd promised. But that was two months ago and promises wouldn't pay the rent that was due. She couldn't expect the landlord to wait indefinitely.

Shopping trips were so much shorter these days. Not for her the leisurely stroll along the High Street, buying best cuts of meat from Marshall's. Now she could barely afford the basics – bread, butter, bones for broth. Soon she'd have to cut down on the milk delivery as well.

Jessie reached into the back of the cupboard for the old cocoa tin that had held their savings fund, which she'd been dipping into since August. With a knife she prised the lid off again and scattered the remaining coins onto the table. By fluke a halfpenny landed upright and Jessie stared as Britannia rolled across the surface, before falling to the stone floor with a clatter.

She glanced upwards, fearing the racket had woken Bill. She stooped to pick the coin up and began putting the money in different piles – seven shillings for the rent, six for food, the gas and coal were all right in the summer but now autumn was here. There was a rap on the door and Jessie flinched, then froze for a second. She threw the tablecloth over the coins and bundled everything up, tin included. As she headed for the door, her mouth was already rehearsing excuses as to why she had to miss another week's rent. *Bill's not back at work yet. As soon as we get the pay-out...*

She opened the door a few inches. Hugh stood jiggling on the pavement, shoulders hunched against the rough September breeze.

'You took your time,' he said, his hands buried in his

armpits. He nodded to the bundle she was still cradling. 'Doing your washing, eh?'

Jessie breathed out. 'I thought you were the rent... never mind. Come in, come in.' She ushered him into the sitting room, feeling light-headed with relief. The pay-out had come just in time.

'So, how're you managing?' Hugh asked, looking around the room casually.

'Oh you know,' she said, perching on the edge on the chair. 'Not so bad.'

'We're missing Bill.' He took the chair on the other side of the fireplace. 'It's not the same at work without him. What's the doctor say?'

Jessie shifted in her seat. 'He hasn't been in yet. Bill just needs a bit more recovery time.'

There was a long pause while Hugh drummed his fingers on his knee.

'Look, Jessie, this isn't just a social call for the infirm.' He took a cream envelope from inside his coat pocket. 'You need to read this.'

The letter was addressed to *Mr William Paignton*. She raised her eyebrows at Hugh.

'It's from the management. Best open it, eh?' he said quietly.

Jessie tried to make her mind go blank. She ripped open the letter. It was on heavyweight cream paper and the firm's ornate logo leapt out at her. *Messrs W. Tressler and Co. Theatre and General Furnishers.* Her eyes darted all over the page. Phrases jumped out at her... *one of our finest workers... tragedy of the accident... caused by a cigarette, carelessly dropped... it would be churlish to proceed with legal action against you ...* and then the words began to dance before her eyes; she clamped them shut.

She felt winded, as though she'd been walloped and had forgotten how to breathe. And cold, too. Icy cold. Standing on the edge of a cliff cold.

Then Hugh was next to her, kneeling on one leg, one hand on the chair for support. 'I asked if I could bring it round. I didn't want you to–'

Eventually, she found her voice, but it sounded strange to her ears – hollow, with an edge of hysteria.

'I don't understand. You came round here to bring me this?' She shook the letter at him. 'What does it mean?'

'They won't pay out because they've decided that Bill was at fault for dropping his cigarette. That's what started the fire. A vat of varnish had been damaged at its base and had leaked under the floorboard of our workroom. It was only a matter of time before–'

'But you said we'd get something. You promised!'

'I know.' Hugh bowed his head. 'They're just wriggling out of it.'

She waited for him to start the union rhetoric, to talk in his blustering way about strikes and industrial action but he looked truly helpless. She struggled to find pity for him.

He warned her that they might not even keep Bill's job open. 'There's a big contract coming in to re-fit The Scala and they're taking on whatever men they can get.'

After Hugh had left Jessie sat down at the table. She had to think, make plans. Other people managed, didn't they? Everyone had periods occasionally when money was tight. Possibilities ran through her mind. Mrs Leigh, who lived a few houses down, took in children for working mothers. But Bill needed peace and quiet, not a load of screaming babies or fractious toddlers. In any case, being around other people's children and then giving them back... No, what about selling something from the house? Jessie stroked the arm of the chair, one of the pair that Bill had made for them and which had brought her so much pleasure when she and Bill sat there peacefully of an evening. She pushed away all thoughts of selling them; she might get enough to cover the bills for a month but what then?

'Jessie!' Bill's cry came from upstairs and she went up, glad for the distraction from her thoughts.

Two weeks later Bill's mother Ann invited Bill and Jessie to the pub for a drink. Jessie tried to get Bill to make the short walk to the alehouse but he'd refused and she ended up going on her own, promising not to be more than an hour.

At the pub her mother-in-law was already there along Johnny, Bill's brother, with his new wife Elizabeth, a slender pale-skinned creature.

'Where's Bill?' Ann said, looking pointedly behind Jessie.

'He said he'd catch me up. Just wanted to sort something out with, er... with a friend who popped in and...'

Ann took out her knitting. Elizabeth caught Jessie's eye and raised her eyebrows, as if trying to tell her something.

'What?' Jessie mouthed.

Johnny reached and squeezed Elizabeth's hand.

'It's for us, what Ann's making,' he said awkwardly. 'Well, the little 'un when it arrives, around spring time.' He sprang to his feet, saying he wanted to get a newspaper.

'Oh, you're... congratulations.' Her voice sounded as hollow as she felt inside. As though she'd been scooped out and was now empty. She looked closely at Elizabeth, unable to help her gaze flitting across her belly, looking signs of swelling. But Elizabeth looked slimmer than ever, only her breasts perhaps fuller and a slight darkness under the eyes. Jessie wondered if she was feeling the early signs – the all-over tenderness and nausea.

'It's next April,' Elizabeth said.

Johnny returned with the paper and while Elizabeth and Ann were fussing over the knitting Jessie stood up, saying:

'Can I have a word?' They moved away from the table.

'Look, I know it's hard with Elizabeth's news...'

'It's not that,' Jessie said. Nevertheless, the fact he remembered brought a lump to her throat and made her eyes begin to smart. She could see him peering at her. It was now or never.

'I hate to ask this, but – I need to borrow some money.'

Johnny looked stunned.

She continued, 'With Bill not working these past two months–'

'Christ, anything. How much do you need?' She adored him for that. He fished in his pocket and brought out a couple of pounds. 'I didn't realise things were so bad. Ann said he'd be getting a pay-out–'

'They're letting him go. I haven't told him yet. And the rent's due. Overdue.' He pressed the money into her hand. Already she was calculating it was enough to feed and house them for a month if they were frugal.

'I'll find a way to pay you back.'

He waved his hand dismissively.

A voice behind her said, 'So where's my son then? You said he was coming in a bit.'

'He's not feeling well, Ann.'

'You've been saying that for weeks. I'm coming back with you to see for myself.'

'No! It's really not necessary.'

Johnny opened the newspaper. 'It's getting serious now. This war with the Kaiser. You won't believe how many hundreds have signed up already. There won't be anyone left in the factories at this rate.'

Elizabeth reached and patted his arm. 'Johnny'll be joining, won't you, love?'

'There's posters down at the Labour Exchange – the factories are desperate for men. You mark my words, they'll be getting the women doing the men's jobs before you know it.'

Jessie saw Elizabeth's alarmed expression. 'Surely not.'

Ann glanced up from her knitting. 'I wouldn't be so sure. Even your old place is running short,' she said, turning to

Jessie. 'They're crying out for machine operators – one of the cooks there told me.'

'What, you mean Cadbury?' She stood up, aware of the idea that had already begun to seed in her mind. 'I've got to check on Bill.'

Back at home, she listened at the bottom of the stairs until she heard Bill stir. Without waking him she went to the cupboard and pulled out the Bible given to her when she'd left Cadbury to get married.

She could picture that day so clearly; telling the forewoman she was now engaged and then being called to the directors' office. Mr Barrow Cadbury had thanked her for her years of service and had written in the blue Bible: *Wishing you well on the occasion of your marriage.* Then he'd reached into his desk for a moneybag with five whole pounds as a gift, as well as a red rose, freshly cut from the works' garden that morning judging by the dew on its petals. When he instructed her to use the money wisely and to be a wifely support to her husband she had nodded fervently. After a lot of discussion with Bill – should they splash out on a few days at the seaside? – they had spent the money on a bedstead, mattress, bed sheets and bedspreads. On their first night together as newly-weds they had bounced on the bed, giggling, feeling like naughty children. She'd said to her husband, 'Do you think Mr Barrow would approve?' In reply he had kissed her solemnly and later brought her to a sweet shock of pleasure.

She tiptoed up the stairs.

'Bill, my darling?' She shook his shoulder gently to wake him up. He groaned and mumbled in his sleep. His eyes opened suddenly with a glassy stare. How much he could comprehend in this drowsy state she didn't know, but she spoke her next words clearly and firmly, as if to give herself courage.

'Bill. Listen. I'm going back to work. At Cadbury. I'm going to get my old job back.'

CHAPTER 3

Leonora closed the director's door behind her and waited until she was in the corridor before she allowed the smile of triumph to spread over her face. She recalled Mr Edward Cadbury's exact words, wanting to preserve them in her mind to savour later on: 'Miss Lime,' he had said, 'we'd like you to be in charge of overseeing the new recruits in your section. With your high standards we consider you the right sort of person to do the job.' The girls in Q block would probably begrudge her this new role, but that didn't matter. The greatest pleasure would be telling her friends, the kindly and supportive Baileys. She warned herself not to brag, but there was no harm in remarking that her hard work had been rewarded. She had been noticed, after all.

With her shoulders back and a warmth radiating through her body she headed to the Works' offices to collect the names and details of the new staff joining the card-cutting department. She scanned the list – only two names were on it: Miss Helen Daw and Mrs Jessie Paignton. The latter was one of the marrieds. Leonora was unsure how she felt about the Cadbury directors inviting married women back to work. At least, she reasoned, the woman would be familiar with the firm and need less help settling in.

She turned her attention to the younger recruit, Miss Daw, quickly reading the director's report and then her school certificate.

'Oh! There's been some mistake,' Leonora said, frowning.

'She's only achieved the fifth standard.' The minimum requirement for working at Cadbury was the sixth standard and, for the last two years, only girls reaching the seventh standard had been recruited.

The Works' officer looked up from her typing machine and gave Leonora a dark look.

'With this war on the directors say we can't afford to run short of workers; we'll be under government orders before long.'

Annoyance surged through her like a bolt of lightning. Perhaps it was genuinely necessary to relax the entry standard, but it was hard not to feel insulted at the poor calibre of this latest recruit. She asked herself whether Eliza Barratt, or any of the other forewomen, would have been put in charge of such workers.

'I suppose I'll have to do my best, then,' she said.

The teacher's report said the fourteen-year-old was hard-working and conscientious but, Leonora surmised, the girl was probably a bit dim. Still, that could suit Leonora. The last thing she needed was another flighty piece like Mary under her supervision. Trying to control the Morris girl was akin to catching a fly with an inkpot.

The officer glanced at the clock. 'She should have finished her medical by now. I asked Dr T. to send her back to the lodge entrance to wait for you.' Dr Townley was the Works' doctor. 'Would you bring her back here when you've finished showing her round? We need to see her birth certificate and proof of address.'

'Yes, thank you. I'm just going.'

Leonora met the girl at the main lodge entrance.

'How do you do?'

'How do you do?' the girl stammered. She was an unfortunate-looking creature: short and slight, with pale – almost grey – skin covered by freckles. Her hay-coloured hair fell over her face, the fringe so outgrown it reached her snub nose. She was buried in a shabby navy raincoat, with sleeves that almost covered her child's hands – probably borrowed from her mother or an older sister, perhaps. When she smiled she showed crooked bottom teeth, but they looked clean.

'Have you been weighed by the doctor, child?' She leaned over her own stout bosom and looked down at the girl. Dr Townley recorded the height and weight of all new workers and the girls were often underweight.

'Yes, Miss. I'm five stone. He said I was to eat as much chocolate as possible and try to get up to six and a half stone.'

Leonora sniffed.

'Good. It's physical work and you'll need to build up your stamina. Eat properly, do the gym classes, enjoy the fresh air and you won't be troubling the doctor every five minutes like some of the girls.' She had in mind Elsie Higgins, who was notorious for her episodes. 'He's there to consult for serious illnesses only.' Leonora prided herself on never having had so much as a headache in her life.

'Now I'll show you round, so listen carefully to all the information I tell you.'

She spoke in a brisk tone. The girl would have a copy of the 'Rules and Regulations' booklet to take home to read with her parents but, Leonora decided, she wouldn't mention that. *Let's see how well you can pay attention.*

'Here's the girls' dressing room. You change into your work clothes in here. You are allowed to come in thirty minutes before you start work. Under no circumstances must you enter this room during working hours. If you feel unwell, come and see me and I'll advise.'

Next they went into the dining room. The girl gazed up at the vaulted ceiling. 'You can buy dinner checks from the library – lunch will only cost you a penny a day. Girls of your age are expected to sit on the terrace at dinner times and avail themselves of the fresh air.'

Leonora studied the girl's doughy complexion, and noticed

a rash around the chin. She wondered what kind of home Helen Daw came from. The sudden whiff of stale biscuit-like odour told her the answer.

'Hygiene is extremely important here. You're entitled to use the shower baths once a week. And, if your work is up to scratch, I'll recommend you have time off for bathing during work hours. Other privileges will be granted as I see fit. But remember this: hard work has its rewards. If you apply yourself fully and follow the rules, you won't fail to thrive here.'

By now they'd come full circle and reached the lodge again. Helen put up her hand, as if she were still in school.

'Miss, what about my uniform?'

The naive gesture suddenly endeared her to Leonora and she began to feel slightly sorry for the girl.

When she'd started at the Bournville Works twenty-five years ago she had thought she'd never master the machine, or find her way to the dining room or the lavatory without having to ask. After her first day she'd gone home so bone-crushingly fatigued she could barely speak. Her father, God rest his soul, had opened his arms and she'd wept on his shoulder, saying she couldn't do it, that she'd never be any good. And he'd said nothing but simply hugged her tight and stroked the back of her neck, easing away all the tension with his strong fingers.

'Don't worry about uniforms for now. Just come to work in your ordinary clothes – clean clothes, please – and if your work and attitude reaches the required standard then you'll be given some fabric to make two pinafores. You have dress-making skills, I presume?'

Helen's eyes widened in alarm. Leonora tutted. Girls today were quite hopeless, it seemed, even the ones who'd been to school.

'Ask your mother or someone to help. If you're really stuck then come to me and I'll find a sewing pattern for you. Now smile – you'll be working at the finest factory in the country, so there's no need to look like a mouse in a trap.'

After a second's pause Helen gave a broken grin and that reminded Leonora to tell her: 'You can collect a tin of tooth powder and a toothbrush from the stores. The Works' dentist will see you free of charge if we take you on.'

Leonora stepped forward and held Helen's jaw, tucking loose strands of hair behind the girl's ears.

'Tie your hair in two plaits, please. Now I'll take you back to the office and you can collect a permission form for your parents to sign so you can attend adult classes at the Stirchley Institute.'

'Thank you, Miss,' Helen said.

'But first you have to pass your probationary period,' she said, her earlier moment of compassion now forgotten. She escorted the girl to the office and walked back to her block, considering just how much work she would need to do to bring this poor creature up to scratch.

Jessie Paignton was first in the queue at the Bournville Works' stores waiting for it to open, scarcely able to believe her luck in getting a job at Cadbury again. On the dot of 10.45 a.m. the wooden shutters were hauled back and a group of women bustled behind the counter. Storage boxes were stacked on open shelves at the back. The queue surged forward like a wave, squashing Jessie against the counter.

'Stand in an orderly line, or I'm not serving you,' one of the women said.

Jessie recognised the Scouse accent immediately – it was Rose Entwistle – but the buxom figure in front of her was barely recognisable as the skinny lass she'd once been.

Rose, in turn, was looking her up and down, and eventually she said, 'Well, if it isn't Jessie Fairfax! They got you back in the old place as well?'

'Hello Rose, it's Jessie Paignton now – as well you know.'

'Course it is. Your old feller signed up too, has he? My John enlisted a month ago.' She spoke the word with pride, as though she'd only just learned it. 'Royal Warwickshire Regiment, he is.' Her bosom lifted a little as she stood up straight.

Jessie smiled in a non-committal way. Rose, she recalled, was a prattler, with a mouth as big as the parish oven. Jessie had made the mistake of confiding in her when she and Bill had got engaged and Rose had spread it round the whole factory. She was about to tell her about Bill's injury, but hesitated. Did she really want Rose Entwistle picking over the details of her life, like a vulture swooping down on a carcass?

Instead, she said, 'Can I have a length of cloth, please?'

'Didn't you keep your old overalls? Me neither. I turned mine into table mats.' She laughed at herself. 'Honestly, I've been rushed off my feet from the moment I started back, what with all the new recruits.' She went off and Jessie turned to look at the queue. Anxious-looking young girls stood with older women, probably their mothers. A few women in their twenties and thirties lined up on their own – they were probably married ones like her. She was curious about what their conversations with their husbands had been like. But if their husbands were at war, like Rose's, then they'd have been told by letter and a fat lot of good it would've done their husbands to object.

Bill had been uncertain about her coming back, judging by his silence when she told him about the interview with Mr Edward Cadbury, and how he'd had praised her excellent work record, asking if she'd be happy to come back and work in the card-cutting section.

She'd held Bill's hand, saying, 'Don't worry, I'll get your ma in to look after you. You won't be alone. And I'll pop back in my lunch-hour, I promise.'

Ann, to her credit, had been wonderful, dismissing all Jessie's fussing about how to care for Bill, with a curt, 'He's my own son. Let me get on with it.'

'It won't be for long, I promise,' Jessie had said. 'Just a few weeks. Until Bill gets back on his feet.'

Yesterday she'd done a practice walk from home to the Works: fifteen minutes door-to-door. She'd do it in ten once she got used to it. Just enough time to pop home in her lunch break and check Bill was all right.

Rose reappeared. 'There you go, my love,' she said, deftly folding up six yards of pristine cream holland and handing the bundle to Jessie. 'Let me know if you need any more.'

The cloth represented a brand new start.

'What department they got you in?'

'Q block, I think. Card cutting.'

'Shame! I'm in the warehouse and running the stores. Still, I'll see you at break times and you can fill me in on all the gossip.' She leaned over the counter to give Jessie a playful nudge.

Rose's colleague thrust a form at her and said, in an impatient tone, 'Will you be needing places for the day nursery?'

'No,' Jessie said, quietly. 'No, thank you.' She turned to go.

Rose exclaimed, 'Don't worry about leaving your kids, Jessie! My little uns are in there and the food is grand. They even give em a bath in the afternoon so they're all nice and clean when you pick em up.'

Jessie tried not to react. It took great concentration but she was practised in keeping calm in this situation. The trick was not to respond, to make her expression bland, until people eventually understood.

'Oh,' Rose said, flushing. 'Thought you'd have had a couple at least by now. Decided not to bother, eh? Can't say I blame you.'

Jessie indicated the queue behind her. 'Better go.'

She heard Rose calling after her. 'It was nice to see you, Jessie!' With the length of holland held tightly to her chest she pushed her way through the queue and into the corridor.

Jessie looked at the factory map she'd been given. Q Block was new to her and over on the north-eastern side of the factory. The entrance was empty of people and the internal doors were locked so she went up a short flight of stairs. She found herself on a raised gangway looking down on a sea of girls all in white caps and overalls, working on benches piled high with brightly-coloured sheets of paper and card. Some girls operated cutting machines, while others pulled trolleys of paper and boxes along the long aisle. Sounds of chatter interrupted the hum of machinery. She couldn't see a way to get down to them.

'Hey!' A girl below was waving at her, grinning. 'The staircase is back that way. Come down and I'll let you in.'

By the time Jessie had found her way down, the girl was waiting with the door open. 'Welcome to Q block. I'm Mary.' A sweep of fringe, the colour of a new conker, showed beneath her cap and she had high cheekbones in a pretty, heart-shaped face.

'Thanks,' Jessie said.

A tall, very upright woman approached them with a harried look on her face, waving a bundle of papers. Her knobbly wrists and bony finger joints reminded Jessie of bolts in a machine, seemingly at odds with her stout, heavy-bosomed figure. Threads of grey were visible in the woman's hair and she gave off a nervous energy as she spoke.

'Good morning, my name is Miss Lime, and I believe you're our married lady. Mrs...?' She looked down at the papers she was holding.

'Jessie will do fine.'

'I'm not sure about that! First names are acceptable for the juniors but for the seniors like ourselves...'

Jessie thought, but didn't say, *I'm closer to them in age than to you.*

The woman was clearly in a quandary. 'There's a spare cutting machine here, but I don't have time to train you just yet. So just observe the others and I'll be back in a few minutes.'

Jessie looked around at the other workers. Some ignored her while one or two smiled shyly.

Miss Lime strode back with a girl of about fourteen in a brown cotton dress, trailing behind her.

'Ladies, this is another of our recruits, Miss Helen Daw. She'll be on trial from today. I trust you'll make her welcome.'

She looked behind her and said, 'Come on, then. You're here to work, not hang around like a wet raincoat. See all that paper next to the machines? I want you to sweep it all up and salvage the good bits.' The girl looked meek.

Someone huffed and Jessie turned to hear Mary mutter, 'Blimey, if that's the standard the bosses are accepting... And to think they turned my Daniel away six months ago.' Jessie stayed silent. Daniel must be a boyfriend who'd tried to get a job here.

The bull sounded three sharp blasts and the girls left their benches. Mary grabbed Jessie by the arm. 'Come on then. It's dinnertime.'

'Wait a minute please,' Miss Lime said to Jessie. 'You need to have your induction and to visit the stores.'

'It's all right, I've already been. Look, I've got the material and I'll make my uniform tonight.'

Miss Lime looked put out. 'Well, have you got your dinner checks?'

'No, I've brought my own lunch.' A slice of bread and a boiled egg, she refrained from adding.

Miss Lime must have read her mind. 'For goodness sake, take advantage of the proper meals here. You can't work if you don't eat properly. Have one of my checks for now.'

Jessie let herself be taken to the girls' dining room by Mary and the other girls. She spotted Helen was in danger of being overlooked, so she beckoned the youngster to come and join them. The building hadn't changed a bit: long tables, with water jugs and vases of flowers down the middle, hard wooden benches to sit on, but if anything the terrific din she remembered was louder than before. Jessie shouted to Mary, 'It never used to be this noisy!'

Jessie chatted with the other girls. Evelyn had a broad, but not unpleasant, face and she spoke with a slight lisp. From the way she was teased Jessie gathered she had a sweetheart and an engagement was imminent. Ruth was blonde, with brown eyes and an olive complexion, and a beauty spot centred perfectly on her left cheek. Mary leaned in and whispered to Jessie, 'We reckon she paints it on every day.' A dollop of beef dropped off Mary's fork and trailed gravy down the front of her overall. 'Bugger it, that was clean on this morning.' She wiped the gravy with her finger and, unsatisfied, licked the remainder off.

'That'll learn you,' Ruth said.

As they all trooped back to their work benches Jessie realised she'd no need to be nervous about returning. Like many of these girls, she'd left school at fourteen, sat a few tests and – because she'd shown an aptitude for art – had been appointed to decorate the chocolates. She'd enjoyed the work a great deal and she was well suited to it. After only a few months she'd won commendations for the neatness of her work. By the time she'd got engaged to Bill and been required to leave under the Cadbury regulations, she'd felt a pang of regret but had been ready to embrace the next adventure: marriage, followed by children. Everything in its natural order. But now she had a curious sense that her life was in reverse.

As she walked down the corridor, laughing along with a joke of Mary's, Jessie stopped short. She'd meant to go back home in her lunch hour and check Bill was all right. How could she have forgotten? She considered asking Miss Lime if she could hurry there and back in half an hour, but decided she couldn't ask – not on her first day.

The afternoon passed at top speed. Miss Lime showed her the correct way to use the cutting machine – how to line up the printed sheets and then pull the lever down hard so it sliced clean through the card. By 7 p.m. her first shift was over. She was exhausted beyond description and Mary had to help her into her coat.

'My arms are so stiff!' she said.

'Just think of Saturday and pay day,' Mary said.

Jessie walked home as fast as her tired legs could carry her, her worry for Bill gnawing away at her sense of achievement. She let herself in, wondering what state he'd be in. Ann was dozing in Bill's armchair.

'I'm sorry I didn't come back at lunchtime! How's he been?'

'Don't fret yourself,' Ann said, struggling to get up. 'He's asleep for the night now.'

CHAPTER 4

Leonora arrived for dinner at the Baileys' cottage at exactly seven-thirty, in time to hear the sleepy chimes of the clock tower in the quandrangle. The elderly couple, who'd been neighbours of her late parents, now lived in one of the single-storey almshouses on the corner of Linden and Mary Vale Road. She tried to visit them most weeks, usually on a Thursday evening, unless she had a church commitment.

They always left the front door on the latch and they liked her to enter without knocking. Leonora ushered herself into their tiny hallway, glad to be out of the evening chill. She was hungry in spite of a substantial lunch at work.

'I'm here!' she called.

'I've baked you a gooseberry pudding,' Mrs Bailey said, by way of greeting. 'Let's have your coat and come in the warm.'

'I've brought some Dairy Milk.' Leonora put the slab down on the side table in the sitting room, along with a copy of the *Bournville Works* magazine for Mr Bailey.

'I know you like the lime fancies,' she said, 'but we've had to stop making them for the time being and concentrate on the main lines. We're under government orders now.'

At the mention of serious business matters, Mr Bailey looked up from his armchair, while Mrs Bailey disappeared into the kitchen to see to the cooking. Like her father Mr Bailey had worked for Cadbury when the firm was at the Bridge Street factory, before they relocated to Bournville in 1879.

'I've never been able to get over the first sight of Bournville,' he said. 'And to think I didn't want to move from the centre! I'd convinced myself that moving out into the countryside would mean the death of the business.'

Leonora had heard him say this a hundred times, but she humoured him. There was something very pleasant about the predictability of the story – his excitement at seeing the new premises, the large dining rooms for the men and the girls, the football pitch where he and her father had practised for the Bournville Works' team. 'We thought we'd found heaven on earth.' After the pressures of the week, Mr Bailey's words washed over her like jets of water from one of the Works' spray baths.

People imagined life at Cadbury was perfect and trouble-free. Even though the working conditions were the best in Birmingham, if not the whole of England – why else would Herr Otto and the others have visited? – there were still pressures. She welcomed her added responsibilities, but the two newcomers, Helen Daw and Mrs Paignton, had also unsettled her equilibrium.

'So have there been many changes in the old place, little Nora?' Mr Bailey said, using his nickname for her.

'I should say so!'

She waited until Mrs Bailey had brought dinner in and then said – knowing it would scandalise the old woman – 'You won't believe this. The directors are asking all the girls who left to get married if they can come back to work. What do you think about that?'

'Dearie me!' Mrs Bailey shook her head. 'The world's gone mad. Them poor husbands!'

'Don't be dropping that stew now,' her husband said, with a wink at Leonora.

'In fact,' Leonora continued, 'I've got a married lady under my supervision.'

They paused to say grace, then Mrs Bailey put a generous

helping of meat and gravy and two suet cobblers on Mr Bailey's plate. He gave her a look of entreaty across the table until she added another ladleful of stew. She served Leonora with a sizeable portion and then a smaller amount for herself.

'So,' Mrs Bailey said, 'they've put you in charge, have they?'

'Of the new recruits, yes,' Leonora said.

'You should put yourself forward for a proper promotion. To forewoman.' She poured her husband a glass of water. 'I reckon she'd be quite good at it, don't you think?'

Mr Bailey stroked his chin. 'I reckon I do. How about it, our Nora? Fancy giving it a go?'

Leonora felt her face go pink. She put her knife and fork back down and reached for the water jug, before speaking. Blithely, the Baileys had said out loud what she'd been dreaming of but hadn't been able to admit, even to herself.

'Oh no, not me,' she found herself saying. 'They've just made the latest round of promotions anyway. Do you remember Miss Barratt? She's now a senior forewoman and very good at it too! Enough of work. Tell me all about this fruit-drying machine you've bought, Mr Bailey.'

The longed-for gooseberry pudding, when it came, may as well have been made of cardboard. Leonora spooned it into her mouth, registering none of its sweet tanginess. Her mind was elsewhere; she saw her earlier triumph for what it was. So what if she'd been given extra responsibility? It was a token recognition of her help with Herr Otto during the town planning tour, but it wasn't a real promotion.

Replete with food, the Baileys sat in their chairs, dozing. The conversation drifted to Mrs Bailey's charity work, which gave Leonora the idea of getting the girls at work to do something for the soldiers now Christmas would soon be here. Perhaps she'd speak to Mr George or Mr Edward about sending the men some Christmas gifts. And that might gain her a little recognition, and even a mention in the Works' magazine. She suddenly felt cheered up.

When it was time for her to leave, Mr Bailey said again, 'Put yourself forward for the forewoman's job, girl. Remember it's only the squeaky wheel that gets the oil.'

'I shouldn't have to *put myself forward*.' How vulgar that sounded to her.

'You're not afraid of the tests, are you?' he said.

She had to stop herself from saying, *certainly not*. She had enough intelligence to pass any exam they wanted her to sit. No, that wasn't the problem. It was the notion of *putting herself forward* that she recoiled from. She believed that a powerful system of justice operated in this world, where hard work and loyalty and patience were rewarded. But then again, she thought, there was nothing wrong with showing the directors what she was capable of, demonstrating her worth, giving things a little nudge.

After a couple of weeks at the Bournville factory Jessie felt like she'd never been away. Her cutting speed was fast, yet she operated the machine with such precision that her cut-out work drew praise from Miss Lime. Not like poor Ruth, whose cutting blades constantly misaligned themselves – resulting in a pile of rejected cards and the threat of docked pay.

On pay day that first Saturday Jessie had broken the wax seal on her wages tin and counted the coins with trembling hands: nineteen shillings. Not even half of Bill's wage at Tressler's, she calculated, but at least she could pay the rent with enough left in the kitty, if she was careful. The sheer relief brought a lightness to her mood that made up for the monotony and physicality of her daily work at the machine. When she went home to Bill each night she found she enjoyed the hour between eight and nine o'clock where she chatted to him about her day. Occasionally, he fell asleep but she didn't mind so long as that sleep and rest helped his body recover.

September rolled into October and brought a bitterness to the evening temperatures, although the daytime weather remained mild. During one afternoon break-time Mary persuaded the girls to wander over to the recreation ground, where they squashed onto the bench near the lily pond.

'Come on, Jessie, there's room for you as well.'

Jessie smiled and sat down on the arm of the bench, closing her eyes and enjoying the warmth of a pale watery sun. Mary and the other girls chattered and she was happy to listen. Break-times had been so awkward at first. The other married women, like Rose Entwistle, had expected her to join their clan, while Miss Lime had lurked around Jessie as though she would like Jessie to sit with her but was too diffident to ask. But Jessie preferred the company of the young girls, like Mary, and Evelyn and Ruth.

'I've been thinking–' Mary began.

'Steady on,' Evelyn said, her lisp as pronounced as ever.

'–about all the men who've signed up for the war. It's going to be Christmas in a couple of months. Why don't we get a group going to make some gifts for the soldiers? Who's in?'

Jessie opened her eyes to see Mary looking around, her eyes bright.

'Oh, I'm not sure I have any spare time,' Jessie said, thinking of Bill. 'But I bet there are loads who would be willing.'

'All right, let's have a poster and get some recruits. Can anyone draw?' Her question was met with silence and much head-shaking.

'I'm not bad at art,' Jessie said, eventually. 'Haven't done it since school, mind you.'

'Can you knock up a poster in your best handwriting, something like... Are you interested in providing treats for our soldiers?

'It's not just soldiers. Sailors too,' Evelyn said. 'A lot of our men are in the navy.' She had recently got engaged and her fiancé was serving as a cook's mate with the crew of a torpedo boat.

'Good point. All right, then – soldiers *and* sailors.'

'Can't we just say servicemen?' Ruth said.

'Sounds a bit... cold. What about "Treats for the Men"? No, wait. Comforts. That's it. "Comforts for the Men" is better.' Mary looked around her and everyone nodded.

'Have you got that, Jessie? I'll talk to Robert in the men's print room. See if we can get some copies made with that fancy machine. If not, you'll have to do about ten by hand.'

'Where can we put them up?' Evelyn asked.

'In all the girls' blocks,' Mary answered. 'What about in the dressing room where everyone will see it?'

'Is that allowed? You'd better ask Miss Lime,' Ruth said.

'You ask her. If I ask she'll say no on principle,' Mary said, pulling a face.

'The library will put one up and what about the baths?'

'Don't we need to have a meeting first?'

'Yes, put that on the poster,' Mary said to Jessie. 'What about next Wednesday?'

Jessie made a mental note of all the details.

The next day Jessie asked, 'What do you think of this, Mary?' She unfurled the sheet of paper and spread it over the workbench. She had drawn on the back of an out-of-date notice taken from the girls' dressing room. 'Will it do?' She felt a flicker of anxiety while Mary studied the red and black poster, the carefully drawn lettering with the heading: *Comforts for the Men.* She'd painted a soldier in silhouette.

'That's blimmin' marvellous. Reminds me of those army recruitment posters. Clever, aren't you? Let's put them up and see if we can get some volunteers.'

Her face clouded over and she said, 'Jessie, I need a huge favour. I need to do something tomorrow morning. It's an appointment, but don't ask me what for.'

'Fair enough. But how can I help?'

'I'm in enough trouble as it is and if I asked Miss Barratt for time off, Miss Lime would only find a way to turn it against me.'

'So?'

'So I need you to cover for me.' She held Jessie's arm and whispered, 'I'll come in as normal, turn my time check over, then I'm going to slip out at dinnertime, and you just need to tell Miss Lime something if I'm late back.'

'What shall I say?'

'Say I've been taken ill and gone to the works' doctor. Anything. She likes you.'

'I don't know... I can't afford to get sacked,' Jessie said. On seeing Mary's face she said, 'All right but come back as quick as you can.' *Was it something to do with that sweetheart of hers, Daniel?* She noticed that Mary's face was pale. 'Are you all right? You're not in some kind of trouble, are you?'

Mary patted her cheeks to bring the colour back. 'Right as rain, honestly,' she said, with a grin.

On her way back home Jessie went past the day nursery and saw the mothers spilling out with their babies. She tried not to look, but her eyes were drawn to a young woman with a toddler at her feet and a baby in her arms. The baby was squalling in collicky pain – making ear-piercing screams for such a tiny thing – and the toddler pulled on his mother's skirts, until she slapped his hand away.

'Leave me alone, will you? I've been at work all day and I don't need you grizzling at me.'

Jessie's feet took on their own momentum as they propelled her over to the woman. She picked up the toddler and he stopped whining immediately. His hair smelled of soap and she caught the sweet scent of banana on his breath. Using her handkerchief, she began to wipe his runny nose.

'There, there,' she said, as she jiggled him on her hip. The mother glared at her, as if she felt judged. Jessie forced herself to smile in a friendly way and the woman muttered, 'Ta.'

Reluctantly, Jessie let the boy slide to the floor. The thought of cuddling that child each night and soothing him to sleep made her throat ache with longing.

She hurried across the bridge over the River Rea and in a couple of minutes she was home. There was no sensation in her fingers as she fumbled with the key in the lock. Ann had left a note on the table to say she'd had to go but had left Bill's dinner to keep warm on the stove.

A while later, Jessie trudged upstairs with the tray of food and some hot water with a dash of lemon and honey, her knees creaking almost as loudly as the stairs. *Please let Ann have emptied the bedpan. I won't ask for anything else.*

'Ma, is that you?' came Bill's voice, in a croak. Jessie opened the door and put the tray on the bedside table. A copy of the *Daily Mirror* lay open on the bedspread and, just visible under the bed, oh joy of joys, was a sparkling clean bedpan. The smell of bleach meant Ann had given it a good scrub as well. *Bless you, Ann.* The newspaper was a good sign, too; it was opened and folded down on the sports fixtures.

'Bournville are playing Oldbury this weekend,' she told him. 'I could take you down to watch.'

'Maybe.' He struggled to sit up, reaching across for the plate. The shadow from that morning's shave was just coming through. Ann was a real angel doing all those chores which she no longer had time for. She bent to kiss him and pointed at the paper.

'So what's happening in the news today? Is it true what they're saying about the king's dog?' Perhaps it was wishful thinking but Bill looked better, a bit brighter than yesterday. She sat on the edge of the bed to undo her boots. She was just about ready to climb into bed with him, but it was only eight o'clock. Another hour should do it.

'You not eating your supper?' He pushed the food around his plate, loading his fork with such a tiny amount that she wanted to say to him, *For heaven's sake – just eat it!*

Instantly, she felt ashamed of the spark of irritation igniting inside. Women were supposed to be infinitely patient, to be natural nurturers. She was a rotten nurse and no mistake.

Maybe that was why our babies hadn't survived, she thought, recalling the loss of her two little ones before she'd even reached full-term. Maybe God had decided she was unfit to be a mother. But that was self-pitying nonsense, she told herself. It wasn't a punishment, just lousy rotten bottom-of-the-barrel luck. And yet some people were blessed with all the luck in the world. Elizabeth married Johnny and was pregnant within a month. Mrs Tops next door had her little boys, so did Rose Entwistle.

Determined to put such thoughts out of her mind, she picked up the paper and turned to the front-page photographs.

Bill said, 'Read us some of that, Jessie. I like it when you read to me in that lovely voice of yours.'

'Flatterer!' She grinned at him and, ignoring the fatigue threatening to overcome her, said, 'Budge up then, I can't get in if you're hogging the bed.' She kicked her loosened boots across the room with a sigh of relief.

'Well, "Daring the Dardenelles", it says here. "British Submarine B11 dives under five mines and torpedoes Turkish battleship." It says it's "one of the most brilliant naval exploits of the war at sea." How about that?' The world was widening for all of them, more so, Jessie thought, since she had returned to the Bournville Works. Countries she'd barely heard of, never mind thought much about, were getting involved in this war. Even Johnny had joined the navy.

She turned to Bill, now dozing at her side, and was glad to be with him. She sent up a prayer for Johnny, reminding herself that she must send him back the money he had lent her.

CHAPTER 5

The response to Jessie's posters was enthusiastic and girls from different departments made enquiries about how they could help. It was decided to pack chocolates and write Christmas cards for the injured servicemen sent home to the British hospitals. Mary had already negotiated the use of the Retirement Room, used normally as a sick room, as a place to store and parcel the chocolate gifts. When the bull sounded for home-time on Saturday afternoon, Mary told Jessie that some of the girls were staying behind.

'We need to get this lot wrapped and into this crate,' she said, pointing to a stack of half-pound Dairy Milk chocolate bars stacked against the wall. 'Can you spare half an hour? No pressure.'

Jessie shook her head. 'I'm sorry, but I can't.' Her curtness hid the fact she wanted to stay and join in with the camaraderie. *I've already helped you out covering for you this week*, she was tempted to say.

Miss Lime appeared, demanding to know what was going on. She harrumphed when Mary explained that Mr Edward had approved the girls' idea. 'If you'd bothered to speak to me first I would have told you *I'd* had a similar idea. Now what exactly are you planning?'

'We're making a Christmas card for every soldier recovering in hospital in England. How does this sound?' Mary pointed to a card and read the words aloud: *With Hearty Christmas Greetings to the Wounded Soldiers and Sailors, and with best wishes for your speedy recovery. From Cadbury Bros. Ltd.* 'Only we've got two hundred to do so they can go out on Monday. Oh well, they'll have to make do with my handwriting...'

Jessie sighed and held out her hand. 'Give me a batch of cards and I'll do some at home.'

'Mrs Paignton has a husband to attend to,' Miss Lime said, in objection. 'Why don't you ask Helen Daw?'

'It's all right.'

Mary grinned and handed her a stack of white offcuts from their section and a pen.

'You've got lovely handwriting, you have. Mine's worse than a spider's.'

That's true, Jessie thought. She was good at handwriting. At school she'd scored top marks for penmanship and her favourite teacher had taught her calligraphy.

She put the bundle of cards and pen in her coat pocket. The dressing room was quiet that afternoon. Evidently many of the girls were staying on after their half-day shift to pack the Comforts. Jessie bent to put on her outdoor boots. They were warm as toast as she wriggled her feet into them. The mild weather of October had turned bitter now and outside the November wind sliced through her coat, taking away her breath. It's all right for girls like Mary, she thought, as she walked down Bournville Lane, under the railway bridge and homewards to Bill. Young and free with all the time in the world.

The sight of a white winter camellia on the ground drew her eye. Jessie stopped and cursed; she'd forgotten to put her pinafore in the Works' laundry. How on earth, she wondered, was she supposed to get it washed and dried for Monday?

'Hello stranger! I don't see you much these days.' Mrs Tops called to Jessie over the garden fence that afternoon while Jessie was pegging out the washing.

Jessie nodded at the cream pinafores on the line. 'Do you think it'll stay dry today?'

'It's windy enough. I reckon so. Come in and have a cuppa with me.'

Jessie glanced towards her house. 'I've got a lot to do,' she said, thinking of the cleaning she planned to do today, as well as keeping Bill company. Saturdays afternoons and Sundays were taken up with all the household chores she had no time to do during the week.

'Come on, you can spare five minutes for a sit-down. Look at you. You've been carrying the grindstone for too long.'

'Go on then.' Jessie put down the washing basket and slipped round the back way. She felt the beginnings of a headache.

The Tops' house was a mirror of their own. Jessie looked around the sitting room while Mrs Tops made the tea, noting the way the brass around the fireplace shone and not a speck of dust to be seen on the skirting boards. Her eye glanced upon a silver cup that sat on the mantelpiece. She peered at the engraving. *Frank Tops, Commendation for Rifle Skills, Territorial Force*. She found Frank Tops overbearing – Bill said he was a pompous pillock. She was just placing the cup back when Mrs Tops came in the room.

'Like that, do you? Frank got it in the summer.' He was away at a training camp somewhere, she explained. 'The government needs all the Territorials now. I don't know how long he'll be gone for. There's talk of shipping them off to France to fight.'

Jessie looked at Mrs Top's face for signs of concern but there appeared to be none as she poured her a cup of tea. A series of thuds and wails from upstairs made Jessie look anxiously at the ceiling.

'Don't mind the boys. They're only playing. Mind you, if their dad was around they wouldn't be leaping on the beds like that. Not unless they wanted a good belting.'

Jessie winced. 'Do you miss him?'

'He won't be home for Christmas, that's certain. We'll make do, I daresay.' She held her cup to her lips, paused, and said: 'I can sit with Bill now and then, if you want to give the mother-in-law a break. I don't mind admitting I could do with a bit of company in the daytime.'

'Would you? I might take you up on that, especially if they want me to stay on in the new year,' Jessie said. Rose Entwistle, that fount of all factory knowledge, had told her the Cadbury bosses would be keeping on all the extra women because the war showed no sign of ending. 'I could give you a bit towards your time.' Jessie had a little pot of money she'd been setting aside with the intention of paying Ann something towards the food and other shopping she brought from home. Ann had been stubborn in her refusal.

Mrs Tops waved her hands. 'It'll get me to cook a proper meal again for me and the kids. With Frank's soldier's wage we've got enough money to get by, but with him away I'm out of the habit of cooking properly.'

Jessie stood up and thanked Mrs Tops for the tea and chat.

'Any time. If it lightens the grindstone for you, just ask.'

Bill was shouting for her when she went in the back door. 'I'm coming,' she said, and hurried up the stairs.

'Where were you?' he said, in his creaking voice.

'I just popped next door for a chat with Mrs Tops.'

'Can you get me a drink, Jessie?' He held up his empty glass.

'Can I dust downstairs first?' she said, through tight lips. Bill clearly wanted her attention. Again, she felt a flare inside. Do you begrudge me five minutes to myself? she wanted to ask.

She trod heavily down the stairs and sat down in the armchair. Her head pounded and she had a pulsating throb above her left eye. Knock, knock, knock, it seemed to demand. Feed Bill. Get him a drink. Wash your pinafore. Change the bed sheets. She needed to calm down, be patient. It wasn't Bill's fault he couldn't care for himself yet. She closed her eyes, making an effort to slow her breathing and reduce her pulse rate.

Halfway through plating Bill's dinner that evening – a stew with swede, prepared by Ann earlier in the week – Jessie suddenly remembered the Christmas cards.

'Damn it,' she cursed. She gave Bill the plate and went to the wardrobe to rummage in her coat pocket.

'What are you looking for?' Bill said.

'I promised I'd write these cards for the soldiers.' She put the bundle of cards on the bed and waited for his reaction – for him to ask, to show an interest – but he said nothing.

Fine, she thought. 'I'll do these downstairs at the table,' she said, feeling as if the atmosphere was infected by her grumpy mood and she would only dampen Bill's evening even more if she stayed in the bedroom.

Downstairs, she spread out the cards and tested the pen before she began to write. *With Hearty Christmas Greetings...* and gradually the repetition of the actions – the inflections on the capital letters, the sweeping round strokes of the pen – began to soothe her. The concentration required was enough to shut out all the angry thoughts and feelings that swirled inside her head.

Halfway through the batch she put the pen down and stretched out her fingers. She pictured Bill upstairs, his dinner half-eaten, probably snoring gently by now. The cleaning could wait, everything could wait; she restarted her task.

Leonora heard the shrieks of laughter half way down the corridor. As she approached the retirement room, it was clear the gathering of girls was already in full swing. She paused outside the door and strained to hear the conversation on the other side, swatting away the twinge of conscience like it was a troublesome fly.

'Come on then, young Sam. Let's see how you measure up.' That sounded like Mary Morris's voice.

Another girl spoke: 'I've seen more flesh on a sparrow's kneecap!' Evelyn, judging by the lisp. Raucous jeering followed.

'Not like that. You'll choke the poor lad.' This voice was calmer and more reasonable. Leonora's heart stuttered in dismay. Surely that wasn't Mrs Paignton in there, she thought. Leonora had heard the woman say she couldn't take part in the Comforts programme, because her husband took up all her spare time. The woman spoke again, saying, 'Loosen the tape measure a bit more. You want a comfort fit.' *That's her! I knew it!* This was more evidence of the easy friendship that was forming between Mrs Paignton and that infernal girl, Mary.

Ruth chimed in, confirming Leonora's suspicions: 'Jessie's right. The men over there are on good rations. Add a couple of inches round his chest.'

'Round his where?' Mary said in a phoney posh accent.

With the unseemly outburst of laughter Leonora told herself, *That's enough!* She turned the handle and flung the door open. The noise tailed off while Mary, with her back to the door, was the only one who was oblivious to her appearance. Samuel Eastwood was stripped down to his vest, with a silly grin on his face, aimed surely at her just as it had been that day on the girls' recreation ground. With Mary's arms around his waist the pair of them looked like they were in a lewd embrace. Mary, now aware of the silence, turned and saw her. The tape measure dropped to her side.

'What on earth is going on in here?' Leonora's voice was shrill with indignation. 'You know men aren't allowed in the ladies' area.'

'It's only Sam,' Mary said. 'We decided to knit some vests for the soldiers and we needed someone as a model. Sam here volunteered to let us size him up.'

'Like I had much choice,' he muttered. 'Oww!' he cried, as Mary pressed his foot with her own.

'Idiot!' she hissed.

She turned to Leonora. 'We're not doing any harm. We just wanted to get the right size before we start making anything for the men.'

Leonora saw the look that passed between Mary and the boy as he pulled his shirt on and adjusted his braces around his shoulders.

'You,' she said, pointing her finger at Sam, 'don't have the authorisation to be in here. Get back to the gardens now. And girls, check your belongings. It's a pity a young man like this hasn't seen fit to sign up for his country instead of, of... fooling around.'

She felt a hand on her arm. Turning, she saw it was Mrs Paignton.

'What Mary said is true, Miss Lime. She was only measuring up so we could make a knitting pattern.'

Leonora drew in a sharp breath. She knew she would have to find a way to deal with this situation before Mary dragged this woman down to her level.

'Mrs Paignton, may I have a word?' She led the way to a quiet spot in the corridor. When she was forewoman she'd have a proper office for dealing with situations like this. Meanwhile, she had to make do with perching herself on a large window seat.

'Do sit down. You've been with us for two months. Is that that correct?'

The woman nodded.

'And how are you getting on? You seem to find the work straightforward.'

'Well, it took a few days to get used to it again, but yes.'

'And if you had any problems, you know the correct procedure would be to bring them to me?'

'Yes.'

'I see that you and Miss Morris have become firm friends,' Leonora said, aware her voice sounded thin and peevish.

'I like her.'

Leonora found these abrupt answers disconcerting. It was time to take the bull by the horns, so to speak. 'I must warn you that Miss Morris has certain qualities that make it inadvisable for you to be too closely associated with her.'

'I don't follow.' Her tone was polite, but cool.

'Let's just say there's a certain standard we expect from girls that are privileged to work here. An attention to detail, a pride in appearance, clean fingernails, these tiny details that speak of self-worth and self-respect. When I see those details lacking it concerns me.'

'There's nothing wrong with Mary's work, or her fingernails for that matter. I think she works hard!'

'We can debate this all day so let me speak straight. I find her moral character to be lacking. There's talk around the Works of certain associations she keeps, a triviality of tongue and of manner that's not quite right. I rather think you witnessed it with today's spectacle, no? Imagine if one of the directors had walked in on that little pantomime instead of me.'

The woman next to her frowned and bit her lip, as if holding back from speaking.

'Let's say no more about it, other than to mention I am very pleased with your work, Mrs Paignton. You have proved yourself industrious and conscientious. If you were to be offered more shifts after Christmas what would your response be? It would please me to know you might consider staying.'

She stood up, 'I'd have to discuss it with my husband, but–'

'Of course, of course. All I ask is that you think about it.'

After Mrs Paignton went down the corridor, Leonora said to herself, *That was well-handled. Well done indeed. A drop of honey was all she needed, after all.* She watched Mary Morris chase after the woman and slip her arm through hers, as if they were a pair of schoolgirls. Leonora's bubble of satisfaction burst.

Jessie shrugged her coat off and threw it over the balustrade, glad to be back. She had walked home in the blackness, the trees stripped of leaves and the ground so hard and icy she had slipped and skidded twice, nearly turning over on her ankle.

Hard to believe it was the middle of December already: the past three months had flown by. The Works would be shut for seven days from next week. And after that? She knew she had to talk to Bill about whether she should stay on at Cadbury – Miss Lime had asked her again since their chat and would keep fussing until she had a firm answer.

'I'm back,' she called.

Ann was sitting up at the table and knitting by candlelight. 'I daresay you want a cup of tea down you.'

Jessie nodded gratefully and picked up the knitting, the beginnings of a strip in lemon yellow. 'This looks nice. Who's it for?'

'It's another one for the baby. Elizabeth's got quite a lump now. She's carrying all out front so it'll be a boy.'

Jessie put the needles down carefully. 'I was just thinking Miss Lime would love you with your knitting skills.'

'Who's Miss Lime when she's at home?'

'My boss. She wants us all knitting for the soldiers. Well, it was Mary's idea but she acts like she thought of it.'

'I could make you some things, I suppose. What do they need, hats and stuff?'

Jessie nodded eagerly. 'Hats, gloves, scarves. And socks.'

'But you'd have to provide the wool.' Ann said, quickly.

Jessie nodded. 'Of course. I'll bring some back from work tomorrow.'

She had joined Mary and the other girls in their break-time unpicking donated woollen jumpers and cardigans, to be sent to the Works' laundry for washing, and then the skeins carded to remove the kinks. The Cadbury directors had promised funds to buy extra wool if needed but judging by the amount crammed into the Comforts room cupboard already they had plenty of wool to spare. Jessie thought how impressed Miss Lime would be if she contributed to the knitting donations, and if she forgot to say she hadn't actually made them herself... well, that wouldn't be a bad thing. All in a good cause. But it was time to talk seriously with Ann.

'How's Bill been today?' Jessie held her breath, hoping to hear that Ann had managed to get him out of bed. The plan had been for him to get dressed and try a short walk on sticks to the tobacconists on the corner. Bill had seemed enthusiastic about the idea when she'd mentioned it last night.

Ann shook her head. 'I couldn't budge him. He flat refused to get up.' Jessie could see the hurt and exhaustion in her eyes; Bill's mother suddenly looked old. She went to the savings tin and delved in it for some coins.

'Please take this. I know you didn't want any money. Just a few shillings for the food you bought.' *And the time you spent.*

'No, I won't have it. I do what I can to help.'

'I know,' Jessie said, 'and I'm more grateful than you can imagine. Bill will get better soon. He bloody well has to –'

'You're stronger than you look, my girl. I doubt if Elizabeth would've coped as well in your situation. I'd never have credited my own son acting like this. A man's job is to provide for his family and he's let you down.' Although Jessie could feel her distress, it felt wrong, misplaced. Unfair.

'Ann, they want me to stay on at Cadbury after Christmas. With you spending all that time with Bill–'

'I won't deny it's hard work, but–'

'Exactly! It's not right,' Jessie jumped in. 'Seeing as you're so determined not to accept anything I was talking to Mrs Tops and she said she'd come in and sit with Bill on some of the days.' Her words came out in a rush.

'Mrs Tops? That one next door with the mizzerlings always a-crying?' Ann said, holding the teapot aloft.

'With the bit of money I've got saved I could give her–'

'Well, good for you, Miss.'

'I thought you'd like the idea! You wouldn't have to work so hard–'

Ann's eyes narrowed with suspicion. 'If you're so well off all of a sudden, why don't you give up that job of yours and stay and nurse Bill yourself? Try as I might, I'm no substitute for his own wife.'

Jessie froze. Where had all *that* come from, she asked herself. 'You're doing a marvellous job, Ann. Honestly, I'd no idea you'd be offended by my idea. It was only a thought. If you're happy to carry on then please, you must.'

A long silence followed, during which Jessie could almost see the workings of Ann's mind. She said, 'It's my pleasure to care for my son.'

'I didn't say it wasn't! Did I?' Jessie felt wrong-footed and more than a little exasperated. She knew she must calm down her jangled nerves.

'Has he had a good day, then?'

'Go and see for yourself.'

'When I've drunk this tea, I will,' Jessie said coolly, staring back until Ann looked away.

She tried to picture spring; it was a blank page. Who knew what would happen? She'd have to decide in the morning. But she knew one thing: she wanted to carry on at Bournville.

CHAPTER 6

Jessie stepped into the slipper bath and the warm water cascaded over her aching ankles and calves. She lowered herself and slid down until she was submerged up to her neck. Her body involuntarily shivered with delight. The wall tiles sparkled, white as the virgin January snow on the ground outside. A towel, freshly-laundered, warmed on the pipe running along the back wall. Jessie's peace was briefly disturbed by Mary hurrying into the cubicle and turning on the taps of the bath next to her. Jessie looked away while Mary undressed.

Earlier that week Eliza Barratt, the forewoman, had sent Miss Lime a message from the Cadbury directors, who were so appreciative of the girls' efforts before Christmas for the soldiers they were to be granted the use of the swimming baths for the whole afternoon.

'And look at this,' Miss Lime had said. 'We even appeared in the newspapers!' She had passed round a cutting from the *Birmingham Daily Mail*, which Jessie and the other girls jostled to read. *Messrs. Cadbury, Bournville, have sent a box of chocolates to each of the wounded soldiers and sailors in British hospitals as a Christmas gift.*

Jessie wriggled in the bath water. That this treat was in work time made the sensation even more pleasurable. Helen Daw was in the spray bath room next to them. Her voice came from inside the cubicle. 'Ooh, it's just like needles sticking in you!'

Underneath the cubicle door Jessie saw the pile of Helen's dingy undergarments. Jessie wondered about helping the girl to use the on-site laundry facilities. Lord knew, it had been a godsend to be able to put her own bed sheets through the Works' wash occasionally.

'Miss Lime would have something to say about the state of her knickers,' she ruminated to Mary, now immersed in the bath next to hers. Then Jessie asked the question that had been on her mind for a long time. 'Why do you let her talk to you like that?'

'Who? Helen? Oh, you mean Miss Lime?'

Jessie began soaping her arms. 'Yes, she really has it in for you. Has she always been like that or did you do something to upset her?'

'Oh, she's had it in for me from the first week I started. Dunno why. Couldn't do right for doing wrong. But the way I see it, Jessie, is let her do her worst. If it wasn't me getting it in the neck all the time it would only be some other poor sod.' Mary chuckled. 'You could say I'm doing a service for my fellow workers.' Grinning, she sat up in the water, her chestnut hair curling in almost-black wisps around her forehead and her high cheeks red and damp. Jessie thought how pretty she was.

'Chuck us the soap, Jessie.'

'You know when Miss Lime had me in for that little interview? She more or less called you a...'

'Let me guess. A loose woman? A tart?'

'She didn't use those words, but doesn't it bother you? I'd be mortified if someone implied that about me.'

'I've got far bigger things to worry about!' Then Mary sighed, as if trying to be patient. 'It would only hurt my feelings if any of it was true.' She lay back again and closed her eyes. 'Now hush a minute while I relax and get the sound of the old cow's droning voice out of my head.'

Jessie shut her eyes too, sensing that she had tried to push gently at the door of Mary's private life to find it was decisively locked. If Mary wanted to tell her about this Daniel chap she'd do so in her own time, Jessie told herself.

In an echo of Mary's words, Jessie had her own life to worry about. Bill had agreed to her coming back to work in the new year, but he promised to find another job, now that his leg was healing. She had been pleased to hear the determination in his voice. Meanwhile, the new arrangements Jessie had put in place were working out, thank goodness. Ann had agreed to come on Tuesdays and Thursdays, before she went off to stay with Elizabeth and the baby in April. Mrs Tops would go in on the remaining days – Mondays, Wednesdays and Fridays – to take Bill his lunch and evening meal. 'He won't be wanting to go back to work with all the fuss over him!' Mrs Tops had joked. And Jessie knew she had stayed on the right side of Miss Lime and the Cadbury directors by agreeing to stay on. An unexpected bonus of ten shillings had appeared in her wage tin on her last day before Christmas.

Now January was here the first of the thank-you letters arrived from the men serving in France. The appeal for knitting donations had been a tremendous success. Girls from all over the factory, and the Works' offices, had made items – vests of various sizes and skill, hats, scarves and mittens, as well as socks. Jessie was not that proficient a knitter but she knew she had a good eye for colour. To begin with, she had divided the gifts as evenly as she could and tried to match the colours, so that each serviceman would have a matching hat and scarf. But Miss Lime, who had appointed herself leader of the Comforts committee, chivvied her so much that in the end Jessie had abandoned any thoughts of colour schemes and bundled hats and scarves of any old shade together. She had wrapped the items in brown paper, tying them with string. Where she *did* take time was to write a note with each parcel. Sitting at a writing table squeezed under the tall narrow sash window she wrote, *To a brave soldier fighting for the cause. All at Cadbury are proud of you.*

It had become a habit at morning break-time for the girls to cram themselves into the Comforts room and fight over who opened the post from the soldiers. The room housed boxes of chocolate bars, left over from Christmas, stacked four-high against the far wall. Jessie took her place on a huge, nearly-filled packing crate that dominated the floor space. Evelyn, her face etched with worry, picked up a half-finished blue scarf chucked onto the writing desk, and began to knit. Pinned to a noticeboard next to the window was a tally of the latest number of parcels sent out, but also postcards and letters of thanks had been haphazardly pinned up there. Occasionally, one of the items was reproduced in the *Bournville Works* magazine.

Miss Lime arrived with a clutch of letters in her hand. 'This morning's post, ladies!' Helen Daw sat cross-legged on the floor, upright and rapt, as if waiting for a story to begin. Jessie was pleased the girl had eventually passed her probationary period, although not without several tongue-lashings from her supervisor.

Miss Lime read out the first letter. 'Private Copeland from the cocoa room sends his best regards and grateful thanks for his Christmas gifts. He says, *The only sight prettier to me than that parcel of chocolate is my memory of you lovely ladies in your white dresses and caps–*' She cleared her throat, and her cheeks went pink. Ruth tapped Jessie on the back and giggled.

'Listen to this one, ladies: *I wanted to write a thank-you for the marvellous hat and scarf you sent. The handiwork was first class and the red, white and blue stripes most patriotic.*'

'Oh, that was mine!' Jessie said out loud, before she could stop herself, and then had to endure good-humoured catcalls from the others. 'It wasn't even that good! I dropped a stitch on the fourth row and I was blowed if I was going to start again, so I sewed it up in matching thread.'

'Cheat!' Ruth said.

She was a cheat, too, Jessie knew. It was the only scarf she'd actually made herself – she'd put Ann's far better creations into the donations box alongside her own paltry effort. But how lovely and sweet that he should write to say thank you. She couldn't help but smile at the irony though.

Miss Lime continued with the letter. 'He says, "Our progress is good, they tell us. Tomorrow, our division's moving north up to ——" Oh, this next bit's crossed through.'

'That'll be the censor,' Evelyn said. 'He sits in his headquarters going through the letters and blanking out anything that would tell us where the men are serving.'

Helen's face, Jessie saw, had fallen with disappointment. The girl looked around the room at them all. Miss Lime pinned the letter to the noticeboard and then led the way back to Q block. Jessie stayed behind in the room and took down the letter, going over to the window so she could read it in the daylight. The script was rounded and generous-looking. Jessie always felt able to tell a lot from a person's handwriting. His was all wide loops and large spaces; a warm-hearted man, she surmised. She turned over the page and read, *Please give warmest thanks to the hands that knitted my scarf. With best wishes, Private Thomas Walker.*

Something in those words, in his tone, excited her curiosity. Up to now, she had given little thought to the men who were fighting – the soldiers were faceless recipients of their charity – but this letter brought home that these were real people, with bodies that felt the cold, and minds that dreamt and hoped and feared, only out in a strange land.

She went back to her machine and turned to Mary, who had been absent from the Comforts room at break-time.

'We had a letter today from one of the soldiers. A Thomas Walker.'

'What about him? Is he one of ours?'

'I don't know. How could you find out if you wanted to know?'

Mary gave her a quizzical look and Jessie continued, 'No reason really. Just wondered.'

'I could ask around. No, I tell you who would know. Dotty Knight, works in the wages office. She'd probably tell you.'

'I thought I might take the letter round to his department.'

'Good idea. Miss Lime will be overjoyed at your initiative. Well done, Mrs Paignton, you're getting the hang of this!' Mary's smile suddenly snapped shut, like a box closing. What's bothering her, Jessie wondered?

On Sunday morning in early March Leonora sat in the Church of Christ on Beaumont Road. Her mind drifted away from the words of Ernest Seddon, presiding that morning, and back towards Mr George Cadbury's address, delivered to the assembled workers the previous Thursday lunch-time.

Mr George had stood in the girls' dining room and said, 'We have accepted our call and will remain under government instruction. We will do our best to support the war effort, whatever our private reservations. Each one of us is required to be flexible in our approach and I know I can rely on every one of you to consider ways you can serve your fellow workers.' Leonora had listened intently, trying to shut out the buzz of chatter going on around her.

Now, she glanced unseeingly round the church until her gaze rested on the words carved into the plaster arch at the front. WORSHIP THE LORD IN THE BEAUTY OF HOLINESS. Suddenly her attention was brought back into focus.

'Fulfil now, O Lord, the desires and petitions of Thy servants...' Ernest Seddon read, and she sat up straighter.

Mrs Wilson, Mrs Ramsay and Tom Fletcher stepped forward ready to do the scripture readings. She studied each of them in turn as they intoned the biblical words. Mrs Wilson made a hash of the Old Testament passage, Leonora thought, with some satisfaction. She had felt overlooked on the readers' rota, ever since the church had moved last year from their old room at Ruskin Hall to this brand new building. Leonora was minded to have a word with one of the elders. Her sense of pique was justified, she reasoned, since her employer, Mr George, had given a generous donation towards the costs of the church they were now sitting in.

Mrs Ramsay raced through the epistle reading at such speed it was as if she were in urgent need of the lavatory. She bolted back to her seat, sitting down so urgently her chair screeched against the newly-laid wooden floor. Leonora winced, imagining a deep gouge in the oak that would need a professional to repair.

Only Tom had the charisma to bring the words of Matthew's gospel to life for her. 'His lord said unto him: Well done, good and faithful servant.' He looked directly at Leonora and she felt as though the words were spoken personally to her, and for her. He continued, 'Thou hast been faithful over a few things, I will make thee ruler over many things.' A shiver of recognition passed through her.

During Ernest's sermon Leonora thought it all through as, again, her thoughts were pulled back to the Works. Ever since the new recruits had arrived, she'd measured each one against her own high standard. Mrs Paignton had adapted well, agreeing to stay on, but warning she would leave when her husband was fit to work again. Helen Daw, by contrast, had needed a great deal of training and guidance which Leonora had resented at first. The child's table manners were non-existent, judging by the way she hunched over her plate and bolted down her lunch. Twice Leonora had gone out onto the dining terrace and silently pulled Helen's back straight. But what if she'd been given this thankless task precisely because her bosses believed she was capable of bring Helen up to standard? Yes, that was it. She smiled with relief at her previous paranoia.

She had been faithful to her employer and one day she would be ruler.

The communion hymn was announced. Her church was the sort that forbade musical instruments to accompany singing. Whilst she sometimes longed for the accompaniment of a piano, she nevertheless thrilled to the sound of the a cappella voices around the congregation. Her own voice was not strong – the choir master at school used to urge her to give it a bit more gusto – but she sang sweetly when the voices softened for the third verse: *Thine was the bitter price, Ours is the free gift given; Thine was the blood of sacrifice, Ours is the wine of heaven!*

A few of the young men – the Taylor twins, the Pincher boy and one or two others had gone to fight in the war – and today the gathering felt the absence of their deep voices.

Kneeling, she took the piece of loaf from the elder and placed it in her mouth; it was still slightly warm from that morning's baking. She then watched through half-closed eyes while the wine was poured from the flagon into the miniature glass cups, waiting tensely in hopes no liquid would spill onto the pristine communion cloth.

After the benediction, Leonora bowed her head in silent prayer and then stood up to leave, squinting up at some visitors in the balcony seats on the upper floor of the church. Surely there wasn't room for more new members, she wondered. She checked her hatpin was secure and buttoned up her coat, nodding to members of the congregation as she made to leave. Everyone was huddled in one group or another – their bursts of laughter and chatter only added to her sense of isolation.

Out in the foyer, the noise of the Sunday School children in the basement reached her. They would come streaming up the stairs in complete pandemonium any minute. On the steps she paused, apparently to redo her buttons, whilst she strained to hear the whispered conversation taking place on the staircase.

She stepped back into the foyer.

'They said he was blown to bits at Neuve Chapelle. You should see the state of poor Nelly. Says they won't tell her what really happened. Imagine losing your son, like–'

'It's against the natural order of things.'

'The good Lord can't believe this war is right.'

She was reminded of Ernest's sermon and the notion that God had spoken to her that morning; he had more work for her to do.

At that moment, a poster tacked to the noticeboard caught her eye. Volunteers were needed at the Southern General Hospital a few miles away on the Bristol Road: first aid skills, and a willingness to serve cups of tea and make conversation with injured servicemen.

'Ah, Miss Lime, how are you today?' Ernest Seddon clasped her hand. His clothes always looked slightly askew, like he needed a good shake-down and the attentions of a clothes-brush. Today his tie was knotted poorly and had a milk stain down it.

'I've been looking at these posters for hospital volunteers,' she said.

'Yes, the men are coming home in droves. It could be quite a harrowing sight.' She heard the question mark in his tone as if he wondered if she was up to the task.

But a strange excitement had taken hold of her. Not since her baptism, the full immersion at the Moseley Road church, had she felt such a rush of pure and startling faith. Tears pressed against her eyelids and she took a deep breath to control herself.

'I shall make enquires there to see if we could be of help. I have plenty of girls under my command at the works.'

'You really are remarkable, Miss Lime. With all your duties

here–' He'd noticed! 'I wouldn't want such a faithful servant of this church to become overburdened.'

'But you said the good Lord calls us in different ways.'

'At least someone pays attention to my sermons,' Ernest said with a twinkle in his eye. He licked a finger and scrubbed ineffectually at the milk stain. 'Before I forget, would you be able to open the church doors on Wednesday night? There's a Band of Hope meeting and with Mrs Wilson going on holiday...'

'Of course,' Leonora said, a little stiffly, affronted that he even had to ask.

'Oh, and another thing ...' He was going to ask her to read in church next week if Mrs Wilson was away. She smiled, willing him to continue.

'Perhaps a batch of your scones for the Band of Hope ladies?'

She said goodbye and stomped down the steps into the street. As she turned into Linden Road she crossed a grass verge, heedless of the snowdrops she trampled on, and all thoughts of hospital visiting forgotten.

CHAPTER 7

'I can't believe how quickly it's come round,' Ann said, standing in the hallway. Jessie hugged her, overcome with fondness for the woman now that she was leaving.

'You've been a wonder, Ann. We couldn't have managed without your help all these months. Could we, Bill?' She signalled with her eyes for him to get up from the armchair. He struggled to his feet, still needing to use the walking stick for support.

As he hobbled over to his mother, Jessie thought how she would miss Ann's twice-weekly visits and the cleaning she kept on top of. But at the same time Jessie looked forward to relaxing in her own home without feeling Ann's constant presence.

'Thank you, ma,' Bill said. And he and his mother shared a long look.

'It's just you two lovebirds now,' Ann said. 'Well, her next door as well.' She was unable to mention Mrs Tops by name.

'Wait a minute,' Jessie said. On impulse, she ran upstairs to their bedroom and knelt in front of the blanket box. She fingered the quilted lid that Bill had made so lovingly. Taking a deep breath she lifted it and inhaled the scent of the lavender bags she had put between the baby blankets. Holding the lemon yellow covering to her face she swallowed down the lump of grief blocking her throat. Jessie's fists tightened around the fabric.

You don't have to do this, she told herself. She made herself jump up with the blanket and walk downstairs, thinking she could turn back at any time. Ann and Bill were staring up at her. As she reached the bottom step, she held out the blanket to Ann, saying, 'Here, take this for Elizabeth, for the baby.'

After Ann had gone, promising to write as soon as there was any news, Bill took Jessie in his arms.

'You didn't have to do that,' Bill whispered. 'I know what it cost you to give that blanket to Elizabeth.'

She was unable to answer. They went to sit down in their armchairs. The pale daffodils in a vase on the mantelpiece were the colour of the blanket she'd just given away.

'We'll have a baby of our own one day,' he said. 'We can try again.'

Unable to stop herself she cried, 'Try again! What's the point of that?'

'Another one might survive this time,' he said, gruffly.

'I mean, what's the point in getting pregnant? I can't afford to give up my job – not while you're still not working. What would we live on? I'm not going back to last year, scrimping and saving, worrying about every blasted penny. You've no idea what it was like!'

Jessie knew she was being harsh but her emotions were starting to unravel now that Ann had gone. She was lost in thought and when she looked up Bill had left the room. She found him in the outhouse with his bag of upholstery tools open. When they had first started courting he was so proud of the tools he had collected over his apprenticeship; he kept them in top condition, carefully wrapping each one in cloth. Now they looked as if they hadn't been touched since the accident. Perhaps it was her imagination but she smelt the aroma of smoke that clung to the bag, taking her back for a moment to that terrible day of the fire. Silently, she picked up the hammer, opened a rusty tin of gimp pins, felt the weight of the mallet, the tack remover, as though by feeling these items she could find a way back to Bill.

He stilled her hands with his own and said, 'I'll write to Mr Tressler; see what he can do. Just you wait, a year from now we'll be back to normal. I promise.' The thought occurred she wasn't sure what normal was any more.

In June Leonora caught Miss Gabriel from Y block soliciting in the Comforts room for girls to join her Entertainments Committee.

The annual Bournville Village Festival, usually in May, had been suspended because of the war, she told her, so she had decided to organise "a little summer show" for the men from the Southern General Hospital. She showed Leonora the programme of music she was planning. Leonora scanned the items: *Now pray we for our country, Empire's Flag, Hurrah for Merry England.*

'What do you think? Our Musical Society is happy with my choices.'

'There's no denying your patriotism,' Leonora said, thrusting the sheet back at her.

'The Bournville Brass Band has agreed to play,' Miss Gabriel continued, 'and we'll put on the CCM–'

'The what?'

'The Comic Cricket Match, of course. It's a hoot if you've never seen it and it'll go down well with the servicemen.'

Mary said, 'Do you want singers? I can do it.'

Evelyn backed her up, 'She's really good.'

Miss Gabriel peered past Leonora. 'We do need someone for a soprano solo...'

'Excuse me,' Leonora said to the girls, 'Miss Gabriel and I are having a private conversation.' She took the woman outside the doorway. 'My girls are busily engaged with the Comforts Committee for the foreseeable future. But thank you for your interest and I'm sure it'll be a splendid success! I just hope the weather stays dry for you. Last summer was such a washout.'

Leonora took a grim satisfaction from wiping the smug expression from Miss Gabriel's face. Shortly afterwards, a feeling of utter dismay came over her. Her shoulders slumped as if all the joy had gone out of the day. She couldn't shake off the suspicion that Miss Gabriel, far from needing her help or opinion, merely wanted to show off. Worse still, here was another contender, another competitor, for the next forewoman's job.

Back in March that time at church she'd felt her calling. Now was the time to seize the initiative and make that visit to the Southern General before she was outdone by Miss Gabriel.

Work that afternoon had been particularly trying. She had given Helen her first try on the cutting machine and she had managed to jam the thing. The Morris girl looked like she hadn't been to bed the night before and was distracted and bothersome. She really was the giddy limit.

Leonora's nerves were fractured as she caught the bus along the Bristol Road, getting off at the stop near the university clock tower, where the military hospital had been set up. It was a quarter to eight.

The reception door of the Great Hall was wide open and the sound of banging and hammering filled her ears. A man's voice behind her barked, 'Move out the way, lady,' and she turned and saw him carrying one end of a metal bedstead. Another man, carrying most of the weight, judging by his red face, held the other end. 'Make way! Make way!' he sang, as the pair negotiated past her into the hall. She followed them and saw the makeshift hospital. The banging had come from a carpenter fitting some shelves along the hallway. Along with the occupied beds already there, two uniformed nurses were busy deftly making up new beds with pristine white sheets. They were too far away for Leonora to hear what they were saying, but they worked swiftly in tandem, and she admired the way they worked. Down the aisle were tables with jugs of fresh flowers and in the far corner she spotted a gramophone and a piano.

The man holding the front of the bed frame said to her, 'Are you looking for someone?' He called, 'Matron! Another volunteer by the looks of things. You've got VADS coming out of your ears!'

The matron turned and gave him a withering look, as if she didn't appreciate being called. She strode over to Leonora and said, 'We interview recruits at 10 a.m. Come back tomorrow morning please.'

'Oh, can't I see you now?'

The matron looked at her watch. 'I could do with a break,' she said, not very graciously. 'Nurse May, carry on please.'

In the matron's office Leonora felt wrong-footed. Surely they should be grateful, not making her feel she was being a nuisance.

'Name?'

'Leonora Elizabeth Lime,' she stated.

'Date of birth?'

'Eleventh of September, 1874.'

Matron raised an eyebrow. 'Experience?'

'Experience?'

'Medical experience. Skills? Any particular expertise?'

She thought back to how she nursed her father in his final days; would that count?

'A little.'

'How many hours can you spare each week?'

'I work full-time for the Cadbury family...'

'You're in service?'

'No, at the Bournville Works. But I could–'

'A factory woman? Most of the VADS are from a class that doesn't need to work, other than to do good works.' She spoke, Leonora thought, with a degree of contempt.

'Are you saying that as a *factory woman* I wouldn't be considered a worthy volunteer? I'll take my offer of help elsewhere. Good evening to you.' Leonora stood up and, not waiting for a reply, walked out with her back ramrod straight. She made her way out of the building, her cheeks reddening. The nerve of that women, she thought, not to say her ingratitude. She caught sight of a man with a tweed jacket thrown over his shoulder marching across the grass. He saw her look of admonition and made a sheepish gesture of apology.

'Don't tell Matron, will you? She'll have me boil washed and hung out to dry if she caught me sneaking across the grass. Still, you don't look like the tell-tale type.' He noticed the grass cuttings stuck to the bottom of his trousers and stood on one leg, then the other, to brush them down. 'Darn it.'

She stepped forward and took his jacket to hold for him.

'I must say, I don't think much of your matron. I came here with the intention of helping her to get some recruits and I barely got beyond the doorstep, before she interrogated me and sent me on my way. I clearly wasn't suitable.'

He frowned. 'I'm sorry to hear that. Truly. We've got another contingent of men arriving tonight, and I'm desperately short of volunteers as it is. Girls who can do practical stuff, not afraid to get their hands mucky, change a few dressings, etc. Not just reading newspapers to the patients or generally getting in the way.'

'That's where I'm able to help! Or would have been, had I not been sent packing.'

He suddenly put his hands on her upper arms and for a terrifying moment she thought he was going to embrace her or, worse, kiss her.

'You're an angel, whoever you are. Can you come tomorrow evening and we'll discuss it then.' Before she could answer he was already on his way.

'Don't forget now. I'm relying on you. Oh, and it's Russell-Morgan,' he called. 'Doctor Russell-Morgan. Up from London.'

He was really rather charming, she thought afterwards, and very easy to talk to. She realised one thing: she must get the girls trained in first aid. There was so much more her girls could offer to the war effort.

'Nineteen, twenty, twenty-one...'

Jessie was on her knees, counting bars of Dairy Milk into batches of thirty. Each pile lay neatly stacked on the floor in front of her. Her neck ached from bending over and pain shot down her back. Just another dozen batches to do for this summer campaign. And if the war was still on by Christmas they would do it all over again.

'Twenty-five, twenty-six–'

'Ow! Ow!' A sudden wail made Jessie lose her place.

'What on earth is it, Mary?'

She glanced up to see Mary with her finger in her mouth, sucking hard. 'These bloody packing crates. I've got another splinter and they're a sod to get out.'

Mary thrust out her forefinger. A fat jagged splinter stuck out of the flesh. Jessie squeezed the flesh around Mary's finger and pinched the minute figment in her fingernails. With a yank it came out clean.

'There. All done.' Mary's dramatics sometimes set her nerves on edge. But she was in a flat mood herself after an enthusiastic letter from Ann that morning raving about what a beautiful little granddaughter she had. Emma was now three months. Wearily, she started counting again and moments later the door was flung open and in came Miss Lime in a state of agitation.

'Ladies! How many of you have your first aid certificates?' She looked around the room. 'Now don't be shy. Evelyn? Ruth? You did the life-saving in your adult classes. And what about you, Mrs... Jessie? There's a new way for us to help the war effort. The local Southern General hospital is looking for volunteers.'

Jessie shook her head.

'I don't know. I've got a lot on at home with Bill–' She also knew she could be leaving as soon as Bill got a job. *If* he got a job, she corrected herself, thinking that she must chivvy him along later.

'Mary, what about you?' Miss Lime ventured.

'What? Working in a hospital. All that blood and guts. No thanks!'

Miss Lime clearly had to bite down a sharp retort.

'Recently I became aware of a situation of desperate need. As some of you know, a contingent of servicemen arrive regularly in Birmingham and the Southern General is overflowing. It wouldn't surprise you to know more of the local buildings are likely to be pressed into service. Mr George has offered the use of Fircroft Adult School on Oak Tree Lane from this October–' She gave a shudder at this example of civic duty.

'Fircroft is a lovely place,' Ruth said. 'My mam used to clean there. It's got a huge lawn and –'

'Yes, quite possibly,' Miss Lime said, 'but to get to the point in question, there's an urgent need for volunteers to go and serve as–'

'What? Nurses?' Mary said. 'But you need qualifications for that.'

'Not exactly. Assistant nurses. Orderlies. Helping the nurses in their duties. Some of you must have taken your St John Ambulance certificates, no?'

She looked around the room. 'So do I have your support? The doctor I met, Russell-Morgan is his name, is looking for volunteers to do an hour or two in the evenings at the Southern General and Fircroft when it opens. We can arrange payment for transport home afterwards,' she added.

Jessie began to feel sorry for her.

'You'd be aiding injured men – men who have given their bodies in sacrifice for us at home. One day this war will end —

and it could be tomorrow for all we know – and here's a chance to serve right here and now.' Jessie noticed a faraway look in the woman's eye.

'Our brothers, our men here at Cadbury, are risking their lives at the Front and doing their bit. Here is an opportunity, yes, an opportunity, to respond to this call and do your bit too. Think of the future.' Miss Lime stepped up onto a little box. 'There will come a time when we women will have our hard work recognised, when we shall claim a right to a voice in the legislation of the country.'

Mary nudged Helen, 'That's the vote, in case you were wondering. Would you credit it, our Miss Lime's turned into one of them suffragettes. She'll be marching in the street before you know it.'

'I don't mind,' Helen said, suddenly. 'I'd like to do it.'

'That's the spirit, my girl. The directors may allow you to volunteer in lieu of evening classes. It could be an excellent opportunity to learn some new practical skills.'

'But Miss Lime,' Mary said. Miss Lime clucked with irritation.

'She's a bit young, ain't she? These men have been through all sorts. It's not like sticking a bandage on your little brother's knee when he's scraped it climbing trees. These are real injuries.'

'You seem very knowledgeable about all of this. It's astonishing that you have such a considered opinion when you've not even seen the men yet.'

'I'm just saying. It's going to be difficult work. I know the sort of thing they'll want us to do. Washing men's privates and all.'

'Mary Morris! Get out and wait in the corridor. I'll deal with you later.'

Mary sloped off, just muttering audibly, 'It ain't right with all those men.'

Miss Lime turned her back and went to go out of the room, but she paused with the door half open.

'Ladies, I have to say I'm disappointed. Miss Gabriel in the Entertainments Committee has girls clamouring to join her group. If she comes round here again, do not, I repeat, do not answer the call to join that committee.'

Jessie smiled, and thought, *That's told us.*

'And casting your eyes up to heaven won't do you any good, either,' Leonora said to Mary. 'If you continue to undermine my efforts I shall have your record card marked for insubordination.' The girl went back to her machine, quietly for once.

Leonora pulled the lever down and sliced through the sheet of paper printed with King George and Queen Mary pictures. What a disappointment that the response to her request had been so lukewarm, she thought, especially when she'd all but promised the doctor she had a supply of girls only too willing to assist at the hospitals. Her speech just then had been rather effective, as well, gleaned from an address she'd heard at one of Mr Edward's lectures.

Mary's reaction had been surprising and it had challenged her thinking. She would never have credited Mary, of all girls, with such a sense of delicacy. Was she right? Surely the girls wouldn't be expected to do the task that Mary described? No, she reassured herself. Dr Russell-Morgan had said it would be a matter of practical tasks like feeding the men and helping them write letters. *No harm in that.* Reassuring herself, she resolved to go across to Fircroft herself before it opened and find out exactly what training would be required. No, wait, she decided. Better to send Jessie Paignton over in a week or so. Once she'd seen the work in action she might change her mind about volunteering and she, in turn, might influence the others. Leonora was reminded of one of her mother's sayings: *slow and steady wins the race.*

CHAPTER 8

A rush of orders before the July break gave Jessie her excuse not to go to Fircroft on Miss Lime's behalf.

'I suppose we can leave it until after the holiday,' Miss Lime had said with ill grace.

When the middle of July came Jessie reflected that it was a whole year since the Tressler fire and Bill's injury. Thinking about that terrible day made her heart clench with fright so instead she looked forward to two whole weeks at home. Because she'd worked for almost a year at Cadbury, her leave was paid.

In previous summers Jessie and Bill had been on works' outings courtesy of Mr Tressler – trips by train to Dorset or Devon. This year Jessie was happy to relax at home. Bill could manage a daytime venture to one of the nearby parks if he used his walking sticks. On the first Tuesday of the break Mrs Tops suggested a picnic with her and her two boys, aged four and seven.

At Kings Heath Park they found a patch of grass to sit on. Jessie lay back on her elbows and tilted her face to catch the sun's warmth.

'I could get used to doing nothing,' she said, smiling.

Bill looked at her uncertainly.

'Oh, I didn't mean that–' she said; she forced the smile to linger on her face.

'Yes, she did,' Mrs Tops said. 'Time you got back to work, Bill – before you lose the habit.'

Bill had rolled up his trouser legs. Jessie stared at the puckered flesh around his right knee and shin dispassionately. But the older of the two boys asked what had happened to his leg. 'It looks like an old parsnip! Did you get it fighting the Germans, like my daddy?'

'Don't be rude, Michael,' Mrs Tops said.

Bill laughed. 'You're right, Michael, it does look a bit like a parsnip,' he said. 'All pale and knobbly and twisted, like it's just been pulled up from the ground. Although my leg's a bit cleaner, I hope.' The younger boy thought this was hilarious and his laughter was infectious.

To begin with, Jessie had itched to do things – 'the house needs an all-over clean for a start' – but by the Friday of the first week she was sufficiently wound down to say, 'I might as well relax and put down the grindstone, as Mrs Tops would say.' Bill replied, 'Been complaining about me to the neighbours, eh?' but she could tell from his tone he was joking. She relished the evenings they spent in their armchairs, Bill reading some of the books Hugh had lent him, she half-heartedly catching up with sewing repairs. Occasionally, they looked up from their tasks at the same time and the flirtatious look or a cheeky grin they shared was imbued with desire that would have to wait until bedtime to be satisfied. The remainder of the holiday passed quickly.

On her first day back Jessie noticed the difference in the atmosphere. The Works was a giant waking from two weeks of slumber, still yawning and rubbing its eyes, unfurling and stretching its limbs. August was blazing hot and, during break-times, the girls spent as much time outdoors as possible. The flowered pergola in the girls' recreation ground shed rose petals as they walked through it; the grass had scorched patches. Even Miss Lime consented to come out with them; she sheltered under the yew tree, standing as stiff and unyielding as its trunk, while she gazed at the girls sprawled out on the grass.

'You wait,' Mary said to Jessie. 'She still wants you for a hospital volunteer. She's biding her time. I know that look.'

The countdown to October and Fircroft hospital's opening loomed in Leonora's mind. *Why ever did I make that promise to Dr Russell-Morgan?* she asked herself. Only Helen Daw had started her first aid classes at the Stirchley Institute. The shine around the doctor was somewhat tarnished since she had discovered King George and Queen Mary had made a secret visit to see the wounded soldiers at the Southern General in July. *And you never thought to tell me!* she had wanted to say to him. She kept silent, speaking only to promise him the girls could make extra bandages from old bed sheets.

As the time passed so the misery and anxiety increased. A pall appeared to have settled over the card-cutting section in Q block, driving Leonora to exasperation.

'Come *on*, Evelyn. Pull your socks up. We'll never make this week's quota with you drooping over your machine.'

Mary said, 'Her fiancé's missing at sea. His mother had a telegram yesterday.' She put her arm around the girl's shoulder.

Evelyn looked up and wailed, 'He could be anywhere. In a hospital or... or dead.'

'Or a prisoner of the Germans,' Leonora ventured.

'Have you no feeling?' Mary said. 'How many more before this bloody war ends?'

Leonora decided to overlook Mary's language in this instance. 'I suppose I'm sorry to have rebuked you, Evelyn, in that case,' she said. 'All this gloom makes me glad I never married. Now let's get back to work.'

At break she said, 'I need a few volunteers for the Comforts room. A little project that won't take up too much of your time.'

She had sent Helen Daw there a few minutes earlier, and when Leonora and the girls arrived, Helen was already tearing bed sheets into strips and rolling them up. Then Leonora's attention was caught by Helen pocketing one of the rolled-up bandages.

'Empty your pocket this instant!'

Helen screamed and ran from the room, knocking over a trolley with a stack of small chocolate tins. All the girls stared after her.

'I'll go,' Mary said.

Leonora heard Mrs Paignton say, 'No, it's all right. I'm ahead with my work. I'll go and find her.'

These girls will be the death of me, she thought. What on earth was Helen doing pocketing the bandages? She hoped Mrs Paignton would find out if they had a thief in their midst.

As Jessie went down the corridor in search of Helen, she reflected on how little she knew of Helen's world. She'd let herself get caught up in Mary's dramas but realised with a pang of guilt how little attention she had paid to Helen. The girl was so easy to forget though; always disappearing into the background.

A faint sound of sobbing made her stop. She pressed her ear to the door of the girls' rest room and listened. There it was again. Jessie opened the door; Helen was seated on the floor beneath the washbasins, her head on her knees as she wept.

'Oh my love, whatever is the matter?' Jessie said, crouching down to the girl.

Helen looked up and revealed puffed-up eyes and blotches on her cheeks; a line of mucus trailed from her turned-up nose to her top lip. Her face was a picture of utter misery.

'Why don't you tell me what's wrong? Is it something at home?'

Helen gave a slow shake of her head, sniffed and swiped the heel of her hand across her nose to clean it. Jessie tried not to recoil.

'Something here at work then? It's not Miss Lime getting you down, is it? I know she can be an old cow but don't let her bother you.' Still silence. Jessie sat down next to the girl and put her arm around her shoulder. 'Is it the ambulance course you signed up for? You're getting on ever so well, I bet. You're not one of those who faints at the sight of blood...'

Helen stared straight ahead. She was a most frustrating child.

'You can't help me so stop asking!' Helen pushed her away and scrambled to her feet.

'Wait!' Jessie called. She put her hand to her tender bosom. She'd have to be patient and try again later when Helen's rage or troubles had subsided.

Then she noticed it – the metallic scent of blood emanating from beneath Helen's overall. Understanding dawned.

'Wait! It's all right,' she said and caught up with the girl.

Jessie put her arms around her and hugged her tight, close to tears herself, as she explained what was happening to Helen.

'I thought I was dying. Are you sure I'm not going to die?' She clutched at Jessie's arm, her eyes wide.

Jessie gently pulled her arm away. 'You're not dying, I promise. It just means you're growing up. Some women call it the curse, but it's normal and natural and nothing to worry about. We'll go to the library and get you some supplies–'

'I didn't mean to steal the bandages. I just wanted to stop the blood–'

'I know, you did the sensible thing. We can explain.'

'But then everyone will know.'

'So what? Every girl has it once a month. Only for a few days. You, me, even Miss Lime.'

Helen looked incredulous. 'But I don't like it.'

'I know, but you'll get used to it.'

A lump had come to Jessie's throat. Pity for Helen competed with anger at the girl's mother for not preparing her. If Helen had been her daughter, she'd have told her everything she ever needed to know. Why do people have children, she wondered, if they neglect them in every way?

Break-time was now over and when she took Helen back to Q block, Miss Lime was waiting for an explanation. Jessie told her the problem briefly and Miss Lime nodded.

'I think an apology is due,' she said to Helen. Jessie frowned and shook her head. 'Well, off you go, child.' She turned to Jessie. 'Thank you, Mrs Paignton. You've been of great assistance.' Jessie remembered what Mary had said about Miss Lime buttering her up.

Her mother begged her not to go to Birmingham centre. It was too late, too dark, it was dangerous, a bomb could drop on her – anything could happen.

Mary hugged her mother as tight as she could, and smelled lavender and weariness. No amount of pleading from her would change Mary's mind. 'Don't worry, Mum,' she said, 'and don't wait up.' She looked directly into her mother's eyes and saw the tear-lines rimmed with pink. Mary's heart contracted. The fear would always be there; etched on her insides like the livid scar on her arm. The scar may have faded but the fear of retribution would mark her expression always.

'Do your coat up,' her mother instructed, and then she put a parcel in her bag. 'Some food to keep your energy up.'

'Mum, I don't need it. There's plenty of sandwiches there.' The clock chimed ten.

'Better leave now. The train's due just before midnight and I said I'd get there early.'

'But how are you getting back tonight?'

'Don't worry, I'll get a lift.' The less she told her mother the better. Her mother managed a smile at least.

Mary shut the back door and went down the alley into the street. Ma Parry's dog came up and sniffed her bag. She bent down to stroke the animal and felt its ribs under the long scraggy coat.

'You don't miss a trick, do you, feller?' She pulled out the packet and unwrapped the sandwiches. 'Ham. It's a criminal waste, this is, so I hope you're grateful, you bloody dog.' It wolfed down the food, then sat obediently, looking at her as if to say, *Is that it?*

'Now bugger off, you pesky mutt,' she said, with a grin on her face. If only people were like dogs, she thought. So gentle and loyal. There'd be no horrible war that's for sure. She didn't even understand why England was fighting. Something to do with the Kaiser bloke and who the hell was he anyway?

The tram swung into the Birmingham centre terminus on Navigation Street. As Mary jumped off, the female clippie shouted after her, 'Mind how you go, chicken!' Under the new War Regs the streetlamps had to be dimmed. Part of the fun of coming into town at night was to see all the bright lights; now the road ahead was black, sinister, as if an ogre waited, unseen, ready to snuff out the smallest chink of light.

She turned left into Temple Street and marched up the hill, her footsteps clattering more loudly in the darkness, her heart thumping from the exertion. Then the cathedral's outline was in sight, the slope evened out and she took the turning into Colmore Row. The sudden evidence of life – people laughing, chattering, a whiff of cigar, a horse clipping past – made light of her earlier fears. She smiled to herself and headed for Snow Hill station.

A bunch of money men sat around a table on the pavement in front of the Grand Hotel. Mary held her head high and straightened her step, suddenly conscious of her worn-down boot heels. One of the men stood up and lumbered towards her.

'I say, old thing, are you looking for trade?' He swayed and peered at her closely, saying, with whiskey breath, 'You're a pretty one, aren't you? Let's go upstairs and find you a nice dress to wear.'

Mary's nails bit into her palms. She pulled her coat tighter and looked him square in the face. She wasn't going to miss the train coming – not for this idiot. Her father's watchword echoed inside her head: *There's only one way to deal with bullies, d'you hear me? Hit once, and hit hard.*

She reached and grabbed the man's ear, yanking his head down so it was level with hers.

'How-about-you-get-lost?' With a shove she sent him sprawling to the ground. His friends made catcalls and jeering whistles as she hurried away.

Hit once. Hit hard. If only Daniel had been able to do that.

She went through the station entrance, past the ticket booths. A dozen or so motor cars sat on the wide concourse, each with a red cross painted on its side.

Down on the platform two men wearing the navy blue tunics of the St John Ambulance struggled to carry an urn with a spout. A group of ladies in white aprons stood in a tight circle, next to a low pull cart serving as a makeshift table, laden with plates of sandwiches and cakes in tins. Jugs, sugar bowls, a huge metal teapot and rows of gleaming white mugs lined up waiting to be filled. As Mary moved closer she caught the sharp scent of oranges. Bananas, too. Her mouth watered and her stomach made an almighty growl. She cleared her throat to cover the sound.

A young woman turned, broke away from the huddle and approached her, evidently relieved.

'Ah, reinforcements! Good-o!' She pointed down the platform. 'See that sign for the cloakroom? Get changed and wash your hands.'

Mary hesitated. 'I haven't got my uniform. I, um, spilt something down it before I came out.'

'Never mind. There's a spare apron somewhere. Put it on

over your coat. It's chilly tonight and we don't want you keeling over with the cold.'

'Okey-dokey.'

On her return from the cloakroom Mary asked, 'What's in the sandwiches then?'

'Only jam. Listen, fancy going on cake-cutting duty?' She held a knife out to Mary, handle first, the blade wrapped in a cloth.

'I'm Amy, by the way.' Before Mary could introduce herself, she'd gone.

The other women ignored her as she cut a fruit loaf into pieces, except for a stout woman with a face like a bulldog, who spoke only to mutter, 'I'd cut those in half again. We don't want to run out.'

A good-looking man in khaki uniform, who'd been pacing up and down the platform, came up to the food table. He wore a red cross armband.

'Ten minutes until the train gets in. The most urgent cases will leave for hospital immediately. If you can keep the not-so-badly injured ones entertained until we get round to them...' Mary nodded, offering him some cake.

Mrs Bulldog reached across and slapped her hand.

'Not yet.' Her brow wrinkled as she glared at Mary. 'What branch did you say you were from?'

Mary crossed her fingers behind her back.

'The Bournville Ambulance Division.'

The man had walked over to join a group of similarly dressed men, all talking earnestly. Mary nodded in their direction.

'Who are they?'

'Them? The FAUs. Friends Ambulance Unit. They're doing all the driving tonight.' Mrs Bulldog lowered her voice. 'They're Quakers, most of them. Can't see the point in it myself,' she said, her lips pinching together. 'It's all very well them not fighting. But some of us have to be willing to make the sacrifice.' Her sagging cheeks drooped even further. 'Still, it makes them feel useful, I expect.'

Mary felt the knife jab that happened every time she heard the word sacrifice. Supposing Daniel didn't come back. She'd never be able to tell him she loved him, that she was sorry.

The ambulance train pulled in and everyone present scattered themselves along the platform ready to open the train doors. The soldiers spilled out onto the platform; arms in slings, heads bandaged, shattered legs needing crutches. Those men who could walk came over to the food station. Others were stretchered up onto the concourse for the Southern General, their bearers yelling instructions.

'Be careful, man, or he'll start bleeding again.'

Five days' worth of grime filled the lines etched into the men's faces. The platform was filling up and Mary dispensed tea and sandwiches before sending them to the waiting room. A man leaned against the railings staring into space. A chunk of flesh was missing from his right cheek.

'Are you hungry?'

He shook his head but accepted a mug of tea from her tray. 'Got a drop of rum in that? No? What's your name, love?'

'Mary.'

She got back to her table to find a queue of men. Amy, the young woman from earlier, dashed in and out, calling names and assigning the soldiers to the various ambulances.

By the time Mary glanced at the station clock it was 2 a.m. The FAU officer came past and nodded. 'Good work, everyone. Let's keep it up and see if we can get these last few dispatched by three.'

Mary went into the waiting room. She sensed the mood of restlessness immediately. An argument had broken out between the cheek man and his soldier friend about who should go in the next ambulance.

'Mary!' he called. 'I've got a song just for you. *That's the wrong way to tickle Mary. That's the wrong way to kiss. Don't you know that over here, lad, they like it best like this.'*

He and his friend pretended to embrace. The other servicemen started banging on the tables and joining in. *'Hooray pour Les Français, farewell Angleterre. We didn't know how to tickle Mary, but we learnt how over there.'*

Mary weaved her way through the sea of khaki to the back of the waiting room, found a crate, stood on it. She had no idea what to do until she remembered a song she'd learned years ago for a city council school competition that had won first prize.

When the men's singing petered out she said, 'You can't beat a singsong, can you? Do you know this one?' She began to sing, *Softly falls the shades of evening.*

When Mary sang she was aware of the stillness of the room; the steamed-up windows, the glow of the candles, and the warmth from the heater bringing pinkness back to the cheeks of the men. They all listened and as she reached the last line, she beckoned them to join in from the beginning. At first they sang raggedly, tunelessly, but then with greater confidence – as if her own voice had infused them with strength and vitality. The sound of a harmonica made heads turn to the middle of the room; it was the cheek man. The soldiers looked back to her.

In the doorway the FAU officer and Amy stood close together, arms touching, smiling at each other as they, too, mouthed the words. The song ended and there came a burst of clapping and cheering. Mary felt light of heart, not from the applause but, as she closed her eyes briefly, because Daniel hadn't been on the train, thank goodness.

CHAPTER 9

Miss Lime sought out Jessie during her lunch-break and asked her to deliver a letter for Dr Russell-Morgan who was at the Fircroft building on Mondays. 'If you don't catch him now,' she said, 'another week will have passed.' Miss Lime had also given her a large box with bundles of St John's Gospel pocket books to give out to the patients.

Jessie left the other girls in the Comforts Room and went out into Bournville Lane. Miss Lime had insisted on sketching her a map, which she balanced on top of the box as she walked. She had to go right at Linden Road, down to the village green, and take the turning into Woodbrooke Road, opposite the Friends Meeting house. The cacophony produced by the infant school children was drowned by the carillon bells.

She hurried down the road and into Oak Tree Lane and saw the grounds of Fircroft on her right. On the wide lawn she counted six or seven men in blue peaked caps dozing on chairs underneath waterproofs that went up to the neck. But it was the nurses that caught her attention the most. They patrolled the lawn in dark dresses with a white pinafore over the top and a cap to hold their hair in place. Jessie's hand automatically went to the bun at the back of her neck.

From nowhere a man jumped out at her. She screamed in shock. The box she carried tumbled to the ground, scattering the gospel pocket books into a puddle. The man wore a blue button-down jacket and a bandage covered one eye. The long branch in his hand pointed weapon-like at her. Her heart hammered.

'Who goes there? Are you a friend of Fritz?'

Not understanding what on earth he meant, she stammered, 'I'm looking for the entrance. I want to see the doctor.'

'Come on then, comrade, let me help you.' He pulled her arm over his shoulder and scooped her up in his arms, marching forward.

She felt silly and a little scared but aware she was not really in danger from this strange man. She became aware of the nurses running towards her, looking alarmed.

'Corporal Watkiss, put down that lady now.' The bellowing voice of one of the nurses did the trick. The man started, as if he'd just woken up from a trance and then all but dropped her onto the stone path. As she scrambled to her feet she was aware of her racing heartbeat.

'I'm very sorry about our corporal. He has a habit of bringing things back to us. Usually it's rabbits but he did find a dead sheep the other day, would you believe?'

Jessie was clearly supposed to smile at the nurse's wry tone. She brushed down her skirt to try to reclaim some dignity.

'And you are?'

'Mrs Paignton. I've come to see the doctor.'

When they were out of the corporal's earshot the nurse began to explain. She walked at such a brisk pace down the corridor that Jessie had to skip to keep up.

'It's the effects of the war. It takes them days or even weeks to adjust. They still think they're out there, poor things, still under bombardment. Can't seem to grasp they're safely back home now.'

A sharp smell of antiseptic came into Jessie's nostrils and then was gone. One door was ajar and Jessie peeped in as they swept past. In the split second she registered a man in a wheelchair, handsome in full uniform, except his legs were missing and the legs of his trousers had been cut short and the excess pinned with a safety pin. The picture was imprinted on her mind.

The nurse came to an abrupt halt outside a door of polished wood and a shiny brass knob. In front of the nameplate was a pinned scrap of paper, with the typed letters, Dr Russell-Morgan. The nurse rapped sharply and a gruff voice said, 'Enter!'

The room smelled of pipe smoke and instantly Jessie was comforted. The man sat behind a large desk that appeared too grand for his slight build.

'Doctor, Mrs Paignton to see you. I'm afraid the final part of her journey was assisted by Corporal Watkiss.'

He put his hand across his mouth as if trying to hide his amusement. 'Awfully sorry about that, Mrs Paignton. He's–'

'I've already explained.' The nurse turned and left.

He gave Jessie a conspiratorial look and invited her to sit down.

'Do you know, the nurses here in Birmingham are really quite terrifying. I find it best just to do as I'm told.'

Jessie warmed to him. She tried to decided how old he was. Older then Bill certainly but not more. Thirty-five or forty perhaps, judging by the deep grooves in his face. He wore a tweed jacket and trousers but she spotted a white overcoat on a stand near the bay window.

She tried to glance outside and when he followed her gaze she turned away and her eyes fell on a watercolour painting of two girls in a wood, aged perhaps seven and nine, one with brown hair and the other a rich strawberry blonde, but similar enough in features to be sisters. The younger child knelt in front of the seated elder girl, tying a bow or a necklace for her. She peered more closely at the tender scene. A wave of sadness overwhelmed her.

'It's a charming picture, don't you think? A local artist, I believe.'

Had her babies survived... They could be my babies, she thought, growing up into beautiful young girls. Hope had flowered and then died, ending in a flow of blood that seemed unstoppable at the time.

You will not cry, don't you *dare* cry, she said to herself. If only he's not kind. Other people's tactlessness, like Rose Entwistle's, she could cope with. Even cruel jibes were fine. But please, she silently begged, please don't be kind.

'It's fine to cry, Mrs Paignton. Sometimes it's better for the mind just to let it out. No-one will hear you in here.'

With the soft tone of his words, the kindness and care imbued in them, she realised that the chord tying her emotions together was fraying. She sensed a snap and then the tears came. At first she struggled against it, not wanting to let herself down in front of this man, but the feeling was impossible to resist. Oh, the luxury of letting go – there was pain but also a queer pleasure as she released all the grief in her body.

After a while, the sobs began to ease and, though her head was still pounding and her cheeks were wet, she felt her equilibrium being restored. She was aware of him standing at her side, a steadying hand on her shoulder, holding out a white triangle of cloth.

'Here, use this,' he said, returning to his chair.

She opened out the handkerchief and held the starched cotton to her face, catching a cologne of some sort, and she blotted the tears away, whilst taking deep breaths in and exhaling loudly. The doctor asked if she was all right. She spoke, gulping for air.

'I'm sorry, I'm so sorry,' she repeated. 'I don't know what...'

'How many?'

'I'm sorry?'

'How many children have you lost?'

'But how did you know?'

'I'm a doctor. I'm sorry. That sounds glib. But you do get to learn something of human emotion and grief in particular.'

'I don't know why I should... after all this time.'

'You had a bad fright earlier. It's probably a delayed reaction. I hope you feel better now. I'm going to leave you in here for a short time while I look in on a patient. Check everything's all right without me. See that door there? There's a room next door with all you need.'

She nodded and closed her eyes, unable to speak yet, but she enjoyed the hand on her shoulder again that seemed to say it's all right. She knew later she would be horribly embarrassed and downright furious with herself for making such a show. Steeling herself, she finally opened her eyes; the doctor had gone and she was alone.

The doorway of the adjoining room was on the same wall as the painting. She tried the handle and the door opened easily. The room was about half the width of the doctor's office, with no window. It was an examination room; a long couch dominated the space and a cabinet with metal instruments. To the side of the couch was an armchair and a wash basin with two taps. Hot as well as cold. She pushed the plug in and turned the hot tap. The water flowed easily and she inhaled the steam to clear her head, before splashing her face. A towel was nearby and she pressed the rough cloth to her face, the tears threatening to come again. Then she plunged her hands into the basin and used the bar of carbolic to soap between her fingers. She dried between each carefully, relishing the roughness of the towel. The simple mechanical routine, combined with the calm atmosphere of the room, told her this could be a place of healing.

When she went through the door, Dr Russell-Morgan was standing looking out of the window. He turned to her with a look of enquiry that said, *Better now?* She nodded.

'Now you had a message from Miss Lime at the Works, I believe. Something to do with you ladies volunteering.'

Jessie said, 'There was a letter to give you. Somewhere.' She searched her coat pockets frantically. Please let it not have fallen out on the walk here or when that mad soldier flung me around. Thank goodness.

'Here it is.' The envelope was a bit crumpled but he took the letter without comment.

'Do sit down a moment.'

She placed herself back down in the chair with a tapestry cushion. She was calmer now and noticing other things apart from the painting that had upset her. On his desk were a couple of trophies: he was a swimmer by the looks of things. She hadn't noticed before but his hair was slightly damp and there was a whiff of chlorine. She wondered if he had used the Stirchley Baths.

She said, 'Has Miss Lime told you we have a little programme providing comforts for the men? We send them parcels of chocolate or things we've knitted, little letters, and so on.'

'I didn't know the details but it sounds excellent for morale. Sometimes possessions are all that they have to cling to.'

'We've started to get letters back. Things are blanked out, especially–'

'–anything that indicates their location or that speaks against the war, yes. It's one of the great frustrations,' he said. 'Are you writing back to the men? I imagine that corresponding with them would keep their spirits up.'

'Well, not me personally, but some of the girls do.' Jessie could picture the noticeboard in the Comforts room as she spoke and remembered with a pang of guilt that she had never written back to Private Thomas Walker.

'Are you all right finding your way out or shall I get the nurse to accompany you? Give my regards to Miss Lime, won't you?' he said, with a hint of a smile. 'She promised to knit me a scarf, you know. Tell her I'm still waiting for it.'

Jessie walked down the corridor. By now it was two o'clock. If she hurried she'd be back to work for two fifteen. Her eyes were a little puffy but she felt lighter of heart as a result of speaking to the doctor.

There was no sign of the mad soldier out on the lawn. An outdoor exercise programme was going on. A male instructor in a leotard was showing the injured men how to flex and straighten their arms, similar to the gym classes the other girls did occasionally. Some of the men wobbled precariously on crutches; others stayed seated in chairs. She thought how grateful she was that Bill was finally getting better.

She found the box with its contents scattered and blown by the wind. She crouched to pick up the gospel pamphlets; one or two could be salvaged but most were ruined.

She met Miss Lime as she went through the door of Q block.

'You were away for ages. I hope you weren't shirking. You did speak to the doctor, didn't you, and not just leave my note?'

'Yes,' Jessie said, putting on the tone of a schoolgirl. 'I delivered the message in person, just as you asked. I had a bit of an accident with these though.' She pointed to the box. 'I'll take some more over.'

Miss Lime tutted. 'Well? What did he say?'

'Oh, just that he was... grateful for your help and he said what an excellent person you were.' It wouldn't do any harm to put Miss Lime in a good mood.

'Oh,' she said, standing a little taller. 'Thank you Mrs Paignton. You see very occasionally the good Lord sees to it that our talents are recognised.'

'And by the way,' Jessie couldn't resist adding, 'he said he's still waiting for the scarf you were going to knit him.'

When Miss Lime left the room, Mary punched her in the arm.

'Mrs P!' she exclaimed, 'that was marvellous. I'd never have expected it of you.'

'What?' said Jessie, innocently.

'Bursting Miss Lime's balloon like that and so sweetly

done. I knew she'd got a crush on that doctor! It's written all over her face. What's he like? Is he a looker? Poor cow doesn't stand a chance if he is. If he's an ugly bugger they can make little monster babies together.'

Jessie flinched. Mary was entertaining but her humour was too cutting, verging on the cruel, at times.

'Don't be mean. Let me think what he looked like.'

'I want a full description from the top of his head to the bottom of his size elevens...'

'Belt up, Mary,' Ruth said, joining in.

'Well, he's not tall, but not short either. About Miss Lime's height.'

'Hmm, that could work. She likes symmetry.'

'A nice friendly face, blue eyes, I think. He smells nice, y'know, clean and refined.'

'She's a stickler for hygiene,' Evelyn said wearily, trying to join in. Helen was watching from the background, her eyes wide.

'Carry on, Jessie,' Mary said. 'I'm trying to build up a picture. See if there's any chance he'll wed Limey and take her off our hands.'

'He's intelligent and kind, well, he has to be, being a doctor–'

'Limey's always swotting up on culture and stuff. All those lectures she goes to.'

'There were some swimming trophies on his desk–' She felt a nudge in her back and turned round to see Miss Lime standing there.

'Since Doctor Russell-Morgan is such a fascinating topic of conversation for you, you may wish to know that he competed in the Paris Olympics. Underwater swimming is a specialism of his. Now I can't understand why we're gossiping like fishwives when there's this consignment to finish, plus the knitted donations that have come in this week, which I'd like sorted out and parcelled up ready to go in the post this evening.'

'Yes, Miss Lime.'

Jessie and Mary worked together. Helen sat quietly, not joining in the occasional fits of laughter between the pair of them. What a day it had been. She had never known this much excitement when she was at home all day. At the thought of heading home she felt like she needed a hug from her husband.

Jessie pushed open the front door and shouted, 'I'm back, Bill.'

His voice replied from the back of the house, 'We're in here, Jessie.' Who would be visiting at this time of night, Jessie wondered. Perhaps it was Hugh; he hadn't been round for a while.

Jessie made her way into the kitchen. Bill was seated at their little table, Mrs Tops standing behind him with scissors in her hand.

'Oh, it's only you,' Jessie said. 'I thought we had a visitor.'

'Thanks a bunch. What do you think of this?'

Spread out on newspaper was a pile of Bill's hair, red brown coils. She'd practically shorn him. Mrs Tops took the towel from his shoulders and gave it a shake, then bent down to admire her handiwork.

'What do you reckon? Will I get the job again?'

Jessie looked at the table. Two tea-cups, two cake plates with crumbs. Suddenly she felt like she was the visitor.

'You're spoiling him, Mrs Tops.'

'You don't mind me coming, do you? I've not heard from Frank for a few weeks and I'm starting to bother.'

Later in bed Bill turned to her. 'What Florrie said earlier wasn't true.'

'What? Who's Florrie?' She was distracted by his haircut. It was like a different man lying next to her.

'Florrie next door.' He saw her look of incomprehension. 'Mrs Tops. Keep up, Jessie!'

'Oh!' Jessie always called her Mrs Tops. She asked herself

if she'd ever known her neighbour's first name. 'What did she say that wasn't true?'

'About Frank. She had a letter from him today. He's in hospital – she doesn't know where.'

Fleetingly, Jessie thought of poor Evelyn out of her mind with worry; at least Florrie Tops knew her husband was safe.

'He's got nervous trouble,' Bill continued.

'Nervous trouble?'

'Nervous debility, I think they call it. Florrie showed me the letter.'

Jessie pushed away the questions in her mind and said, 'What did the letter say?'

'How he never knew what it was like to be completely fit on the outside and feel perfectly bloody on the inside.'

'Poor Frank,' Jessie said. She remembered how she and Bill used to laugh at him and his pompous manner.

'Poor Florrie, too,' Bill said.

Jessie felt the slightest chill, the source of which she couldn't locate. She leaned towards him, saying, 'Night Bill.'

'You haven't asked me. Why Florrie cut my hair.' He ran his hand over his scalp.

'Why?'

'She's taking me to the BSA factory tomorrow. In Small Heath. Her cousin might be able to get me in there.'

'What, a job?'

'No, a holiday.' He sounded exasperated with her. 'Of course I mean a job!'

CHAPTER 10

Leonora popped home after her Saturday half-day shift and then set out for the village green. It had been a week of bad news at work, like an unstoppable tide: Private Copeland killed by a falling shell; Evelyn's fiancé still missing, presumed drowned, his torpedo boat apparently sunk by gunfire. The girls had wandered around with pale, pinched faces, muttering words of disbelief. Yet on Wednesday that anguished scene was swept away by Eliza Barratt approaching her at her bench, whispering, *Your efforts haven't gone unnoticed by the management, Leonora.*

Miss Barratt's words had given her the sign: it was time to get prepared.

She had the rest house in her sights now; a small octagonal building that the Bournville workers had commissioned to celebrate the wedding anniversary of Mr George and his wife Elizabeth. Leonora found a nearby bench and, feeling puffed, sat down for a few moments. Every Saturday, before church the following day, she carried out a little reckoning of the week's events and occasionally looked at things on a larger scale. She was ruminating on her new recruits. Jessie Paignton had proved to be a level-headed sort and for that she was thankful. Never late for work and no days off sick, and acting like a mother to Helen over that silly business brought on by the girl's pubescence. She hadn't yet seen fit to volunteer at Fircroft but she was working on that. The greater disappointment was Leonora's hope that they might become

94

friends. She had pictured Mrs Paignton coming round to her house for Sunday afternoon tea and, from that, building into a camaraderie at work. But it had not transpired. Mary Morris had brought the woman into her own orbit and that was that.

She stood up and headed for the row of shops where Underwood's, the drapery and haberdashery, was located. She glanced round to make sure no-one she knew was watching. The bell clanged loudly as she entered and Mr Underwood, perched on a stool sorting some buttons on the counter-top, looked up and said, 'Good afternoon.'

Reluctant to reveal her true purpose for coming in, she began with, 'Hello. I've run out of some embroidery silks.' She allowed him to show her the selection he had in stock. Pretending to spot one of the bales of fabric behind him, she said, 'Oh, that green cotton is rather nice. Might I have a look?'

Just as he was pulling the bale out Leonora heard the bell behind her as the door opened. She turned. Blast. It was Miss Fox from the library. The nosiest parker of them all.

'It's all right. I've changed my mind. I don't want it. Let me see those buttons you've got.' He suppressed his look of annoyance and, with a weary air, put the bale back.

'How do you do, Miss Fox?'

'Good afternoon, Miss Lime,' said Miss Fox with unusual enthusiasm, almost glee. 'And how are you?'

Leonora inclined her head. 'Very well, thank you.'

'This war is taking its toll. Quite dreadful. But some of your girls at the Works are making quite a contribution.'

Leonora smiled, attempting modesty. It was always gratifying to receive recognition for one's services.

'They have shown themselves equal to the task,' she replied. 'We must all pull together and do our bit in these troubled times.'

'Do our bit? You can say that again.' Miss Fox tilted her head, and Leonora heard the chuckle in her voice. Miss Fox told her precisely what she'd heard from her St John

Ambulance friend, about a girl purporting to be from the
Bournville Ambulance Division that had sung songs for the
soldiers like a performer in a club; the description given, of 'a
dark-haired pretty piece who went down a treat with the men',
fitted that of Mary Morris exactly.

Leonora's heartbeat quickened; her mind leapt. She would
take action first thing on Monday morning.

Jessie overheard the dressing down. All the girls did. They sat
at their machines trying not to listen but it was impossible.

'At Snow Hill station!' Miss Lime said in a hissing voice.
'In the middle of the night! Singing! Like some common street
woman!'

'Yes,' Mary said, standing up from her bench. 'I don't know
who your spies are, but it was all very proper, believe me. I
met the night train. Made sandwiches and tea for the men.
They were in a right state – travelling for days – in pain as
well. They needed cheering up something rotten, so I sang a
couple of songs while they waited. It was no different from
Miss Gabriel's musical concert.'

'It most certainly is different! You may not care about your
own standing but have you no thought for the reputation of
the company you work for?'

Mary said, with steel in her voice, 'You can rule me here,
but what I do in my spare time is my affair.'

Jessie grabbed Mary afterwards and asked her outright.

'What were you really doing at Snow Hill?'

Mary sighed heavily. 'I told you, I was making refreshments
for the soldiers off the ambulance train.'

'But you hate the sight of blood! Who said she wasn't
volunteering for any first aid?'

'Okay, if you want the truth, I was there to sing.'

'Sing?'

'You remember Limey wouldn't let me go in the summer

show? Well, I heard they needed a singer for the men while they waited for the ambulance to take them to the hospitals.'

Jessie didn't believe her – her tone was too flat and unconvincing. Still, she thought, as she returned to her work, she had enough concerns of her own to think about.

Yesterday Bill had passed the medical for working at the BSA munitions factory in Small Heath. The doctor had declared his lungs clear and his limp 'no impediment' to a job in the shell-making department. They had offered him just under full-time hours.

Jessie had seen in Bill's eyes the boost the news had given him. Yet she hadn't been able to stop herself saying, 'But it's in Small Heath. How will you get there?'

'They have these things called buses, Jessie.'

'And what'll you be doing exactly?'

'I've just told you, munitions – making guns and bombs and stuff to blow the Germans to kingdom come.'

At Bill's tone Jessie had felt a finger of unease tap along her spine. 'What about Tressler's?' She had thought of his bag of upholstery tools in the outhouse.

'Huh, Tressler's will have gone to the wall by Christmas! Munitions is the only industry making any profit at the moment. Oh Jessie, I can't tell you how grand it feels to be back in the game. Come here, my girl, and give us a hug.' She had gone into his arms, feeling like a shop mannequin.

'The money's not bad either,' he had said, trying to spin her round but his leg made it awkward. 'Wartime wages aren't quite what we're used to, at least not till I build up to full hours, but it's a darn sight more than you're getting at Cadbury.'

She had pulled away so she could stare into his face. 'Cadbury has kept us out of a hole this past year.'

'Hey, don't be so tetchy. You know I didn't mean anything. What do you say, my girl?' He had looked at her so expectantly, so full of hope, she felt ashamed.

'Bill, that's brilliant news,' she said, and she had hugged him properly so he wouldn't see the look on her face.

'Best of all, you can put your feet up now. You won't be needing that job anymore, will you? You can stay home and look after me. Jessie, I knew we'd get things back to normal in the end. Didn't I tell you?'

Jessie found Mary coming out of the dressing room on her way to the gym class. Miss Lime had decided the girls had been cooped up for too long and she had made it compulsory for the card-making section to do more exercise.

'Mary, I have to talk to you. I don't know what to do. Bill's got another job–'

'That's great news. Isn't it?'

'He wants me to give up working here.'

'What's the problem?' Mary said. 'All this married women working stuff. It won't last anyway.'

'I don't want to leave. I can't leave. Suppose his job doesn't work out and then we'll be struggling to manage.'

'I don't get you. Most women would love to be at home with a husband flogging himself to bring home the bacon.'

'Would you, Mary? Honestly?'

'Well, no, but then I'm–'

'Different? Well, I'm different too.'

'I was going to say, *I'm* never getting married.' She left through the lodge door, leaving Jessie staring after her. Some help she had been.

Later, when Mary came back red-cheeked, she found Jessie.

'I was thinking about you while I was doing my waist twists. I swear that gym instructor is evil. Here's what I'd do. You know they'll be introducing conscription for single men after Christmas? If this blasted war carries on much longer you can bet they'll call on married men and there won't be any choice in the matter. If Bill gets called up then won't you be better off having stayed here where we need you – okay, where *I* need you – than leaving only to come back again?'

Jessie considered the logic of this somewhat convoluted argument and decided it was sound.

'Thanks Mary.'

'I've just told you what you wanted to hear. That's the only reason you asked me and not Miss Lime or that opinionated mother-in-law of yours. I'm not having a go at you Jessie, honestly. It's just that–'

'You think I've got so much to be grateful for. I know.' That night she went home and persuaded Bill she should stay on for a few more weeks. Mercifully, he agreed.

In late October the official opening of Fircroft convalescent hospital was announced in the local *Evening Dispatch*. All the college students had already been relocated to rooms in nearby Holland House. A second hospital in Bournville, at The Beeches, would also be opened to accommodate wounded soldiers.

Helen Daw had by now completed her 12-week first aid course at Stirchley Institute. Jessie, sensing the girl's nervousness, agreed to accompany Helen for her first volunteer session at Fircroft. She tried to engage Helen in conversation on the way to Fircroft, and discovered she was one of six children, but not much else. The girl was almost mute with nerves.

When they arrived Dr Russell-Morgan nodded at Jessie, and then she and Helen lined up with a group of about ten other female volunteers. The doctor explained there was room for up to twenty-four patients.

'Many of these men have been through a trauma you cannot possibly imagine; indeed, it would be futile even to try.' He closed his eyes briefly and Jessie wondered what images were flashing through his mind. He'd served in the Boer War, it was rumoured, so perhaps he drew on personal experience.

'They need the gentlest of care, given with a warm yet practical attitude. Try not to show any emotion or make a comment, even if you are distressed by what you see. Ask yourself, are you ready for the challenge?'

Jessie felt a movement behind her. A girl had picked up her bag and was slipping out, her head down, blushing scarlet.

'There's no shame in not being up to the task,' the doctor said.

Two more girls left and the remainder shuffled closer together. He explained further.

'You'll be doing the work of an orderly. The best way to learn is to follow the nurses around, anticipate what needs doing, without,' he looked sternly at them all, 'cluttering up the place. Do you understand?' These men, they were told, would be in varying degrees of recovery. Jessie saw relief on Helen's face when the doctor said the more severely injured men would be going to the specialist hospitals, for facial reconstruction and spinal injuries.

Someone behind them whispered, 'Ooh I feel a bit sick!'

Then matron, a stern, capable woman, took over from the doctor.

'A good orderly provides companionship and conversation. Little tasks like helping them to wash their faces, or writing letters home, even playing a simple game of cards.'

Jessie, Helen and the other volunteers followed as the doctor and matron moved over to the first bed. A man of about thirty, still in his khaki uniform, was lying flat out. Jessie watched out for the rise and fall of his chest, but he was breathing in such a shallow way she worried he was dead.

They all moved on but she lingered, went up close to him and leaned over. Suddenly her arm was grabbed and she cried out in fear and shock.

'Ow, you're hurting me. Please let go,' she said, as gently as she could.

His eyes were vacant; he looked at her without seeing. She

prised his fingers off her arm, aware from the tenderness that he had bruised the flesh. She moved away from the bed, straightening her ruffled sleeve as she did.

'Good of you to rejoin us, Miss...'

'Mrs Paignton.'

The matron raised an eyebrow. Jessie wanted to explain she was only there to keep Helen company but she kept quiet and then matron threw out a question to the group.

'What needs doing? Look around you. Think about the men you've seen.'

The matron's eyes bored into each of them in turn. With difficulty Jessie held the woman's iron gaze until it passed onto the next girl. After a long pause, Helen raised her hand.

'Yes?'

'Well, the man in the bed over there...' Helen pointed to the man in the far right corner of the room. 'He needs a shave.'

Guffaws of laughter came from the girls. Helen's cheeks turned a deep pink and she dropped her head. Bless her, thought Jessie.

'Good girl!' the matron exclaimed. 'That's exactly what he needs. Think you're equal to it?'

'Pardon?'

'Do you think you can shave him without slitting his throat? We've seen enough blood, thank you, and my ward is to be kept nice and clean.'

Helen was rooted to the spot.

'Come on,' Jessie urged her. 'Shall I help her? She can do it under my supervision.'

'Very well. The men's supplies are in that corner,' matron said, indicating a wash basin and cupboard near the bay window.

Jessie and Helen collected supplies: soap and towel, a bowl, and from a box of personal effects labelled with his name, Callum Fullerton, they found a shaving brush and razor. Jessie ran her fingertip over the blade. A little blunt, but it would do.

Helen was astounded by the warm water. 'It comes warm from the tap. I wish I could live here, don't you? All those lovely clean white sheets. Imagine going to sleep on a bed like that all to yourself.'

Jessie didn't know much about Helen's home life but she guessed that her parents were poor, given the speed with which they'd pushed her into a job at just fourteen.

'Does matron think I'm stupid?' Helen asked as they walked to the man's bed.

'Of course she doesn't. She just has a job to do and she wants to do it as efficiently as possible. She reminds me a bit of Miss Lime. Do you think there's a special factory somewhere that produces copies of Miss Lime?'

They began giggling, which earned them a dark look from one of the nurses. They laughed even more after that.

Jessie approached the man, saying, 'It's time for a shave. Can we help sit you up?' Helen went round to the other side of the bed and hooked her arm under his. They pulled him upright.

'Does your arm hurt a lot?' Helen asked.

'A bit,' the man conceded. Jessie put the bowl of water down on Helen's side and watched as Helen deftly dabbed the brush into the soap and applied it to the man's chin in confident circles. With a steady hand, Helen began to shave. The man flinched and Jessie drew in a sharp breath.

'It's all right,' Helen said, wiping clean the blade with a towel. 'I haven't cut you, honest.'

'Sorry love, I'm just a bit... my nerves, you know. How about I close my eyes and let you get on with it?'

Helen looked at Jessie, who nodded. Helen shaved the man methodically, scraping away at his stubble, using her fingers to stretch the skin taut. She left his moustache in place.

'There you are,' she said, handing him a towel to wipe the residue from his face.

'Better than any French barber, I can tell you.' He flashed

Helen a grin. 'Smashing that is.' He stroked his cheek and smiled. 'Will you come again tomorrow?'

Helen looked at Jessie. 'Maybe. I don't know.'

Jessie saw the time, almost eight o'clock. Bill would be home from work by now. Still, she knew Florrie Tops would sort him out with supper if she was late back. 'I could do with going now, Helen. Are you coming with me? Come on, I'll walk you home.'

As she was saying goodbye to the doctor Jessie noticed a man sitting up in bed reading. On his bed table there was a glass of water, a pack of cigarettes or playing cards, but looped around the iron bedstead was a knitted scarf in stripes of red, white and blue. Jessie squinted and she was just able to see the hole she'd stitched up on the fourth-from-bottom row.

CHAPTER 11

Jessie turned away from the man. She remembered his name easily – Private Thomas Walker – and the letter Miss Lime had read out in the Comforts room saying thank you for the scarf. He had kept her gift and brought it back to England with him. Jessie was unsure what to do. Helen was waiting so she took the girl outside and walked her home.

She felt bad that she'd never written to him; too busy with work and looking after Bill. Now November was here Miss Lime began another campaign for the troops, but the atmosphere was changing as Christmas 1915 approached. News had come through that day of another three deaths of Cadbury men. Jessie didn't know them personally but when she walked around the Works, there were pockets of distraught women and girls being comforted by their friends.

The latest issue of the *Bournville Works* came out, and Jessie read an announcement of a meeting for the entire workforce. She and the other Q block girls went to the men's dining room and stood on the opposite side to the men.

George Cadbury senior stood on a platform with his eldest son Edward at his side. Mr George spoke in his sonorous voice.

'Whatever private reservations I have about this war,' he said, 'it is clear we must do all in our power to support the war effort. I have been instructed by our government that we must expand our operations and make a number of adaptations to our product lines and to the way we operate. I want to explain to you what will happen and to reassure you that your jobs will be safe. From next week we will be stopping production of all of our luxury lines to concentrate on government demand for Dairy Milk and Bournville drinking chocolate. In the coming weeks we will be producing a wider range of foodstuffs. Our milk processing plant at Knighton will be involved in producing milk powder, cheese and biscuits. I personally have spoken to the foremen and forewomen of all the departments and I am encouraged, indeed humbled, by your willingness to co-operate and serve in these terrible times. We have heard news today of yet more casualties. We have lost valued men who worked here – esteemed colleagues, who were also sons, brothers, sweethearts and fiancés. My heart goes out to them, and to all of you. Now let us return to work with renewed vigour.'

There were subdued murmurs of approval from a small group at the front, which soon faded out when they caught the generally sombre mood of the meeting.

Jessie wondered about their efforts in the Comforts room. What good was a knitted hat or a bar of chocolate in the face of such slaughter?

'That was some speech, weren't it?' Ruth said. 'And with all he's got on his plate – one of his sons has gone off to fight.'

Jessie was surprised. 'But they're Quakers, aren't they? I thought they didn't fight.'

'Yes,' Ruth butted in. 'But he always said to the men who work here they must act according to their own conscience, and it must be the same for his sons. He's got another one in the Friends Ambulance Unit helping out all the injured soldiers. That must sit better with his conscience.'

'Not necessarily. He might feel like he should have signed up properly too.' Mary said.

'Miss Lime,' Ruth asked, 'what will happen to the Comforts programme if the war's still on at Christmas? Will we carry on sending the chocolates?'

'Yes, of course, I'm sure Mr George and the other directors

would want us to continue. Never underestimate the value of our little gifts. And don't forget the hospitals too, girls.'

Jessie thought of Thomas Walker and decided she would go and see him, just once, before Christmas.

When her shift finished that Saturday she went across to Fircroft. She peered through the bay window. Thomas was sitting up in bed reading as he had been before. Jessie went inside and stopped one of the nurses to ask where Helen was.

'She's been sent to The Beeches this afternoon. They're short of staff.'

'Is it all right if I go in?' The nurse nodded and Jessie crept into the ward. She approached his bed, no words prepared, and not even a gift for him. Why didn't I bring some chocolate at least, she cursed. Thomas glanced up, caught her eye and went back to his book. She walked straight past and approached the man two beds down.

'Hey love,' he said, 'have you come to plump my pillows?' A low jeer of approval came from the man next to him.

Precious minutes were being wasted, minutes she didn't have. A male orderly on his knees scrubbed at a stain on the floor. Someone snored and rolled over with a groan.

She turned sharply, took a deep breath and went to stand at the side of Thomas Walker's bed. A look of impatience flashed across his face as he lay down the book he was reading. Her courage almost failed.

'Sorry,' she said. 'Are you at a good bit?'

'I am.' He pushed himself up a bit further and grimaced with pain. 'But I'm always glad for real-life company.'

'Hello, I'm Mrs Paignton.'

'How do you do, Mrs Paignton? I'd stand up and shake your hand, like a gentleman, only...' He leant forward and lifted the bed cover to reveal a fruit box. Through the slats she saw his bandaged and splinted leg underneath.

'Does it hurt?'

'Of course it blooming does. It's driving me insane!'

The man in the next bed spoke to her.

'Don't mind him, love. He's got the grumps. Come and sit with me instead, or go and talk to Mad Tony over in the corner.'

The other men cheered. She locked eyes with Thomas; she saw pale-green, brown-flecked irises.

'God, these men,' he said. 'It's worse than being back at school. Sorry if I was a bit short. Yesterday, one of the volunteers sat by my bedside for two hours and I swear she didn't stop talking the whole time.'

Jessie chuckled. 'What on earth did she talk about?'

'All the charity works she and her band of ladies have been doing. How she'd turned around one of the young lads in trouble, reformed him and got him to sign up. So there I was, a captive audience,' he continued, 'wondering if she'd notice if I picked up my novel. I was halfway through a chapter before she stopped for breath.'

She burst out laughing and thought how good it felt.

'In that case I'll leave you to it. I can take a hint. I wouldn't want to come between you and,' she picked up the book, 'The Adventures of the Scarlet Pimpernel'.

'No, stay,' he said, urgently. 'I want to talk to you. I can't get a game of snooker until tomorrow. Someone's donated a snooker table for billiards.'

He saw her glance at his leg. 'They'll stick me in a wheelchair to play.'

They chatted until 3 p.m. It would be black outside in half an hour. Matron came past a few times and looked but didn't say anything. Other patients had visitors, too. She looked around the room – some women were writing letters for the men; others were holding one-sided conversations of the kind Thomas had described.

'Do you play rummy? I'll teach you.' He reached for the pack of cards. Miss Lime suddenly appeared in her mind's eye, rebuking her for playing cards games with a man. Not the done thing!

'No, actually I'd better go.' She saw his crestfallen expression and said, 'Go on then, a quick game.'

The game absorbed all her attention and she won three times. When it was time to go he said, 'All right. But you will come again, won't you? You've cheered me up no end.'

'Yes,' she said, without thinking. 'I'll bring you a book next time.'

She walked back home, an extra ten minutes added to her journey. Her heart felt lightened as if she'd righted the wrong of not writing to him. Playing rummy had been fun as well. The feeling of letting her hair down felt like a novelty. When she got home she said to Bill, 'Sorry there was an extra order and we had to work late.' A white lie wouldn't hurt.

'How are you getting on, little Nora?' Mr Bailey leafed through his copy of the *Bournville Works*.

'Oh, you know, we struggle on.' Her tone was so weary and flat that Mrs Bailey put her arms around Leonora's shoulders.

'So the November show at the Southern General was a success, I hear.'

'Yes, it was tremendous.' All credit to Miss Gabriel for that, she thought. Oh yes, Miss Gabriel had pulled off a spectacular event and was planning a Christmas theatre trip for the wounded men. And she'd heard today that Miss Gabriel was also putting herself forward for forewoman in her block. Leonora remembered her little pat on the head from Eliza Barratt but the forewoman's job seemed as remote as ever.

'One of my girls is off work at the moment. Evelyn Jackson. Her fiancé is now missing presumed dead.'

Mrs Bailey was full of sympathy. 'The poor thing.'

Leonora felt differently. 'I can never understand why these young girls rush to get engaged. Poor Evelyn indeed, but she could have saved herself a lot of heartache by not getting involved with a boy in the first place.'

'Ah, but matters of the heart are never straightforward,' Mr Bailey said. 'If Mrs Bailey had saved herself, chances are she'd be on the mantelpiece instead of sitting here with me now. Remember when we started courting?' And then he launched into one of his reminiscences that would take fifteen minutes.

Oh Lord, Leonora said to herself. Please help me. *Just give me a sign about what I should do next.* Later on, she realised Mr Bailey's next words were just that.

'I'm reading a smashing book from the library at the moment. Them lads in the army would enjoy it.'

That's it, she thought. *A books scheme for the soldiers.* It was so obvious once one thought about it. They were already dealing with requests from individual soldiers for fresh reading material, but how about a proper loaning service? With books from the Works' library and donations from the workforce. She was suddenly supremely grateful to Mr Bailey.

'I think that's an excellent idea, Miss Lime,' Eliza Barratt had said. 'I'll bring it up at our next Works Committee meeting. What a pity the Suggestions Scheme is no longer running – that's the sort of idea that may have earned a prize.'

The money didn't matter to Leonora.

A week later she was given the nod of approval. Mr George senior was so impressed with the idea he had pledged not only to cover the postage costs of the scheme, but also to order the most-requested books wholesale from the publisher. Eliza had said, 'The Education department will deal with the book requests but if your girls could help with packing...' Even better, Eliza Barratt had asked her to take her place in the next one or two Works' committee meetings. How silly she was to doubt the good Lord.

Leonora beamed as she explained the scheme to the girls. 'That's where your organisational skills come in, ladies,' she told them gleefully as they sat at their machines. 'We need to compile a list of the most requested fiction and non-fiction books so far. Ruth, can you tackle that? Good girl. When a request comes in we need to find the book as quickly as possible – so check if the library has copies or see if it's been donated.'

When she had finished her research task, Ruth reported that adventure books like *King Solomon's Mines* and *The Scarlet Pimpernel* were the most popular. The girls in the Comforts room would be required to parcel up the books.

'Have you read any of these?' Mrs Paignton said to her. She held up a compilation, *The Adventures of Sherlock Holmes*. 'Could I take this to Fircroft next time I go?'

'I have no time for stories,' Leonora said. 'I'm surprised to see so many requests for novels. What about practical books like this one?' She showed the girls a gardening manual: *Beeton's Dictionary of Every-Day Gardening*.

Mary, who'd been silent up to then, suddenly burst out, 'Gardening! As if they're going to be growing flowers out there in the trenches!'

Leonora spoke in a cool voice. 'We've had a few requests for gardening books, you may like to know. According to a family friend of mine the men will be able grow vegetables if there are food shortages.' She continued, 'Or maybe they're thinking ahead for when they return home.'

'They won't *be* coming home!' Mary said. 'But why not? Let them grow some flowers for their own gravestones. Is that efficient enough for you? Better still, get them to dig their own graves in advance. How about that?' She left the room and slammed the door so hard the room vibrated.

Jessie went after her and found her sitting on the window seat in the corridor, where she had sat with Miss Lime a year ago, being warned off Mary Morris. Mary was staring straight ahead and when Jessie approached her hostile expression softened, but not without effort. Jessie peered at her – her face was so pale.

'What's wrong?'

Mary looked down at her feet. 'I'm sorry about my little outburst earlier. Miss Lime, she's so bloody naive, she hasn't a clue what's going on out there. I'm just fed up with it all.'

'Can I help?'

Mary shook her head. 'No, just keep being you. The calm level-headed person you always are.' Her eyes suddenly filled with tears. 'I won't be in tomorrow, by the way. I've told Miss Barratt. I've a funeral to attend.'

Poor Mary, she must have lost someone important.

'Is it the boy Daniel you mentioned once?'

'Jesus, no! Not Daniel. It's my father.'

'Oh Mary, I'm sorry. You must all be–'

'Don't be sorry,' she said, through a shuddering breath. 'He was a pigging bastard and I'm glad he's dead.'

But Mary refused to say more and Jessie, having tried once before, knew it was pointless to keep pushing at a door that was bolted shut.

CHAPTER 12

There's no need to go to Fircroft this evening, she told herself. She stood outside the Lodge on the path. Go left and home to Bill, or go right in the direction of the hospital? The wind was getting up and she shivered.

Other girls streamed past her. 'Goodnight, Jessie,' Ruth called. She felt the warmth of their friendship.

A few minutes later, after the main stream of girls had died down, she heard a voice behind her, 'Have you taken root, Mrs Paignton?'

She turned quickly. 'I was debating about going to Fircroft for an hour.'

'That's most commendable.' Miss Lime beamed. 'I'll be sure to mention your sterling work at the next committee meeting. Good evening to you!'

Jessie took a deep breath and headed right. Thomas's smile, when he saw her, lit up his face and and she was glad she had come.

Jessie became a frequent visitor to Fircroft, often managing to go in her lunch break. Thomas's appreciation of her visits and the books she brought was evident.

She was sitting at his bedside on one occasion when she heard the voice of Dr Russell-Morgan behind her. She hadn't seen him during her last couple of visits to Thomas. She surmised from the conversation the doctor was having with matron that he wanted to send Helen Daw on a home visit to change Bert Cathcart's dressing. Bert Cathcart, Jessie gathered, had come back from the war severely injured and was at home recuperating.

The doctor caught her eye. 'Hmm, you're frowning, Mrs Paignton. You don't like the idea.'

'She's only fifteen.'

'Is she? I had no idea. Bit too young for district nursing. Mind you, I can't tell what age girls are these days.'

It was an easy mistake to make, Jessie thought. Helen had grown and blossomed, shooting up in height by a head in the last year and a bit. Her complexion was healthy, the once-grey pallor gone.

'Where does this patient live?'

'Stirchley.' He named one of the side roads in the poorer part.

'That's just around the corner from me. I'll go.'

Dr Russell-Morgan explained, 'He's an amputee.' He saw Jessie's brief look of confusion. 'His arm had to be cut off just below the elbow. Dreadful thing for a man. Any chance you could go round tonight and change his dressing? But don't expect a royal welcome or a thank you.'

Thomas had stared at her afterwards, and she saw his respect for her in his green-brown eyes. 'You're a regular angel, aren't you? Why do I suddenly feel jealous of this Cathcart bloke?'

Jessie blushed, and felt warm inside. 'Don't be daft. I'll come in a few days and bring you a Christmas paper hat.'

'Can't you come tomorrow? Please,' he said with a pleading expression.

Jessie did her afternoon shift at the Works and went straight to Bert Cathcart's house at 7 p.m. The matron had given her bandages and other medical supplies. Bert's wife, Beth, let her in and Bert was sitting at a dining table, the remains of his dinner on a plate, ignoring Jessie as if she wasn't there. She kept her voice light.

'Good evening, Mr Cathcart. I'm just going to have a look at your arm.'

She unwound the bandage on the stump that ended halfway between his wrist and elbow. Determined not to flinch she had imagined it to be a smooth repair, but whoever had stitched him up had taken little care or time: the flesh at the end of his arm puckered. The dim light did little to soften the ugliness of the remaining stump.

'Lucky, they told me,' Bert said, with violence seeping out of his voice. 'Lucky it's not the one you write with, they kept on saying. Lucky?' he shouted, his face so close that Jessie felt his hot sour breath on her cheek.

He nodded in the direction of the scullery. 'As for her, she thinks she's helping by cutting my dinner into pieces like I was a two-year-old. If it's a nice piece of steak you still can't get a purchase on it.'

'Steak, eh?' Jessie said. 'I'm coming round tomorrow if steak's on the menu.'

'You can cut that false cheeriness. I'm sick of it, I tell you,' and with a sweep of his good arm he flung his plate off the table where it crashed to the stone floor and shattered into pieces. The noise made Bert cover his head with his arms, his good hand protecting the stump.

Jessie knew his state of mind was fragile, that something was wrong beyond his physical injury. Bert Cathcart's next words brought her out of her thoughts.

'They don't tell you about making love to a woman, do they?' Jessie blushed and wound the soiled dressing up into a ball to dispose of. She took a fresh bandage out of her bag and rolled it over his injured arm. 'Go on, tell me that, Miss Pretty. Still, at least I can still wipe my own backside.'

Jessie stooped as if to clear up the pieces of broken plate.

'For goodness sake, leave it. Shout back, woman! I'd love a

good ding dong, I can't stand all this pussyfooting around. Her out there is ten times worse. All soft voice and wifely concern, when I know she's really wishing I'd been blown to pieces. At least she'd have got a decent pension out of it, but what use am I now? How am I going to get a job like this?' The new dressing had come off entirely and he waved the injured limb at her.

'I need to dress that wound again. Immediately. Before it gets infected.'

'In the old days,' he said, calmer now, 'me and Beth used to have some right old belters. Used to get the neighbours round sometimes, we did.' He chuckled. 'She'd give back as good as anything, that's what I loved about her, the spark, the energy, proper little firebrand, she was, and now look at her.'

A woman's voice, presumably Beth's, said meekly, 'Is everything all right?'

Jessie looked up from the dressing she'd nearly finished applying.

'I'm sorry. I was going to clear that mess up–'

'It's all right. I'll do it,' his wife said. 'I'm sure you've got other patients to see.'

'There,' she said, tying the bandage neatly. 'That's quite a good job, even though I say it myself.' Bert glowered at her. She needed to get outside before his temper flared again.

Out on the doorstep, his wife whispered to Jessie.

'I'm going spare. He's not the man I married, it's like he's given up. He just sits there brooding and then he flips. I'm not sure what's worse really. I just want the old Bert back, but I don't suppose you can help with that, can you?'

'Look after yourself, Mrs Cathcart. And I mean you, as well as your husband.'

The woman tried to smile.

'Why did the silly sod have to go and volunteer? Just showing off, he was. Trying to keep up with the lads on the street, like some boys' adventure. The Kaiser gave him an adventure all right.' She held onto Jessie's arm. 'He won't talk about it, won't tell me the details. How can I help him if he clams up? Did he say anything about what really happened?'

Jessie shook her head. 'Not really.' She glanced down at the pristine front step, newly scrubbed that morning and every morning, no doubt. It was a matter of pride for most women. Her own doorstep hadn't been cleaned in weeks; she no longer had the time or energy to keep up the routine.

'They changed, you know, friends of ours, they don't come round no more. Maybe they're afraid of seeing Bert's arm. Lord knows I was when he first came back, but it's me they're shunning too. It's as if... no, it's nothing.'

Even though Jessie was conscious of getting home before Bill returned from work, she said, 'Go on.'

'It's as if they need to watch their husbands now. Like they think you're going to steal their man because your own's not fit.'

'I'm sure that's not the case. I must be off now. All the best. One of the other district nurses will see you in a week's time. I've left a supply of bandages so if you feel like it, you can change the dressing yourself – if you think the wound needs it.'

'How much do I owe you?'

'I'm a volunteer, and I'm glad to do it. Goodnight.'

'Tara. And thank you.'

As Jessie walked over the cobbles she felt unsteady and nearly turned her ankle. A group of children streamed out of the alleyway. She stopped to watch them as they shoved and teased each other. She was moved, not just by their poverty but their lives forever blighted – how many had already lost fathers and brothers? How many more would? She opened her case and fished in it for something to give them. She found a roll of bandage. It was a waste but she could restock next time she went to Fircroft.

'Here,' she said, holding it out to the boys. They looked at her as if she carried the authority of a policemen, half in awe, half in terror.

'I thought you might want this to play with.' The tallest of the group, a boy of about seven, reached out and grabbed it.

'Can we really have it, Miss?' He turned to his mates. 'Come on, let's go and hang a cat from a tree.'

'You will not,' Jessie said fiercely, unable to stand any more evidence of human cruelty.

She trudged home to Bill, suddenly grateful he hadn't been called up to the war. When she got in he was gone. He had disappeared. After a few minutes searching the house she ran next door to Mrs Tops.

'What's your hurry, Jessie?'

'It's Bill. He's gone.'

Mrs Tops laughed. 'You daft so-and-so. He's in here with me having a bit of supper.' Mugs of cocoa and a plate with a few cake crumbs were on the table. 'We all needed a bit of company tonight.'

Jessie looked at the scene in front of her. Bill was sitting on the rug and the oldest of her boys was clambering over him. He was protesting but she could tell from his voice that he was enjoying it.

'If you're going to keep giving Bill his dinner I ought to give you some money.' She put her hand in her pocket.

Mrs Tops shook her head. 'Get away with you. Bill's back to his old self so if I pop round to yours or invite him here for his dinner when you're out, then it's my choice. If you want to give me a copper now and then I daresay I'll take it but I won't expect it.'

'Are you coming, Bill?' Jessie said, turning to the door.

He looked at her and his expression was hard to read. Then he said, 'I'll be along in a minute, Jess. Just playing with this little rascal.' He suddenly grabbed the child and tickled him.

And to think she'd felt guilty about neglecting him!

The following week, before the Christmas break, snow came down and Bill looked up from the letter he'd received to say Ann was coming to stay over the holiday. Jessie took the letter from him and scanned it, skipping over the news about how wonderful her granddaughter Emma was and getting to the reason.

'Ah, that explains it. Johnny's home on leave and she wants to leave the two of them together.'

That week was frantically busy at work. Every break and lunchtime was spent in the Comforts room leaving Jessie little time to see Thomas for the last time before Christmas. On the Friday evening she took him a copy of *A Christmas Carol*. The ward was decorated with paper chains and the mood was festive. One of the men banged out a tune on the piano and she and Thomas giggled every time he hit the wrong note.

Thomas's leg had mended now and he was generally more cheerful, but she could tell something was bothering him.

'I'll see you after the holiday,' she said.

'I'll have gone by then.'

Her heart lurched. 'Gone? What do you mean?'

'I'm fit enough to go back, they've said. Looks like I'll be spending Christmas Day with my section. What's left of it, anyway.' He reached into the pocket of his jacket and handed her an envelope.

'What's this?'

'Open it later.'

She couldn't wait. She ripped apart the envelope, pulled out the sheet of paper. An address in France. Army Post Office.

'Write to me, Mrs Paignton.'

'I will,' she said, nodding. 'Of course I will. And Private Walker – please keep safe.' They stared at each other until matron came bustling past to hang a piece of holly from one of the picture frames. 'Happy Christmas,' she whispered to him and got up to walk away.

When she had left the building, she looked back for a

moment at the snow-covered roof, and the illuminated bay windows. 'Happy Christmas, my love,' she said, under her breath, although no-one was present to hear her.

She raced home to try to shake off the feeling of doom surrounding her. By the time she burst through the front door, her lungs ached. The sound of Ann's voice made her heart sink. Christ, she'd forgotten Ann was coming tonight. She quickly shed her coat and smoothed her hair down and opened the door. Bill and Ann were sitting up at the table, dinner half-eaten in front of them. The tension in the air was tangible.

'I'm sorry, Ann. Sorry Bill. I had to do a visit to the new auxiliary hospital. It took longer than I thought.' It was absolutely the wrong thing to say.

Ann's face was red, her mouth working as though gathering spittle before she spoke.

'From what I hear there's always some reason for you to be late. "Oh, we had to pack some chocolates, oh, we had to knit some socks," and now it's, "oh, we had to go and help at the hospital".'

'That's not fair.'

'Leave it, Ma,' Bill said. 'I asked you not to say anything.'

Jessie flared. 'What do you mean? What have you been saying about me?'

He stared into the fire; she sensed his fury bubbling beneath the surface.

'Oh, come on now,' she said, unable to stop the cruelty in her tone. 'Don't hold back now you've found your tongue at last.'

Ann stood up and poked her hard on the shoulder. 'You just pipe down, madam. You think you're on the moral high ground just because you swan around doing your good works at the factory, passing my knitting off as your own, I bet. Now you fancy yourself as a nurse!'

'No-one asked you to come back and stick your nose in,'

Jessie said. 'Why didn't you stay in Wolverhampton? We're managing fine without you.'

'Fine, she says! Have you seen the state of your front step? And I spent the day turning out your cupboards and sweeping all the dust from the corners. I'll not see Bill live in squalor.'

'Squalor? Don't be so ridiculous.'

'If you can't keep house for your man then I'll do it for you.'

'Is that the real reason you're back or has Elizabeth got fed-up with you?'

Ann turned to Bill. 'I told you I didn't mind coming here to help out. I'm happy to do it for the child that came out of my womb, but you,' she said, turning to Jessie, 'you wouldn't understand that.'

'That's low, even for you.'

'I didn't mean that, you silly girl.'

'Anyway, what's so wrong with wanting to help out? It's not a crime, is it?' Jessie was close to tears now. She went into the pantry and shut the door behind her. In the dark she took deep breaths and pulled at her wedding ring until it came over the knuckle. She slid it almost to the end of her finger and then pushed it back over the knuckle into place again.

'How many of them girls at work have got husbands that want looking after? None, that's how many!' Ann shouted. Jessie heard Bill shushing his mother. 'She doesn't even need to work, son! That's what I don't understand.'

The pair of them could go hang, she told herself.

That Christmas was a miserable affair. Ann, Bill, Florrie Tops and Jessie sat around the table, while the little boys played with the puppets Bill had made them. Not even the sight of their pleasure could dispel the mood of gloom.

Jessie was glad to return to work in the new year and Bill, she guessed, was equally glad of his job at the BSA factory. Sundays were the only days where they shared any common ground and Bill was happy to rest in bed for the morning or sit in the armchair reading. She felt shut out of his life in the way that he had probably felt before Christmas.

As Mary had predicted conscription was introduced at the end of January for single men. When the time came for married men Jessie knew that Bill would be able to get exemption from the war on the grounds of his injury. She often thought of Thomas and had written him a brief letter wishing him well; up to now there had been no reply. As the weeks passed it became clear that any hope of an end to the war was a pipe dream.

That spring George Cadbury addressed the workforce again. Jessie was sure she could see the signs of stress taking its toll on the kindly man. His eyes were watery with tears.

'It has been a brutal and bloody war. And we have lost over ninety men so far. But this statistic does not tell the story of your grieving hearts. Should this war continue, it is likely that many more men will be required to sign up. For you, your families and loved ones, this will be devastating, so I can only repeat my sincerest thanks for your continued efforts to serve the company so faithfully and loyally in the face of such adversity.'

Jessie felt her heart chill as she thought of Thomas as one of those statistics. She trooped out silently with Mary to go back to work. In front of them Eliza Barratt appeared at Miss Lime's elbow and Jessie couldn't help but hear their conversation.

'Did you know Mr George's daughter Mollie has joined the war relief effort? She's serving in the Friends Ambulance Unit in a hospital near Dunkirk.'

Miss Lime put her hand to her throat. 'We must send her a parcel as well.'

'I was thinking much the same thing, Leonora. Apparently, she has a weakness for those Neapolitans, but we're not making them anymore, which is a pity.'

'Has anybody checked if there's some in the warehouse? Let me see if I can find some.'

Jessie and Mary were sent by Miss Lime to track down the Neapolitans. In the warehouse Jessie encountered Rose Entwistle, whom she'd only seen half a dozen times to wave at since her first day.

'How's your husband getting on?' Jessie asked her.

Rose said, 'It wouldn't be so bad if they were equipped properly. It's an absolute disgrace. The cold is bad, Lord knows his rheumatism's playing up rotten, but the wet is ten times worse. He's got what they call trench foot.'

'What's that?' Jessie asked, curious. She hadn't come across it on her district nursing rounds so far. Rose hesitated, as if not wanting to offend or upset her.

Mary said, 'It's all right. She's a district nurse. A volunteer anyway. There's probably nothing she hasn't seen.'

'Of all the things! What on earth do you want to go and do district nursing for? Don't you have enough on your plate?' She began to describe trench foot to her. 'Basically, it's where your feet go mouldy and they get infected. One man had to have his feet cut off. Anyway, the chocolates. What did you want and who's it for?'

'We wanted to send some Neapolitans to Mollie Cadbury – they're her favourites, so I'm told.'

When Rose had disappeared, Jessie said: 'Mr George must be worried sick about his daughter.'

Rose came back with two boxes.

'And don't let on I've given you these. It'll cause an uproar. Oh and Jessie, don't be a stranger.'

'Two boxes,' Jessie walked off gleefully. *One for Miss Cadbury and the other for Thomas.*

"I'll get them packed, shall I?' Mary said.

'It's all right, I'll do it.'

By the time Thomas's letter arrived Jessie had given up hope. It was now March and Jessie sat in the Comforts room on a crate knitting another scarf when the delivery boy put his head around the door.

'A few more letters from the men,' he said. 'Calm yourselves, ladies.'

Miss Lime took them out of his hands, and said, 'Run along, now.'

'And thank you to you, too,' they heard him mutter. Mary and Jessie grinned at each other.

Miss Lime told them to take a break while she opened and read the letters. There were more thank-you notes from the soldiers, plus another death notice, which Ruth pinned on the noticeboard.

'Oh, there's a letter addressed to you: *Mrs Jessie Paignton, c/o Bournville Works*. That's no way to address a married lady!' Miss Lime tutted. 'Surely you know personal letters are not to be sent to the Works? The rules are very clear on that.'

'I'm sorry. It won't happen again.' Jessie put down her knitting and held out her hand for the letter. Her heart pounded until, after what seemed like an age, Miss Lime deigned to hand it over. She put it in her pocket. There was no need to open it to find out who it was from. She recognised the handwriting immediately. Thomas.

After an agonised wait that was probably only five minutes, Jessie excused herself to go to the ladies' room. She walked along the corridor, praying she wouldn't see anyone who would delay her. One of the lavatory cubicles was occupied so she went to the other end, sat down and waited. The other occupant left and Jessie heard the sound of her scrubbing with the nailbrush that was supplied for the girls.

Her hands were trembling as she slid her finger under the letter flap, trying to ensure she didn't make a sound. The door banged and footsteps retreated down the corridor. *At last!* She unfolded the flimsy sheets, counting three in all. At first glance the censor hadn't been too heavy handed this time and she found the final page and read: *Warmest love from your friend, Thomas.*

She settled down to read. *My dear Jessie,* he began (causing her to flush with embarrassed excitement). *I can't tell you what a pleasure it was to receive your letter and the chocolates. I was quite the envy of the other men, and inevitably the recipient of a bit of leg-pulling! We have stopped being men, we are more like animals. Being out here it's astonishing how quickly something horrifying or something one would once have recoiled at becomes the norm. I was never a bold boy at school, never one of the bullies, though I am sad to say never brave enough to challenge the bullies either. But one day I stood up to a bully and got beaten to smithereens. I'm not telling you this to make you sorry for me but to say how good it felt, giving him what for. But back then I knew who the bully was. Out here I'm not so sure. Is it Fritz, as we call him, or is it the Commanding Officer, who delights in savagery? Anyway, I was feeling somewhat sorry for myself the day when your letter arrived and it cheered me up no end. Just hearing you talk about your life and the Comforts room takes me back to your kindness in visiting me so often at Fircroft. It was selfish of me to monopolise you the way I did and for that I apologise. If only you knew how I long to be in that bed again, albeit with my smashed leg, just to have your company. My fellow colleagues heard me chuckling and wanted to know what the fuss was about. They said I'd cheered up and wanted to know the source of my improved mood. I'm afraid I passed you off as my aged aunt. Tell me how you really are. Not the polite Mrs Paington, but the real you. Are you happy? You'll have to forgive me. We have seen too much out here and it makes one free with one's emotions, just in case – well, in case one is never coming back. It's morbid to say it but this could be my last letter. I'd like to see you when I return. Do you think that would be possible? But anyway let's pray for a happy outcome to this infernal conflict. I live in hope.*

Jessie put the letter down in her lap. She'd read it again later, knowing she'd devour every single word. She imagined his hand in the act of writing; she tried to picture the conditions under which he'd written those words to her. In her mind's eye she imagined him inside a trench with drizzling rain. No, she thought, let him have sunshine on a warm spring day like this one. Let the sun's rays ooze deep into his bones and joints. Let the sun bring him love, the feeling that he really matters.

She put the letter back inside. Her fingernail caught against something inside the envelope. A small square of card fell out; a photograph. She studied the portrait closely. This was him.

Clutching it in her hand, she stood and held the photograph up to the window, the better to see him. He was in a soldier's uniform – a head and shoulders picture, taken professionally in a studio. The date on the reverse said June 1915. She studied his physical details. He looked very young in the picture, innocent of the conflict, a handsome, beautiful face with wide-set eyes that seemed to communicate directly with her, even though it had been taken months before they met. She gazed at the firm jawline and the sensitive mouth. Not a trace of arrogance in that stare. He was a gentle man.

Something inside her jolted, like a jigsaw piece pressed firmly into place, a sudden recognition. She clutched the picture to her chest; for the moment she felt no fear or apprehension, only a glorious exhilaration as she said, 'Thomas. Thomas'. Just speaking his name brought her a bright, sparkling pleasure.

The slam of the main door brought her back to reality. With trembling fingers she put the photo and letter back inside the envelope, which she put inside her camisole. She left the cubicle, and didn't use the wash basin; she wanted to preserve the connection that came from him writing the letter and her receiving it. A link had been made between them, one person to another, crossing an emotional as well as a geographical chasm. She had the sense of a hunger gnawing, a thirst beginning to build.

Out in the corridor a crowd of girls streamed past. Jessie

hadn't registered the sound of the bull for dinner-time. She joined the flow, content to be swept along by the sea of bodies and the terrific din, absorbed by them, yet feeling entirely alone in her own precious whirlpool of yearning.

CHAPTER 13

Eliza Barratt asked Leonora if she could attend the next meeting of the Women's Works sub-committee. She was, she explained, increasingly busy with other committees at the Works and it would give her peace of mind to know Leonora could attend in her stead.

'Of course – I'd be delighted,' Leonora said and wrote down the details of the date, time and meeting room on her calendar at home. She was sent an envelope containing the agenda for the meeting, which she opened and read with trembling hands. There was something exciting about being privy to all these Works' matters, like being let into a secret society. The items included: the transfer of the girls to the men's departments, Relief Work, Manufacturing Matters, and – she was gratified to see – the Comforts programme.

Miss Carter, one of the most senior forewomen, was to chair the meeting. She was a large woman, whose formidable bosom almost rested on the table in front of her. A plate of biscuits was being passed around the women, none of whom Leonora knew, apart from Miss Gabriel, who bit delicately into a shortbread.

Leonora was eager to get started. She thought, I don't know where all this business of eating between meals comes from. She was certain Mr George wouldn't approve of this unnecessary snacking.

'A biscuit, Miss Lime?' Miss Carter asked her, after taking

two for herself, although she was hardly in need of the extra calories.

'I don't think so, thank you. It seems an extravagance in the present circumstances.'

As Leonora had been the last to be offered the plate the others looked askance at one another. Good, she thought.

Miss Carter tapped the sheet of paper on the table. 'To begin with, the Cadbury board of directors has met and agreed a slight increase to the women's wages. There was some question over whether this applied to the married women also. The firm has agreed, somewhat generously in my view, that the married women should be compensated so there will be an increase of 5% across the board.'

A quiet woman with spectacles spoke, 'What with trying to manage a home when there are food shortages–'

'Yes,' Miss Carter said, 'that's true. I went past the queue for the greengrocers this morning and it stretched the length of the village green.'

'Anyway, to move onto the main item: the transfer of women to the men's departments. The latest tally is that just over twelve hundred men have now signed up or been conscripted and we can expect many more to follow, especially married men. I'd like you to think about which girls you could spare to go and boost the men's departments. The print room is in particular difficulty, as is the fruit processing section. They're also short in the Cocoa room.'

'On what criteria should we recommend them?' Miss Gabriel asked.

Miss Carter said, 'Obviously, physical strength and general robustness.'

'That rules out Elsie Higgins then,' one of the others said. Everyone laughed. Elsie was notorious for claiming stomach cramps, usually after lunch and then recovering miraculously after an hour's rest in the retirement room.

'Dr T. cottoned onto her,' Miss Carter said. 'She claimed

it was, ahem, "ladies' problems". He said, and I quote, "My dear Miss Higgins, you were here only last week with the same problem. Have you any idea of the length of your menstrual cycle?" And the silly girl had looked baffled and replied, "I don't know. About three inches?"' She beamed around the room as there was more laughter. 'But enough of this. Back to the agenda.'

As if she wasn't responsible for driving the conversation away, Leonora thought. She wrote 'Mrs Paignton?' in the margin of her agenda. Jessie Paignton might be willing to move departments. A good worker, although lately she'd seemed distracted, making silly mistakes with her cutting-out work. Leonora would mention it to the woman first.

The committee covered the next two items quickly. Miss Carter said, 'Finally, Item 4. The Comforts programme. Shall we have an update?'

Leonora cleared her throat to tell them about her girls and their activities, as well as the work at Fircroft, but Miss Gabriel had caught the chair's eye and got in first with the Entertainments Committee report.

'We held a fundraising concert in the Cadbury hall for the servicemen from the Southern General hospital and two of its annexes. Over one hundred men came and it was all rather marvellous. All those hours of rehearsals paid off and it was even reported in the *Gazette*.' Miss Gabriel handed round a cutting from the newspaper and Leonora glanced at it briefly before passing it on. All the committee members made congratulatory noises.

Miss Carter said, 'Can we record in the minutes our appreciation of the work Miss Gabriel has done?' Nods of approval all round.

'Of course,' Miss Gabriel continued, 'we're always looking for new members. Singers, pianists, violinists.'

Leonora knew Miss Gabriel was an accomplished pianist but she played with too much gusto. She kept her face passive until Miss Gabriel said, 'I rather hope you can help me, Miss Lime. We're short of voices for the party at Fircroft.'

'A party? At Fircroft? I don't know anything about a party!' Leonora said. Surely Dr Russell-Morgan would have told her, would have kept her informed.

'We, the Entertainments Committee, felt the men there needed cheering up. We've got a troupe of singers with quite a number of sopranos but no altos since Fanny Fletcher left us to train as a full-time nurse.' She looked around the room. 'Do you know anyone who might fit the bill?'

'I wouldn't recommend any of my lot,' the forewoman from B Block said. 'I've heard better voices from cats quarrelling in the alleyway.'

'Pity. Miss Lime – what about your section? There was that girl of yours who made a stir down at Snow Hill station last year.'

Leonora shot her as blank a look as she dared.

'Mary, her name was. Mary Morris, no?'

'Well,' Leonora replied, pretending to consider the matter, a studious look on her face. 'It's true she has a fine voice, but, well...'

'For heaven's sake, there's no need to be coy,' Miss Carter said. 'Let's hear what you have to say.'

Leonora thought hard. Why did she still harbour an animosity towards Mary Morris? Perhaps it was time to let go of the prejudice that she had built up. It would be the Christian thing to do.

'No, nothing. I'm sure the Morris girl would be pleased to get involved.' Rather than have Miss Gabriel poach the girl, surely it would be better to have her warm recommendation. Leonora smiled at her own generosity. At last it was time for her to speak.

'I took the liberty of writing a little report of our activities in the Comforts programme.' She handed out copies. 'Since January we've successfully mobilised the workforce to knit two hundred pairs of socks and one hundred vests. The girls in the wages' office have been especially productive and my team have parcelled and sent all the items. They have packed over three hundred crates of chocolate. We've also been running a books request service where our servicemen can order books to read. The most popular are French and German phrase books and gardening manuals, and,' she coughed, 'the odd novel. It's good to know the men are thinking of their future and making plans to rebuild their lives when they return. I find that rather encouraging.'

She continued, vaguely aware that interest was waning, but she was determined to get to the end, even though dusk was arriving. At the back of her mind a little plan was bubbling on the stove. If Miss Gabriel was organising a party at Fircroft then she, Leonora, needed to do something spectacular to make the party memorable. A surprise of some sort. Whatever she decided she knew she would need some assistance. And that scoundrel Samuel Eastwood, with his network of contacts, might be just the person to help.

The next day, Eliza Barratt sought her out. 'Thank you for standing in for me. How was the meeting?'

'I was a little put out to learn that Miss Gabriel is planning a party at Fircroft in November. Had I not been at the meeting, would anyone have told me?'

Eliza said, 'Oh, Leonora. Can't you find a way to work together?'

Leonora walked away disgruntled. She was unable to escape the feeling that other people's efforts would always be recognised and rewarded over hers. No matter. She would find a way to make a splash at the party.

Since Thomas's letter with the photograph Jessie had puzzled over her intense feelings but also, more practically, where she should ask him to write back to. Miss Lime had warned her that letters at the Works were forbidden. Her home address was impossible. Whilst she hated duplicity she could not explain her feelings to herself, never mind to her husband. The only other person she could trust was Mary but she balked at the idea of sharing her dilemma. It pained her to do it but she parcelled a bar of Mexican chocolate to Thomas with a quick note asking him not to write to her at the Works.

She also made more of an effort with Bill at home, reducing her district nursing nights to one night a week. He was coming home from work exhausted but she could see he'd got his inner sparkle back, along with his sense of self-worth. Since the awfulness of Christmas when they had frozen out each other there had been no formal declaration of the ending of hostilities but a gradual thawing of the block of ice between them. By that July the awful reports came through in the newspapers of casualties in the Somme. Bill was reading the *Birmingham Gazette* one evening.

'There's an article on the wounded men coming back to Birmingham for treatment in the local military hospitals.'

Jessie took the paper from him and looked at the front page photograph. It showed about twelve men with various injuries, smiling for the camera. Underneath the picture, a caption commented on the remarkable cheerfulness of the men as they bravely walked to the ambulances. She scanned the faces, as she did for any photos, looking for Thomas. She had begun to understand the fretfulness experienced by so many women with loved ones at war.

'Is that someone knocking?' Bill said.

Jessie lifted up her head and listened. 'No, it's next door.' She went back to the newspaper and felt heavy of heart. She must have sighed because Bill asked her what was wrong.

'I was just thinking that no-one questions the sheer awfulness of it.'

Then there was a knock at the door. Jessie got up to open it and on her front step was Florrie Tops, a telegram in her hand, to say Frank was dead.

Bill brought the children inside and took them into the front room. This was women's talk, his look seemed to say to her as he closed the door. Jessie had no idea what to say to her neighbour.

She offered her brandy, but Florrie shook her head slowly and continued to stare at a fixed point in front of her, her arms clutched around her waist. Jessie tried touching her shoulder. There was a statue-like quality about her, as if her flesh had turned to marble.

Although it was a hot evening outside, their houses often stayed cool in the summer and Florrie had brought an extra chill in with her. Jessie went upstairs and found a blanket. Before going back in the room she opened the door to check on the boys and Bill. They all stared up at her, like three street beggars, imploring her to help them.

She put the blanket round her neighbour's legs and tucked it in.

'I'm not an invalid,' she said in a flat voice.

'Do you want us to look after the boys tonight?'

Florrie shook her head. She pulled the blanket off her, stood up and announced she was going back home with the boys.

When she'd left Bill said, 'Do you think she's in shock? I know the boys haven't taken it in properly.' He paused, clearly thinking.

'You know, there's a summer pageant in Small Heath this Sunday. I could take the boys to it.'

'You're a good man, William Paignton.' Then without knowing why she burst into tears. His shoulder was a good place to cry on. Was she crying for Bill or for Thomas?

'Why are you crying?'

'I don't know. I feel like I don't know anything anymore.'

The summer break came and went and she thought nostalgically about the previous July's languid atmosphere.

Now they were all sick with worry. Mary was fretting; Jessie was fretting over Thomas. She wrote numerous letters, and sent him treats of books and chocolates. 'I don't know why, but I want to spoil you,' she wrote. Only Miss Lime seemed impervious to all the strains. She had asked Jessie if she would move to a different department and Jessie had agreed to think about it.

One October afternoon when she had been home from her Saturday shift for an hour, she heard a loud rap on the door. Bill went to answer it and came back saying, there's a young woman called Helen to see her.

'Oh?' What did she want? 'Have you asked her in?'

'She wouldn't come in.'

Helen was on the front step looking flustered.

'One of the patients is asking for you.'

'What patient? Where?'

'At Fircroft. One of the soldiers who was here last year. He's back again. Did I do the wrong thing? I nearly didn't come. But he really wants to see you.'

Jessie stood out on the doorstep pulling the door to, so Bill wouldn't hear. Her throat felt thick with longing; her stomach ached.

'Is it Thomas Walker? Is he all right?'

Helen nodded.

'Go back,' she said to the girl. 'I'll come over in a minute. Oh and don't say anything to anyone else, will you?' Helen's eyes were wide as she shook her head.

I wasn't prepared for this, Jessie said to herself. She took a deep breath and went up to Bill. He was dozing but his eyes opened when she went in.

'That was Helen from work. They need some people in this evening. Big order from the government's come in and they need as many people as possible.' For a moment she was tempted to tell a half-truth, that she was helping at the hospital but she decided against it.

She held her breath. *Please don't make a fuss.*

'Tell them no. It's not like we need the money,' Bill said.

'I know, but I've said I'll do it. Why don't you go round and see Florrie?'

Closing the door she tried to ignore the feeling of treachery inside her heart.

Thomas Walker was asleep when she got there. She went to the head of the bed and gazed down at him. His arm was in a sling and his ankle was heavily bandaged. She thought again how his photo hadn't done justice to the pale pink of his cheek. His jawline was covered in reddish blond stubble. She would shave him tonight.

Helen was behind her. 'It's all right,' Jessie said on seeing her anxious face. 'You did the right thing in coming to get me.'

'I wasn't sure what to do, whether I should wait until I saw you at work on Monday.'

Jessie was glad, without fully understanding why, that Helen hadn't involved Miss Lime.

'This man,' she said, 'he's a... a friend of my husband. They go back a long way, and ...' She curtailed her explanation, not wanting to utter more untruths.

'Are you coming to the party next month?' Helen said.

'The party?' She remembered hearing chatter about the party from Mary and Miss Lime but she hadn't paid much attention.

'Yes, Miss Lime's really excited about it. She said it will be a night to remember but she won't tell us why.'

'Yes, I'll be there.'

'That's good. We've got so much to do.' Helen's eyes were shining. 'We're having an evening of entertainments for the men. There's going to be some music, and Tess is reading a poem, and Mary's singing–'

'What about you, Helen? Are you reading or singing?' She glanced sideway at Thomas, still sleeping peacefully.

'Me? On no, never,' she said with a shudder. 'I couldn't

do what Tess is doing. Reading out loud in front of all those people. But matron says...' she screwed her face up trying to remember 'that we all have our talents, and that mine is looking after people. She thinks I could be a nurse, a proper nurse, one day if only I can read and write a bit better. When I have to fetch the medicines I can recognise most of the writing on the bottles now.'

On and on she chatted. It was heartwarming to see this animated side of Helen. Meanwhile, Jessie considered what to do about Thomas. She decided to stay until he woke up, reasoning that Florrie Tops would be glad of some company on a Saturday evening.

Jessie marvelled at how Thomas could sleep through all the hubbub around them. Men wandered around in their blue hospital uniforms. A raucous game of cards was going on between three men in one corner. She sat by his bedside, picked up a book and began to read, waiting for him to awaken. She must have nodded off because she suddenly jerked upright to see Thomas Walker staring at her.

'You came,' he said. His voice was husky but the smile was just the same.

'Hello, you,' she said. 'Nice of you to come back.'

On the night of the party the food planning was like its own military operation. They were cooking sausages and roast potatoes for the men, with plenty of onion gravy. Vegetables were in good supply now since the conversion of the flower beds at Bournville. Miss Gabriel's plan was for some entertainments – songs and sketches – followed by the supper, and then some skits from the soldiers if they weren't too crude. Miss Lime had been cock-a-hoop about a surprise she was planning. Jessie thought it was a professional brass band – "anything to trump Miss Gabriel", Mary had said.

Jessie smelled burning and opened the kitchen door. Black smoke billowed out of the oven and Miss Lime stood by looking helpless. Jessie wrapped a towel around her hand and pulled out the baking tray, with charred blackened sausages on it.

What the hell's going on?

'Why have you put the sausages in to cook already? You know Miss Gabriel's ladies are doing the cooking.'

'Oh dear, I was merely giving a hand,' Miss Lime said. 'I thought I'd get started early, only this darned oven.' She flapped her hands.

'But it's not time yet.'

'Well, I beg your pardon.'

A team of women arrived at that moment and Jessie left the kitchen. Let Miss Lime explain her way out of the mess she'd created. She had Thomas to think about.

Miss Gabriel intercepted her on the way to Thomas's ward and asked if she could help to escort the men outside.

A handful of men were already out on the Fircroft lawn, which had been decorated prettily with bunting and candles in jars. There was space for thirty-five men – mainly from Fircroft, but a few from The Beeches and even the Southern General. Miss Gabriel had coordinated the transport from the other hospitals. The fittest men could sit on blankets on the grass, she said, while the less mobile could go on chairs or in wheelchairs.

Jessie began with the most disabled men. 'Come on,' she said, leading a man named Wally who was blind.

'Don't hold his arm and drag him,' the matron chided her. 'Put your arm out and let him hold onto you. Keep talking as well. Don't walk too fast, but don't dawdle either.'

'Yes matron,' Jessie said, humbled.

As they shuffled down the hallway and out onto the grass, she wondered what it would be like to lose your sight. Would that be worse than losing a limb or your hearing? She guided Wally out of the door and down the slight slope to the grass.

'Just a few more steps and we'll get you seated.' A soldier in a wheelchair was lounging backwards with a vacant look in his eye.

Jessie gave him a tight smile, intending sympathy, but he jeered.

'What's up, nursey? Don't you like the freak show?'

Ignoring him, she turned her back and said, 'You sit here, Wally.'

'Why are you giving him a front row seat, eh? It's not like he can see!' The man cackled at his joke.

Jessie sighed with exasperation and bent low so no-one else could hear her, 'Will you shut up, or I'll have matron send you back to your room and you'll miss the show and the supper.'

The man slumped in his wheelchair saying, 'All right. I was only having a laugh.'

'Well, don't.' Jessie turned and went back inside, until all the men except for Thomas were seated. She was leaving him until last in hopes of chatting with him alone, even if it were only for a few minutes.

'I can't wait to be out of this wretched bed,' Thomas said.

'I can. They'll send you back again if you're better. I wish you could stay here until the war's over.'

They were silent for a few moments. He ran his finger down the middle of a ruck in the blanket. 'That reminds me of that trench and just how hellish it was. Four days on, four days off.'

'What was it like there?'

'Oh, you know. Terror but then awful boredom. Sometimes the time passes so slowly you almost long for... no, it's not so bad really.' He looked around the room, saw that it was empty except for the two of them. He held her chin and Jessie knew her eyes were sparkling with tears.

She wanted to take all the thoughts from inside his mind – all the horrors he must have seen – and bury them deep underground. If only she could do that then perhaps she could cope with not seeing him again. *Who am I fooling?*

'I don't want you to go back,' she whispered. 'Not this time.'

Footsteps sounded behind her and she stood up quickly, grabbed the water jug and made over to the sink. The tap stuck and she couldn't turn off the wretched thing. Water splashed down her front.

'Oh hell.' She looked around her and beckoned to the male orderly, who had come in.

He looked at her drenched clothes and said, 'You don't want to be taking a splash at this time of night.' She smiled thinly and carried the full jug back to Thomas.

'We can't stay long,' he said. 'People will wonder where we've got to.' His words, though well-intended, had the effect of spoiling the intimacy between them.

'To hell with them,' she argued. 'People can think what they like. I want to see you and people can get lost if they don't like it.'

He smiled at her outburst and looked around to see if the orderly was nearby. Pulling himself into a seated position Thomas said, 'Let's walk. Can you help me?' He grabbed onto her before she had time to answer.

'Wait, let me get your crutches. Hold onto the bed while I get some from the rehab room.'

She prayed she wouldn't see anyone she knew on the way. Everyone was now outside. She could hear the words of a poetry recitation and muted applause. The rehabilitation room was dark and empty. She relied on the moonlight to help her find what she was looking for. The crutches were all different lengths so she picked two that she thought would be right for his height and took them back.

Thomas struggled to his feet and tried them out.

'Good guess,' he said.

'Ready?' She smiled brightly although her heart was heavy.

He took his arm out of the sling and with his weight on the crutches he hobbled next to her. She felt helpless. 'Maybe a wheelchair?' He looked at her as if to say, *no thanks*. They went slowly down the ward and into the corridor. They were almost at the rehab room when he stopped, wincing with pain.

'This wasn't such a good idea. I'm going to get you a wheelchair.'

'No,' he said loudly, 'I just need to sit down somewhere.'

'Let's go in here. It was empty a moment ago.' She held the door open and went in, checking behind her that they hadn't been seen. The door had a lock on the inside and, with her hands behind her, she turned the key. It barely made a sound.

At last, some privacy. She guided him over to the window – the lower half of which was shuttered – and they sat on the seat. The moon was high, almost full tonight, and it cast a glow over his face. He stretched out his injured ankle and she fetched a stool for him, placing a cushion on top to rest his leg. She scanned the room. It was eerie at this time of night. Crutches, false limbs, a machine of some kind.

'You don't want to know what that's for,' he said, pointing to a pulley hanging from the wall. 'It's a torture so bad the men cry out to be sent back.' She flashed a look at him to say his joke was in bad taste and he grinned at her.

He shifted in his seat awkwardly and turned to face her.

'I don't know what I'd have done with you. Your letters … well, they saved me. Seriously. When you're out there, every time there's an attack, every time a bomb drops you're thinking, is this it? Is this how it ends? Then it's not you, it's some other poor sod, and it mixes everything up inside.

'Every time the post came and my name was called out it was grand. Your heart soars knowing I'd hear all about you and what you'd been doing. I understood you didn't want me to write back but oh, there was so much to say. I talked to you all the time in my head.'

Jessie swallowed, her mouth suddenly dry. In a moment the air between them changed. His eyes roamed her face: her forehead, eyes, nose, cheeks, hair, mouth, like he was committing each detail to memory. With the force of a blow she realised the significance: he was memorising her because he wasn't coming back. They said it happened sometimes. Jessie remembered an anecdote Mary had told her recently about a neighbour who claimed she knew as soon as her son was conscripted she would never see him again. She'd waved him off at New Street station and six weeks later he was dead. Killed in action.

'I can't bear–' Jessie stopped, her voice breaking. She lowered her head.

'Can't bear what?' He forced her chin up so she had to look at him. His eyes were still searching, grey in the moonlight, and his chest rose and fell as if he were out of breath.

'I couldn't bear it if I didn't ever see you again.' Silence. He was leaning closer. She clamped her hands to the hard edge of the window seat and shut her eyes. His lips were on hers, first with the lightest of touches and then they pressed their mouths together hard. Jessie's head swirled, emptied of thoughts, no past, no future, just a pure and delicious delight. He touched her upper arm and felt his way down until he found her hand still clutching the seat. Her grip loosened and their fingers interlocked tightly. Music came from outside.

'Oh Jessie,' he said.

'Thomas. Beautiful Thomas.'

His fingers let go and explored the fabric of her dress. He bunched the material in his hand as if not knowing quite what he was searching for. Am I his first, she wondered. She took his hand and guided it to the top of her breast; he cupped it and her breath drew in sharply, like an inward sigh. It had been so long since she felt desired by Bill this was a heady feeling.

She stood up in front of him and he pressed his head against her stomach. Stroking his rough, soft hair she said, 'Let's find somewhere quieter.' She was taking charge. She helped him stand and she put her arm around his waist. He draped his arm on her shoulder and limped to the cupboard room with a bed in it, which was used for occasional massage.

He guided her to the bed and she made him lie down first, careful of his arm and ankle, before she squeezed up next to him. He put his arm under her neck. It was uncomfortable but she didn't want to say anything or move out of his grasp. He pulled her body close to his and tentatively they began to adjust their clothing.

Suddenly a blast sounded over their heads. The tiny window near the ceiling rattled, a flare of light exploded and then came a *put-put-put* sound. Thomas reacted by rolling off the bed and onto the floor, crying out with the pain of his leg. He pulled Jessie down with him and tried to crawl under the bed.

She reached out of his grasp and went to stand on tiptoe to try and see out of the window, whilst buttoning up her dress. She ran next door and went to the large window where she opened the shutter slightly. Men ran across the lawn as if in a panic.

Jessie watched the scene developing in front of her. A man darted one way and then another as the nurses tried to catch him. It was matron who succeeded, wrapping him in her powerful arms, until he thrust his elbow out and winded her so badly that she fell to the ground. Another explosion sounded and a blast of light shot into the air, peaked and then rained down golden droplets. A patient spun his wheelchair, looking round fruitlessly for help.

'Fireworks,' she said, under her breath. She ran back to Thomas who still cowered on the floor. She cradled his head and said, 'Look at me, my love. It's only fireworks. You're all right, you're all right.'

CHAPTER 14

Leonora trudged homewards from the party, shoulders slumped, her legs heavy as if weighted with sand. She felt like an old woman. *Stupid, stupid, stupid.*

That serviceman had run wild across the lawn. She'd watched in horror as he careered into the table and turned it over on its side, sending their carefully prepared food to the floor with a crash of china.

Sunday, the warden's dog, had dived on the sausages although they were still hot. She had heard one of the nurses exclaim, 'Serves you right if you burn your tongue, you little bugger!' as she crouched to pick up the ruined potatoes and vegetables that had been trodden into the grass. Some of the men were crying, clearly distressed by the sound of the exploding fireworks. Sparks and fragments of ash had continued to rain down on them. Just when Leonora thought it had finished another rocket burst into the night sky.

Another man had run at full speed and collided with her on the lawn. She had stayed on her back, winded, waiting for the pain in her stomach to subside. A hand had appeared over her and she had stretched out her own. Someone was pulling her upright. Dr Russell-Morgan. His look had told of his fury.

'I was busy in my office, catching up with work then all of a sudden I heard mayhem. What the hell is going on? No, don't answer. I can see what's happening. Some fool thought it a good idea to set off fireworks to group of men whose minds and nerves have been shattered, almost destroyed, by their recent experiences.'

Leonora's instinct was to deny all responsibility. She had looked down at the wasted food and put her hands to her head.

'Don't tell me this is your doing? Christ, have you no sense at all, woman?' he had said and stalked off.

She'd felt so proud of herself after having had the idea of a pyrotechnic display to end the evening. Miss Gabriel had wrong-footed her completely by arranging the party at Fircroft without asking her. So she'd sought out Samuel Eastwood and given him some money to buy some fireworks, knowing he'd be able to get hold of some without too many questions. He'd agreed on her signal to light them at the back of the house to entertain the men on the front lawn. And now? It had been a disaster and she would be a laughing stock on the committee. Worse still, Dr Russell-Morgan would never take her seriously again.

The rain had started to spatter on the ground but she barely noticed the splodges on her coat and gloves. A drunken man came past.

'Are you all right, love? You look like you've had the stuffing knocked out of you.'

Normally her response would have been to reprimand him for his impertinence. But she closed her eyes, hoping he would move away.

'Please yourself,' he said. 'Only enquiring.' He moved down the road muttering.

What to do next? First, she would redouble her efforts on the Comforts programme – although they had achieved a great deal she felt the momentum had been slipping lately. The initial burst of enthusiasm had waned and it was up to her to keep their spirits going. She knew she could rely on Helen Daw. Perhaps the girl could do more shifts at Fircroft or the Southern General hospital instead of the adult classes. She was much better suited to practical work of the vocational kind, rather than academic study. Yes, that would suit her better.

Mrs Paignton, Leonora had decided, was better off in the men's department. She was sensible and it would be best to have her and Mary separated. Feeling slightly better, she quickened her step and marched home, her arms swinging in rhythm. A cup of cocoa and a teeny drop of her father's whiskey – untouched since his passing – would see her through to tomorrow when she would take all her problems to the dear Lord at the Church of Christ.

Jessie had said goodbye to Thomas hastily. 'I have to go. Are you sure you're all right?'

'I can get back to bed on my own.'

In all the confusion and distress she was unsure whether the mood between them had been broken permanently. Part of her was grateful for the interruption – who knows what would've happened. Oh, she knew all right – she'd have made love to him. She felt she had just avoided a calamity, yet part of her still yearned for his lips to touch hers.

After she watched Thomas hobble back to bed, she turned and collided with Mary. All her stage make-up was smeared over her face. Her eyes were huge with black smudges. 'I didn't even get to sing!' she said.

Mary slipped her arm through Jessie's as they walked back from the party.

'Poor Miss Lime,' Mary said. 'I almost felt sorry for the cow. But you've got to laugh.'

Jessie didn't reply. She was lost in the thoughts of what had happened with Thomas. Much as she liked Mary she really wanted to be alone. Her body was trembling with shock and she didn't want to explain her state to Mary when she couldn't comprehend it herself.

'Are you listening to me?'

Mary's voice brought her back to the present and Jessie was aware of being steered down Bournville Lane.

'There's something I need to tell you and I'm only saying it because you're my friend.'

Jessie tensed. *Had Mary guessed about her feelings for Thomas?* She wouldn't be surprised if her feelings were written all over her face.

'You know everyone thinks I've got a sweetheart out in France?'

Jessie sighed with relief and nodded. 'It's Daniel, isn't it? I didn't want to pry.'

'It is, only it's not what you think. Anyway, I'm going out there to bring him back home.'

'Wait a minute.' Jessie stopped and pulled her arm out of Mary's. 'Going where? To France? But when? And how?'

Mary nodded. 'You know the night train comes in to Snow Hill with the injured soldiers? Most times it carried on north.' Jessie stared, a little confused now. 'Well, sometimes the train goes back to Portsmouth with some of the ambulance staff and any returning servicemen. I worked it out when I was there serving sandwiches and cakes before.'

'I always wondered what you were doing there that night. You told me you went there to sing.'

'Sorry about that. So listen, I heard word yesterday that in two days time there's a train going straight back to Portsmouth with the Friends Ambulance Unit people and the VADs, you know, the volunteer nurses, on board. I'm going to get myself on that train.'

'But that's... insane. They'll know you aren't supposed to be there. You're not qualified, you're not...'

'Neither are the VADs.'

'Yes, but they're–'

'A cut above me? A better class? I know that. I'll think of something. I'll say I'm from one of their fancy entertainment societies and I missed my train.'

'I still say it's mad. What about your mother?'

Mary's face suddenly turned solemn. 'That's where I need a favour. Will you keep an eye on her? She can't read very well so if I write you with news will you promise to go and see her from time to time? Here's my address.' She gave Jessie a slip of paper, hugged her tight and then slipped off into the darkness.

With trepidation Jessie crept in through the front door. The lights were off downstairs and the hallway was pitch dark. She felt her way into the kitchen. She couldn't face anything to eat or drink; she just wanted to sit undisturbed before going up to bed. But how could she sleep next to Bill after such treachery? She tested her feelings. Guilt hadn't set in yet. Surely it would do – like the harsh winter that was forecast – but not yet. Right now she wanted to rejoice and relive every moment she had shared with Thomas. She closed her eyes and imagined how the evening could have ended – she found herself having to take a very deep breath.

Eventually, the cold seeped into her bones and with it a creeping sense of despair. She shivered as she hung her coat on the balustrade and finally climbed the stairs.

Bill was fast asleep, still in his clothes, lying on top of the bed. He must have come up, intending to stay awake for her but succumbing to sleep. She eased open the drawer and found an extra blanket to cover him.

She undressed and lay in bed. Too much had happened for her mind to make sense of – the kiss with Thomas, the disaster of the fireworks, and then Mary's news. She'd have to deal with it in the morning.

But sleep refused to come. She lay on her back, staring at the ceiling, tempted to wake Bill and say, 'We have to talk.' But apart from a stirring now and then, muttering in his sleep, *I love you, Jessie*, he remained in a heavy and righteous slumber.

In the dressing room Leonora heard a voice behind: 'I hear the Fircroft party was something spectacular.' With a sinking heart she turned and saw one of the B block girls nudging her friend, saying, 'Quite a spectacle.'

The room had gone silent; none of the usual hustle and bustle. The chatter and gossip was suddenly suspended while they watched her ready to be baited like a bear.

She held her head up high. What choice did she have? But tears pressed dangerously against her eyes. She turned her back to the girls and fished in her coat pocket to check she had a handkerchief. She would never let the girls see her crying.

'Yes, at least the evening ended with a bang!' one of the others said.

Jessie Paignton came into the room. 'Leave it, you lot. Don't tell me you've never made a mistake.'

That was the last thing Leonora wanted to hear. She could cope with derision, but pity? Oh no! She bent to put her shoes in the metal cage to warm and in doing so the friendly hand about to be placed on her shoulder missed its mark.

'I'm all right, thank you. It's quite all right,' she said. 'You don't need to concern yourself.' Mrs Paignton was evidently taken aback by her brusque attitude.

'If you're sure,' she muttered and put her coat on the hook.

Before the woman could say anything else, a head popped around the door. It was Miss Gabriel.

'Miss Lime? Miss Dorothy Cadbury wants to see you in her office.'

With dread in her heart she went.

The carpet was a functional green but the rug on top was colourful and exotic. Miss Dorothy Cadbury was the daughter of Barrow Cadbury, Richard Cadbury's son, and there was talk of her becoming one of the directors of the company. She had started working on the factory floor, 'just as my father did' she would say, but had been promoted to a senior role.

'Would you like to tell me what happened?' she said, gently, her crossed hands resting on the desk.

Leonora pushed her knees together and explained as calmly as she could how she had been working on the Comforts programme. 'The girls have worked up a storm – over four hundred vests so far!'

'And the night of the party?' Miss Dorothy said, with a hint of impatience.

She slumped a little in her seat as she recalled the debacle.

'My team had worked like billy-o – doing posters, making tickets for the men to buy. They wanted the party to entertain the men, but without making them feel pitied, or like charity cases.'

'I see that. That's sound thinking. Go on.'

'I had the idea – disastrous in retrospect – of a surprise firework display.'

'And you didn't think to discuss it with Dr Russell-Morgan or Miss Gabriel. Or even the matron?'

'No, I didn't. I don't know why I didn't. I discussed many of the men's other requirements.' But she knew why. She had to admit she wanted the glory to be hers, the triumph and the success to be enjoyed gleefully by her alone. To have people talking about the party in years to come; her work colleagues, the Baileys, her church fellowship. To have people recognise *her* for once. These thoughts were difficult to admit to the efficient, earnest young woman in front of her.

Miss Dorothy spoke quietly: 'There is something of a lesson to be learned here. Sometimes in pleasing God we may also please ourselves, but it is precisely when we please ourselves that we must watch our motives don't become vainglorious.'

Leonora felt the unpleasant sensation of this woman's gentle rebuke all up her neck. Her skin was almost crawling; she shuddered involuntarily, as if she could shake off this feeling. She fought back the urge to respond, to justify, because deep down she understood that this rebuke, her punishment, had been designed to teach her a lesson.

'All things considered, we will wait a while to consider your fitness for the forewoman's role. Let me reassure you, you are a very diligent and most conscientious worker, who gives freely of her spare time.'

Leonora closed her eyes briefly, committing the words to memory, knowing she would need them as a balm later.

'However, the work is also about our relations with our co-workers. We are all working together as a team: that means sharing information freely so that in your *collaborations*,' she gave the word heavy emphasis, 'we might learn tolerance and respect of others.'

'Does this mean I am to lose all chance of...?' She couldn't bring herself to say "promotion".

'Not at all. I am merely suggesting a few extra months to give you sufficient time to prepare your mind and heart. Now I'm sure you're keen to get back to work.'

Leonora rose from her seat, feeling like someone who had been in an accident. She tried to smile but her mouth was strangely frozen. Walking felt odd, too. Miss Dorothy was suddenly at her side.

'You will be ready one day. Now go and face those girls and put it out of your mind.' Leonora stumbled out into the corridor. She adjusted her hair, checking it was still in place and smoothed down her clothes. Taking a deep breath, she exhaled loudly and made her way to Q block.

She'd just got there, full of resolve, to hear the news that Mary Morris had gone to France.

CHAPTER 15

It was one of those life-changing moments, she reflected, as she packed her bag for France. Mary had been at work when she'd heard news of the latest crisis in Dunkirk. The Friends Ambulance Unit, organised by Laurence Cadbury, George Cadbury's eldest, had sent a telegram to the Bournville Works asking for assistance from any Cadbury men who had not yet signed up.

Jim the lodge-keeper had told her, 'They need stretcher bearers in particular to transfer the injured men from the battlefield to the hospitals. They're based in a town near Dunkirk.'

'Are they like doctors?' Mary had asked. She was certain Daniel was serving in that region.

'As good as,' Jim had replied. 'Only the Red Cross people don't think much of them.'

Mary had nodded, remembering her time at Snow Hill Station, where she'd noticed the hostility between the St John Ambulance woman with the bullfrog face and the FAU officer. How she'd slapped Mary's hand and denied the man a piece of cake.

Jim had told her a group of Bournville men had volunteered. They had forty-eight hours to get ready and to be at Snow Hill station for 10 p.m. on Monday night. Mary processed all of this and decided.

When she arrived at Snow Hill she had no trouble spotting the FAU officer she'd seen before. He was in khaki uniform again, addressing a small group of men. If they were the Bournville factory men she didn't recognise any of them. Her small case contained two dresses, her work pinafores, underwear, soap, tooth powder and brush. She wore her lace-up work boots, her best coat; fingers crossed it would be enough. In her pocket was a box of Neapolitan chocolates she had stolen from the Comforts room. She had wedged her hat firmly on her head.

The FAU man broke away from the group and surveyed the station platform. The train was already in, she noticed. His gaze landed on her and he nodded – he looked as if he had recognised her but couldn't quite place her. He gave a quick glance behind and strode over to her.

'Good evening. We're not serving refreshments tonight.'

'I know.'

'Have you come to wave someone off? The train leaves in thirty minutes, or as soon as we get the signal.' Should she sneak on board or come clean now? She decided the latter.

She took a deep breath to fortify her nerves. 'No, I've come to volunteer. The call went round Bournville that you urgently needed people, so here I am.'

There was silence. She almost felt for him when she saw the look of embarrassment on his face.

'There's been some mistake.'

'You don't want volunteers?' Look him in the eye, she told herself. The way she'd told Daniel to do with the recruitment officer.

'We do, but we didn't ask for women. It's the men we want. For driving the ambulances and getting the injured men to the clearing stations.'

'I can drive – or I can learn if someone will teach me.'

He gave a harsh laugh. 'You don't understand. This isn't some school trip, some picnic at the seaside. We can't afford to carry anyone. Unless they've got skills we're not interested.

Now why don't you go home? It's cold.' He stamped his feet to emphasise the point.

Mary paused, looked down and then up.

'The work you're doing is wonderful, it really is. I want to be part of it. I can help, I can do whatever you need.'

He softened a little at her words. 'You're about the only one who thinks so. The Royal Army Medical Corps tell us off for getting in the way. They hate us because we're not regulated. Or else they lump us in with the conscientious objectors. Look, it's just not possible. I really have to go.'

He made to leave and then looked at her closely. 'I've seen you before, haven't I? You sang for the soldiers. Calmed them down that night when they were getting fractious. Lovely sweet voice. Stay here and visit the soldiers in the convalescent homes and sing them songs.'

She stood still on the platform, her case clutched tightly in front of her as she watched him walk away. She'd been so close, she sensed, to making a connection with him. She should have known it was a terrible idea but she just couldn't shake off the thought of being nearer to Daniel. He could have been transferred anywhere in France, she reasoned with herself; he could have been injured and on the next ambulance train home for all she knew. But the bond between them was strong and it told her that he was cold and frightened and she must do all she could to find him.

It was time to play her trump card. She called out, 'Excuse me –'

'Look, I thought I made it clear–'

'Can you give a message to Mollie Cadbury for me?'

'You know Mollie, Laurence's sister? She's a darn fine nurse.'

'Tell her I'll be posting some Neapolitan chocolates for her. How is she?'

'Working hard at the Queen Alexandra. It's very basic. Not exactly home from home.'

'You must need nurses there.'

'Trained, yes. Mollie did her prep at the Q.E.'

'I've got my St John Ambulance certificates. I can give you references.'

He sighed impatiently and held out his hand.

'Not with me, but you could telegraph through to Fircroft hospital and ask them to send them.' She gambled that by the time he found out she had lied it would be too late and she'd be in France. Her love for Daniel overrode any scruple, any conscience. *Did mothers feel like that about their children?*

'What do you say?' She sensed him weakening.

'Well...'

Yes! 'How about I get on this train and you turn a blind eye? You can act all surprised when you get there.'

He hesitated for two seconds, during which time she climbed on board the train.

Jessie passed the week after the party in a confused whirl. Mary's disappearance had caused a hullabaloo, coming close on the news of Miss Lime's dressing down. There would be an enquiry into Mary's disappearance, according to Miss Lime, who – whilst claiming to be indignant at Mary's 'midnight flit' – was clearly grateful to have someone take the attention away from her.

Opinion was divided amongst the girls as they dissected Mary's story, easily the most exciting thing to have happened since the war started.

'Isn't she brave?' Evelyn said, her face still pale with grief.

'Or mad. She could have said something, though.' Ruth was clearly hurt so Jessie kept Mary's confession to herself.

'Is she really going to drive an ambulance?'

'I heard she was pregnant with Sam Eastwood's baby,' one of the girls speculated.

'That's rubbish, and you know it.' Jessie couldn't help but intervene. 'When we get her address we'll send her some treats.' Afterwards Jessie reflected on how easy it was to sort out other people's problems while her own life was in turmoil.

The crossing to Calais was rough. The ship seemed to lurch constantly, Mary thought, as she vomited for the hundredth time into a bucket. She sat on a hard bench on deck, empty-stomach and dehydrated with a terrible shiver that she couldn't stop. Others were in the same condition: mostly men in uniforms as well as a few nurses. They all ignored her, too concerned with their own wretchedness.

By the time Mary sat on the waiting room bench at Calais train station, her bag clutched to her lap, she feared she might actually die from cold. A ragbag of men waited with her: a few soldiers returning, a handful of FAU men and their officer, whose name she had finally found out by asking one of the others.

'His name's Richard Ockwell. I'd stay out of his way though. He's bloody furious with you. Moaned about you the whole train journey from Birmingham.'

It was hours until the next train.

'Sod this for a lark,' said one of the men, standing up. 'Let's go and find something to eat in town. I've got some francs in my pocket and I need somewhere to thaw out.' He'd been squatting against the Brazier, and shivered as soon as he pushed himself away from it. The other men stood up preparing to join him. At least they had overcoats, Mary thought; her thin wool coat was hardly adequate. Her lips were turning blue. How she'd kill for a cup of tea or cocoa.

All the men were leaving, as if she didn't exist. She closed her eyes, not bearing to watch them abandon her. The open door let in another icy draft and then it was silence. Great, she thought. *Pigs, the lot of them. I left the security of home for this?* Snow had started falling outside. She brought her knees up to her chest and cradled them with her arms, as she pressed her face into her coat. She couldn't speak French – she'd had the chance to learn at day continuation school, but she hadn't seen the point. She wanted to cry but thought the tears would freeze on her face. She opened her eyes.

Richard, the FAU officer, leaned against the door. He had a rueful smile on his face.

'I thought you'd left me.'

'I was tempted to, believe me, you darned nuisance, but it wouldn't have been right.' He held up his arms as she opened her mouth to protest. 'I know you can look after yourself – the way you handled those soldiers was brilliant.' She knew he was talking about the night at Snow Hill Station.

Now the tears did come, hot on her frozen cheeks. She wiped them away quickly.

'Thank you,' she said, smiling. 'For staying.'

He didn't reply, just sat down at the other end of the bench. The station manager came in to turn the gas lamp on. Richard spoke to him in French. Their conversation was rapid, fluent, she couldn't catch a single word. When he left Richard said, 'The next train isn't for another three hours.'

'Three hours?'

'But there's another train back to Bologne harbour coming soon.'

She focused on the steam coming out of his mouth as he spoke. 'Why are you telling me that?'

'Look, this was a silly idea. Why don't you catch the boat back home? I can telegraph to say you're coming.'

'You just said you knew I could look after myself.'

'I know, but you wouldn't do this if you had any choice. The hospitals here are nothing like the ones at home. They won't be nicely patched up, pottering around in the garden, playing games of cards. Once you've seen it, you can't un-see it.' He shook his head slightly. Mary sensed him retreating into a darker place in his mind, but knew she had to carry on.

'You chose to do it. You had a choice.'

'It's my calling – if that doesn't sound so bloody pious.'

'It's my calling too. I want to help.' He paused, as if he were considering what to say. For a moment she wondered about confiding in him about Daniel, but no, she couldn't trust him, not yet.

He got out writing paper and a pen from his kit bag. 'Just letting the folks back home know I'm all right. Trying to give them something to brag about to their friends. It's different when you're not actually fighting though. My mother is always telling me about so-and-so's son who's been awarded a bravery medal.'

'I'm sure she's proud of you.'

'I sometimes think she'd prefer it if I died a hero's death.'

Mary recoiled from the bitterness of his words. 'That's a wicked thing to say.'

'I know. I don't mean it.' He screwed up his face and ran a hand over his forehead in a scrubbing action. 'It's just that... Forget it. Do you want to write home too?'

'Yes, please.' She would write to Jessie and ask her to give news to her ma. Richard put the writing set on the bench between them so she could use the pot of ink. She dipped her pen in.

Dear Jessie,

Please tell mother I'm fine and safely in France. How are you? Right now I'm sitting in a freezing cold train station in a place called Callay (I don't think the spelling's right but that's how they say it) before we get to Dunkirk.

The crossing was horrible. I was sick the whole time. When I eventually went on deck I saw a lovely string of birds in a V shape flying to France ahead of us. It felt like a good sign, like they were pointing me to Daniel.

I almost didn't get here. There was an almighty row at Snow Hill with the FAU bloke determined not to let me on the train. Let's just say I managed to persuade him. I think he's regretting it. Even now he's trying to get me on the boat back home!

Must go now as I don't want to use up all of his paper and ink.

Will write again soon as I get to the hospital where they're putting me. Please look after mother for me and give the twins a kiss.

Your loving friend, Mary

P.S. Tell Miss Lime I'll be away for the foreseeable. She'll be glad to see the back of me, no doubt.

She folded the sheet into an envelope and wrote *Jessie Paignton* and her friend's home address. Richard took it off her and said, 'I'll see it gets posted.'

An hour later the men burst into the waiting room, brushing snow from their overcoats and hats, and tapping their boots against the legs of the bench. Their faces were merry and they staggered around, clearly fuelled by alcohol.

'We found a hotel. They let us bathe and shave and gave us dinner, all for 2 1/2 francs. I'm stuffed.' He patted his stomach and belched.

'What happened to you?' he said to Richard. 'We thought you'd come with us.'

'I had some paperwork to do,' he said. Was it her imagination, Mary wondered, or was there a slight flame to his cheeks?

The man looked at Mary and fished inside his jacket pocket, bringing out a bag. 'I got you some penny rolls.' He gave one to her awkwardly, then passed the bag to Richard. The smell of yeast made her salivate. She broke off a piece of bread and ate it. Meat inside. Stringy, salty meat. She didn't care if it was horsemeat. She was thirsty and she watched as a hip flask was passed around. Richard refused it but she took a swig of the liquid – it burned her throat and chest but it was welcome. The kindness of Richard and now the other men added to her sense of well-being.

The train journey to Dunkirk was better. It was all flatlands, as she gazed out of the window, watching as gulls flew and swooped down, making a racket, crying.

'We're at the seaside but this is no holiday,' said one of the men. Once they got off the train the men dispersed and it was just her and Richard trooping down the streets of Malo Les Bains heading for the FAU headquarters. The road was carpeted with slushy mud. They arrived at a large town square with a row of hotels and cafes. Her boots were wet through and her skirts were sodden and muddy. It looked like a parade was going on. She saw FAU men marching and noticed a fleet of ambulances with canvas covers lined up outside a hotel.

'Here we are.'

Mary glanced up to see the frontage. Underneath the name of the hotel's proprietor, A. Pyl, a freshly-painted wooden sign declared that this was the Friends Ambulance Unit Headquarters.

Richard said, 'I'll report for duty and then get someone to escort you to the Queen Alexandra hospital. It's just up the road.'

She felt disappointment and also a fear that Richard wouldn't be there to introduce her and vouch for her. But it was silly. She'd got this far on her own wits. For her nerves to fail at this stage would be ridiculous. Just think of Daniel, she told herself.

She held out her hand. 'Well, thank you, you've been a big help. Just point me in the right direction and I'll go there by myself.' She wondered if she would see him again.

He told her to look out for a group of wooden huts. 'Like I said, it's a pretty basic hospital but the staff are very good. You'll be fine. I'll drop in now and then, but for the moment I'm off manning the ambulance train.'

The Queen Alexandra was opened in 1915. The huts could accommodate 150 patients, the superintendent explained. 'Mostly French civilians but we're seeing more British servicemen by the day.' Pinned to the noticeboard there was a sign saying *Hello* in different languages, like French, German, Chinese and Japanese. Mary saw dark-skinned men walking around with spades and pick-axes.

'Are they the Chinese?' she asked.

'Ah, we're a medley of races here. There are Chinese labour battalions here. West Indians too. And Algerians. Do you have any French? Pity. The men are building new dugouts all the time.'

'What are dugouts?'

'When there's a bomb raid – believe me, they're shelling daily at the moment – we get the patients into the dugout shelter.'

Mary reeled. No-one had mentioned bombs to her. No wonder Richard didn't want her coming. If she got killed by a falling shell this whole enterprise would have been for nothing.

The superintendent narrowed her eyes and then looked Mary up and down. 'Are you sure you've been properly trained? Only you don't seem like our usual sort.'

'I came over with Mr Ockwell from the FAU. He'll give me a personal recommendation.'

'Your papers?'

'I... lost them on the way.'

'But are you sure you've done the training?'

Mary beamed. 'Of course.'

The superintendent gave her a quick tour. 'Each of the wooden huts has its own gardening plot for growing vegetables.'

Mary allowed herself a moment of humour. *So Miss Lime was right after all!*

'See those tents over there? Stay away. Those are for infectious cases. We had a typhoid epidemic last year and we don't want a repeat.'

So if the bombs don't get me then the typhoid will.

'I'll take you to your sleeping quarters.'

CHAPTER 16

The sleeping quarters turned out to be an old villa nearby run by a sour-faced patron, who did not return Mary's smile. The superintendent beckoned her up the stairs to a landing and a room with two beds in it. Two nurses' uniforms hung on the outside of the large wardrobe.

'I'll put you in with C.D. and her colleague.'

Mary went to put her case on the bed.

'Not there. You'll have to sleep on the floor for now.'

The superintendent left her alone. The room was square, functional, and the floor space between the two metal beds was no wider than the bedside table separating them. Sleeping down there will be interesting, she thought.

There had been some attempt to make it homely. The bed coverings were fancy – silk by the feel of it. Photographs had been pushed through nails in the wall. She moved closer to look at them. A man in uniform. Another of a large house and garden. A bit like Fircroft, only bigger, and a family of girls in fancy clothes. The eldest of the girls stood behind her seated sisters. She looked confident, haughty, a tall drink of water, as her granddad used to say of any girl above average height.

Mary moved over to the bedside table and opened the drawer. On top of a bundle of silk clothes was an envelope marked *Camilla Dungate: documents*. She peeked inside the opening. It looked like official papers of some kind. Beneath the underwear there was a collection of small cases. She picked one up and tried to prise it open.

'If you've quite finished snooping–' a voice said from behind her.

Mary turned quickly, dropping the case, and shutting the drawer with her hip. The tall girl from the photograph was glaring at her. 'Perhaps you'd like to tell me who you are and what the hell you're doing in my room.'

Mary stared back. The girl was in a nurse's uniform, soiled badly, with mud and bloodstains.

'Nothing to say, huh? Well, come with me then.' She approached her and Mary recoiled, falling back on the bed. 'I warn you, after the night I've had I'm in no mood for any fun and games.' Her grip of Mary's arm was strong and the girl hauled her into the corridor, ignoring Mary's pleas for her to stop. Doors opened on the landing and other girls came out, curious to see what was going on. Mary bowed her head to avoid the hostile faces in front of her, thinking, how can I explain? Then a solution came to her.

'I was looking for Mollie. Mollie Cadbury.' The faces around her relaxed. 'I've got some of her favourite chocolates. The Neapolitans she likes.'

'So why were you rummaging through my things?'

'I thought if it was her room I could leave them on her bed as a surprise.'

The haughty girl said, 'Mollie is on leave at the moment – back in Blighty for a few weeks. But I can help you out with the chocolates. Camilla Dungate at your service.'

Mary laughed with relief and held out her hand. 'Mary Morris, Supplier of Emergency Chocolate Rations,' she said, imitating the clipped tones of the woman.

Camilla pulled her filthy apron over her head. 'I'm so hungry I could eat a scabby donkey. Let's get changed and see what slop is on the menu today. Coming to the canteen?'

She took Mary back in the direction of the hospital. The canteen was in a wooden hut identical to the hospital wards.

They queued for a bowl of soup and a bread roll doled out by exhausted women. Camilla led them to a bench.

She slurped the soup and pulled a face, knocking the stale bread on the table for effect. 'She's a good egg, that Mollie. How long have you been friends?'

'More acquaintances, really.' Mary said. 'We did some charity work together at Bournville. And I know her father very well. Such a kind gentleman.' *Well, that last bit is true.* Mary tried the soup. It was mainly beef stock with shreds of meat and some grey dumplings.

'Look I'm sorry I was so vile just now. What a welcome, eh! I'd only just come off a day-and-a-half shift. We had the most bloody time in the ambulance last night. We went into a ditch and–' She touched her left arm and winced at the bruising. 'Luckily, it wasn't worse. We got the men in safely, just about.'

'You were travelling in the ambulance?' Mary felt a spark of excitement.

'I was driving the thing.' Her chest stuck out a little. 'We went out to the CCS, that's the Casualty Clearing Station, in Dunkirk. They're supposed to be two of us in the front but my partner got called out to deal with a civilian emergency in the town. She's gone down with flu this morning. I hope she doesn't pass it on.'

'Where did you learn to drive?' Mary asked.

'Daddy let me have a go on the family car when I was fourteen. As he didn't have any sons he said he wasn't going to miss out on teaching me to drive.'

Mary thought of her father, bullying, hectoring and shuddered.

'When the war started,' Camilla continued, 'he said I could jolly well sign up and do something useful. Once they found out I could drive they put me on ambulance duties. I should have kept my mouth shut.' She looked at Mary. 'Where are they sticking you?'

'I don't know.'

'Come in the ambulance with me. The only thing I'd say is don't expect a routine. You might get days where not much happens – then you're expected to talk to the patients on the wards – all sorts of nationalities here, so if you got languages you'll be snapped up.'

Mary shook her head. 'To tell you the truth, I don't even have my first aid certificate.'

The girl slapped the table and laughed heartily, causing heads to turn. 'Lord, you'll end up doing the washing up in the labour quarters. Wouldn't wish that on anyone.'

'That's not all. Have they told you we're sharing a room now?' Mary said, waiting for the young woman's reaction. More laughter came and beneath the jolly exterior Mary could tell her nerves were exhausted.

Mary was suddenly grateful for her luck. She'd taken a risk coming out here but if she tried to settle down and blend in she would amass the information that could lead her to Daniel.

After much agonising Jessie had made a decision. She would make every effort to strengthen her marriage again.

She put the episode with Thomas down to a kind of insanity. She felt tainted and blemished, although glad it hadn't gone further than a kiss. She cursed the naiveté through which she had fallen heedless into the arms of another man. His expression of feelings for her had turned her head, that was all, and she had confused the care she felt for him with a baser kind of desire.

Jessie pulled the machine down and cut through the straw card. The repetition of the same movement, day in, day out was giving her pain. So when Miss Lime mentioned again the idea of moving her to the Men's department because they were so short, she simply shrugged and said, 'All right.'

She told Bill that night.

'What do you think, Jess?'

'I don't mind. It's not the same without Mary, not so much

of a laugh.' She hadn't been to see Thomas since the night of the party. Her feelings for him were all mixed up.

She looked across at Bill. 'You look so much better now you're back at work.' His hair had grown back to its normal length and she preferred it that way.

'Are you district nursing tonight?'

'No, let's stay in and talk.'

She resolved there and then not to go back to Fircroft.

She and Bill had a good night. He told her some jokes he'd picked up at work and they laughed to the point of hysteria. When she reached into a cupboard Bill noticed her wince with pain. She sat down at his feet while he rubbed her aching shoulder with firm thumbs. He took her hair pins out and unwound her locks, letting them cascade over his hands. She'd forgotten what it was like to be touched by him. And when Florrie Tops knocked to see if Bill wanted supper, Jessie said, 'It's all right – he's with me tonight.' And she took pleasure in shutting the door and adding more coal to the fire.

Their Christmas was spent with just the two of them and she managed not to think of Thomas alone in his hospital bed. Most of the time.

The new year brought a proper winter; heavy snow fell and kept falling all through February and even into early March. They were all glad when the thaw arrived.

One break time Jessie spotted Helen Daw out on the terrace. She hadn't seen much of her since the disastrous party. She wanted to avoid the temptation to find out about Thomas, to check he was all right. As she approached Helen she noticed the girl didn't look terribly well – she was deathly pale and she picked at her dry biscuit without appetite.

'The food's rotten, isn't it,' Jessie said, 'with all these shortages.' They were all missing the sugar rations.

Helen didn't reply, just pulled the yoke of the pinafore away from her neck and blew down it. She tugged at the cloth underneath, clearly uncomfortable, as though it was restricting her.

'Are you all right? You look awfully hot.' Jessie was concerned. 'You're not sickening for flu, are you? Helen, I wanted to ask how Thomas Walker was.' The words were out before she could stop them. But, she told herself, she was only asking how he was, not going to see him. Her resolve was like sand trickling through an hourglass.

'He's all right. His ankle's getting better. He can walk without a stick in mobility training and Dr Russell-Morgan has got him on the electrical therapy.'

Jessie let out a deep breath. He was still there. They hadn't sent him back yet. Thank goodness. 'Oh, what's that?' she said, feigning interest.

Helen explained how it worked.

'And has Thomas been having this therapy?'

'Oh yes.' Jessie felt a stab of envy at Helen. She pictured herself rolling up his trouser leg, and undoing his bandages, tentatively touching the raised red scar before strapping on the machine. *But that's all in the past. New year, fresh start.* She realised with sadness that Thomas hadn't asked after her. Perhaps he was embarrassed.

The next few weeks passed quickly and one morning Bill announced, 'There's a work's outing to Weston at the weekend. Shall I get us tickets?' Jessie nodded, with a strong sense everything was going to be all right. After her half-day shift on Saturday she was to come straight back to catch the coach at 1 p.m. The plan was to stay over until Sunday.

Bill hugged her, saying: 'All the people in my section are going and you can't blame a man for wanting to show off his wife.'

Saturday came and Jessie prepared sandwiches before setting off for work. Perhaps it was time to think about leaving Cadbury for good to concentrate on Bill, now he was back at work full-time. She would mention it when they were on Weston beach or in a cafe if the wind drove them indoors.

At midday when the shift ended, Jessie lined up for her wages tin. She pocketed the twenty shillings and reflected that Bill had been right that her wage didn't compare to his.

'Are you coming to the shop?' Ruth asked.

'I'm off to the seaside,' Jessie answered, pulling on her coat.

Just as she was leaving Helen Daw dashed into the dressing room. She'd just come from Fircroft. Breathless, she gave Jessie an envelope addressed to *Mrs Paignton* and said, 'Sorry, I can't stop.' Jessie immediately recognised the handwriting – the wide open loop of the 'g'. She pocketed the note to avoid questions from the other girls, although Ruth looked curious.

I've tried to stay away, she told herself, as she left the Works through the lodge. Turning right, she ran in the direction of Thomas. Just to see him one last time.

Jessie arrived there just as the patients were taking part in an exercise class on the lawn. He wasn't amongst the men. She hurried through reception and past the appliances room where Thomas had kissed her. Matron was seated at her desk and there was a hush, most of the men being outdoors.

Jessie's shoes clacked on the wooden floor and matron, without glancing up and said, 'No visitors until 6 p.m.'

Jessie went up and stood right in front of her desk. She put her hand on it, to steady herself, aware of the matron's gaze slowly going up her arm until she stared into her face. Jessie's mouth was dry.

'Is Thomas... Private Walker still here?' The matron closed the ledger she had been writing in with a thud.

'Mrs Paignton? We thought you'd abandoned us. Not a word from you about your district nursing duties and you left us high and dry over Christmas when we needed you most.'

'Oh, I'm sorry I haven't been lately. My husband–'

'An explanation, even a short note, would have been appreciated.' Her voice was pure acid.

'Yes, of course. I'm sorry. I wondered if he's still here. I have a letter to give him,' she improvised. 'From his mother.'

'Give it to me and I'll ensure it's passed on.'

Jessie made a show of patting her clothes and pretending she'd lost the letter.

'I must've dropped it. Can I speak to him in person?'

Matron gave her a withering look. 'Very well,' she said, with a huff. She lifted her bulk out of the chair and led the way to Thomas's ward.

Jessie felt jubilant – she tried to suppress the jaunt in her step. She didn't care if matron stood by the entire time. Just to see him one last time and whisper goodbye.

The second before they arrived at the bed, she felt a shudder go through her. The bed, she knew, would be empty. Furthermore, matron, who had turned with a supercilious smile on her face to face Jessie, had known all along that Thomas was not there. A petty revenge.

'But–' Jessie started to say. No further words came.

'Oh, dear me,' Matron said. 'Private Walker appears to have taken himself off back to the Front.'

Jessie walked unsteadily to the bed and touched the foot of it. The sheets and pillows were fresh on the bed, the over blanket drawn tight and tucked in. No trace at all of Thomas. It was as if he'd never been there. The male orderly leaned on his mop and said, 'Looks like lover boy's gone.'

Feeling faint, she sat down on the edge of the bed. Matron tutted in exasperation and then Jessie was aware of the click of her heels as she marched back to her desk.

Somehow Jessie managed to walk outside. The sunlight, still bright, was an assault on her eyes. She shivered and felt she would never feel warm again. The sun would never bring comfort to her bones. Despite the temperature a trembling feeling had started up inside her; her teeth chattered and a slow, animal-like howl emanated from her.

He had gone.

She couldn't bear to go home yet. After leaving Fircroft she walked past the village green and into Bournville Park. She down on a bench. Parents and children strolled past. A young man pushed a wounded soldier wearing hospital blues in his wheelchair. Why had she never thought to bring Thomas here?

She remembered the unopened letter in her pocket. His note was written on the back on an old army postcard, the message curt. *They're sending me back. Did I mean anything to you? T.A.W.*

That's when the hurt had flooded through her body and her heart had ached.

At five o'clock she had thought of the forgotten seaside trip. Too late now. With any luck Bill would have caught the coach without her.

By the time she arrived home it was past seven and dark. The moment she opened the door and stepped into the hallway she sensed the house was occupied, although no lights burned downstairs. She took off her hat and coat, and tiptoed along the floor, glancing upstairs to listen for signs of Bill.

She stepped forward in the hallway and heard a shredding sound and smelled burning. She went into the kitchen and took in the scene in front of her. Bill was sitting at the table in the dark, his bowed, still figure somehow corpse-like. The only movement was in his hands. The candle in front of him was burnt almost to a stump and he held a fragment of paper to the stuttering flame, where it caught, flamed and disintegrated into ash. She realised that tearing sound she'd heard earlier was coming from Bill as he ripped a page out of a book and tore that into shreds. Not aggressively. Quite the opposite. His slow and careful manner frightened her before she could analyse why. He began to make smaller and smaller pieces, in a repetitive, manic action – feeding each piece one-by-one to the flame, staring as though he were in a trance. He finally looked up at her and the candle died.

The room was icy cold.

'What are you doing, Bill?' He didn't reply. She lit the gas lamp and saw ashes on his fingers, a black smudge down his vest, and finally the mess on the table: the stump of the candle, ashes in its saucer, an empty tumbler and an open book. She wondered idly if it was one of Hugh's books but that made no sense. He tore another page from it.

'Do you still love me, Jessie?'

His voice was so soft and casual it shocked her, like a knife jabbing and twisting beneath her ribs.

'Bill,' she said, 'I'm sorry I'm so late. I'm sorry I missed the trip. There was a crisis at work and... Let me make us a drink and then I'll tell you all about it.'

He continued tearing strips. With horror she realised that the book, with its flimsy pages, was her Bible. He was tearing her Bible to pieces. The Bible she'd been given by the Cadburys.

'How dare you? Stop it. It's mine,' she said, with a childlike sense of injustice.

Jessie wasn't a frequent churchgoer; she hardly believed in God. But this was awful. The Bible was sacred. *Haven't we had enough calamity in this house and now you're inviting more?*

'I know it's yours.' He hauled himself to his feet, using the table for support, and limped over to her. He shoved the book in her face. 'Read that: *On the occasion of your marriage.* I never should've let you go back to that place. Where are you, Jessie?' He spread his hands wide and looked around as if appealing to an audience.

'What do you mean? I'm here, aren't I? And I said I was sorry for being late.'

'I went there, you know, to meet you today.'

'Where?'

'The Works.' Her heart contracted. *This is it.* 'I couldn't find you. No-one knew where you were. I thought you'd had an accident. Then someone said they'd seen you go in the direction of the hospital.' He stared at her, and shook his head. 'You've changed. Even my mam said–'

'Oh, I can remember what your mam said,' Jessie said bitterly. 'She's never held back from giving us her opinions.'

'That's not fair. If it hadn't been for her–'

'You'd have been left to fend for yourself by your selfish wife. Never mind that your selfish wife had no choice about going back to work. But why let the truth get in the way of a good sob story, eh?' He reached towards her in a gesture of conciliation. She stepped back, but not so quickly that she didn't catch the alcohol on his breath.

'Don't,' she said. She was bubbling inside. 'Perhaps I should have let us starve. Would that have been better?' His expression told her she had gone too far.

'I know you've had a hard couple of years caring for me, but I don't want a nursemaid. I want a wife. My wife. The way it used to be.' He touched her face and she looked downwards. Please don't kiss me, she urged silently. After the intimacy of the other night he was a stranger to her again.

A lump formed in her throat, preventing her from speaking. He gathered the fragments of paper into his hand, came close to her and very slowly sprinkled them over her head. She closed her eyes as he spoke the words. 'Let no man put asunder. You remember our marriage, do you?' She heard him roar and opened her eyes to see him tear the Bible in two and fling both parts against the wall.

'That's what our marriage is.'

He slumped and stumbled back to his chair. Jessie realised she'd been cowering from him and relief flooded her veins.

'I get more interest from her next door than from you,' he said, jerking his head towards the wall behind him.

Say something, she urged herself. *Soothe him, pacify him, tell him he's wrong.* She opened her mouth. The words froze and died inside her throat before she could utter a single sound.

There was no reasoning with him. She turned to fetch a

broom to sweep up the pieces, picking fragments out of her hair. She was incapable of thought or speech, but this simple action of clearing up was easy.

'For God sake, leave it!' he thundered and she dropped the broom where it clattered to the floor. His outburst seemed to have shocked him too and punctured all his rage. He sagged a little, then came over to her again.

'Jessie, it's time you left that job. Come back to me. Back home.'

And, as if she were an invalid, he put his arm around her and hauled her upstairs.

I can't do this, she said to herself. I thought I could but I can't.

Next morning she gathered a few things: clothes, her cleanest uniform still hanging on the line. She picked up the two halves of the bible and dropped them in the grate. Let Bill have the pleasure of burning it later. The voice of reason said, *You don't have to leave. Thomas has gone. Stay here and repair your marriage.* But it wasn't just about Thomas. She didn't know yet if the damage was irrevocable, only that she had no choice but to pick up her bag and tell Bill she was leaving.

'Where will you go?' he said. He seemed resigned, making no attempt to stop her.

'To stay with a friend.'

'A friend? You mean another man?'

She shook her head. 'I promised a friend. She's had to go away. I'm going to stay with her mother.'

'Let me get this straight.' His eyes were cold and bored into her like a stick. 'You're going to move in with the mother of this friend of yours?'

She could no longer meet his gaze. But she had to face up to her feelings: where there was once love and tenderness she felt only a hard resolution.

CHAPTER 17

Jessie had rehearsed what she was going to say. She would explain to Mrs Morris that she was a friend of her daughter and could she lodge with her for a short time. 'I can pay you rent, I wouldn't expect any favours,' she would say. But when the door opened and Mrs Morris, a tiny, birdlike figure, looked up at her with such concern, Jessie could do nothing more than sob. She was aware of Mary's twin sisters, aged nine, watching her as she let herself be steadied by the woman and led into the tiny house.

'I've made a mess of everything,' she said.

'Don't cry, lovely,' Mrs Morris said, soothingly. 'Whatever it is, we can sort it out,' She made up Mary's bed for her and told Jessie the twins would sleep in with her. Compared to her comfortable home in Fordhouse Lane, this was primitive. Not quite a slum but dark and dank with a tiny back room. Well, she had made her bed and she must lie in it.

Mary put the VAD nurse's apron on. It was freshly laundered and sparkling white and she deftly tied the strings at the side. She double-checked the items in her front pocket: scissors, notebook and pencil, thermometer. The daily routine at the hospital had become second nature now that spring had arrived.

It was only now, after four months, that Mary realised how ill-equipped she had been when she first arrived at the Queen Alexandra. She lacked every skill needed for a nursing job: she was tickle-stomached, nearly fainting at the sight of blood;

she'd had no training, no induction, and – she had quickly intuited – she was not part of their social class. Listening in on conversations taught her about the fairytale world of the volunteer nurses: big houses with huge gardens, maidservants, Mummy and Daddy, French lessons, musical instruments and private tutors. That Mary succeeded at all was down to her energy and years of hard work at Cadbury. Her warm and friendly manner with the patients meant she was a big hit.

She remembered her second day on the hospital ward where she was left on her own to change a dressing when one of the VADS was called away. A soldier named Hughes was recovering from a shrapnel wound to his arm. The army surgeon at the CCS ('Casualty Clearing Station – don't you girls know anything?') had removed the six-inch piece and Hughes had kept it proudly under his pillow.

'What do you reckon to this then? Sticking right out of my arm it was, like the Eiffel Tower. This is coming back to Blighty with me. I'll take you and all if you play your cards right,' he said to Mary.

'Doctor, can't you remove this man's sense of humour. It's rotten.'

The men whistled and Mary grinned. She unwound the stained, seeping bandage. 'Phewee, that stinks,' she said.

The wound was yellow. She pressed an absorbent pad on it and tried to remember the pictures from the manual she had studied the night before. The bandage kept slipping down, no matter which way she tried it.

'I'm sorry, I'm sorry, I just can't seem to get it... Oh.' It had fallen off.

'You're not like the rest of them, are you?' Hughes said with a grin. He had spotted it right away but Mary had managed to convince Camilla she was the real thing.

After a week she stank herself. There was barely a minute in the day to take a personal wash. Only cold baths were available in the villa's sleeping quarters. Mary longed for the girls' swimming baths at Bournville.

Camilla took her to the 'luxury bathing facilities' down in Hotel Pyl where, for a franc, Mary had the dubious pleasure of showering in a bathroom so cold that ice had formed on the floor between bathers.

The water that eventually gushed out of the overhead shower spray was piping hot. Camilla had said, 'Watch out. One end of you will freeze to death while the other gets scalded.' Mary hadn't minded. She'd hopped between feet until the ice melted and she relished the hot water down her hair and back, staying in there for so long, Camilla remarked afterwards, 'I thought you'd fallen down the drain.'

The first quarter of 1917 was one of the coldest winters that region of France had ever experienced. Mary had known icy winters in Birmingham but this coldness was something else. It was like being bitten all over or having your limbs in a vice. She rued the thinness of her nurse's uniform and thought with nostalgia about the Works' dressing room with its steel hot pipe and the metal cages where she could warm her boots.

'Didn't you bring any woollens?' Camilla asked, chipping away at the frozen surface of a jug of water with the end of a stick.

Mary shook her head and rubbed her freezing nose. She found it ironic to think of how many vests she'd knitted for the men and yet hadn't thought to send any for the nurses or women like Camilla, never mind bringing some for herself.

'Here, have one of my vests. Your lips are going blue.'

Her aim to start with had been to do enough to survive in France without getting sent back home. She wondered if Richard would come and see her but apparently he was away in Ypres. On the train to Malo Les Bains he had told her the Friends Ambulance Unit's unofficial motto: *Find work that needs doing. Regularise it later, if possible.* That was what she had done – found work that needed doing. In her case that work was trying to find Daniel.

Back in Bournville the early months of 1917 also sped by. Mr George announced that, owing to problems with the supply of milk, all milk chocolate production was to cease for the time being. The news sent shockwaves around the factory.

Miss Lime recovered something of her composure, Jessie thought, but whereas she once spoke her opinions freely, she now reined herself in.

She was also determined to change her manner with the girls. She'd give an order, adding 'if you'd be so kind'. Jessie, hearing her, thought of telling her it made her sound sarcastic.

Helen said, 'I preferred Miss Lime the way she used to be. I know she'd be harsh and all that but it's like she's a different person now.'

'I know,' Jessie said, seeking to reassure the young girl.

'Why did you have to go to another department, Jessie?' Helen had tears in her eyes. 'I wish you hadn't gone.'

Her new block, the fruit-drying section, took an extra ten minutes to walk to. But she didn't care where she worked. What was another move after the upheaval of leaving her home? Nothing could ever be as bad as that day when she had turned up on Mary's doorstep and fallen into Mrs Morris's arms. She had deliberately told no-one at work about her personal circumstances, but now it was time.

She spotted her former supervisor in the dining room. 'Miss Lime, can I speak with you please? In private.'

Jessie explained that she had moved out of her home and was lodging with Mary's mother. She expected Miss Lime to shout or to complain about her loose morals. She expected every reaction apart from the subdued response she received, where the woman said, 'Judge not lest ye be judged. Now, tell me how you're getting on in your new department.'

The atmosphere, Jessie told her, was completely different.

The workers were a mixture of men and other older married women. There was none of the frivolity engendered by Mary and her friends. Jessie preferred it this way, although she wouldn't say that to Miss Lime. She immersed herself in her work, took up her district nursing again for three nights a week and then went home to Mrs Morris, sometimes as late as 10 p.m.

'You haven't got to stay out on my account,' Mary's mother pleaded.

'I feel bad. I've already had one of your rooms. It's not right you and the twins having to sleep altogether.'

'It's all right, love. With Mary and her brother away I like having the girls in with me.'

Jessie was about to ask about Mary's brother, but the girls were buzzing around her now, sniffing out the treats that Jessie brought from the Works. Tonight she had dried fruit strips for the twins and they had pounced on them. She found the nine-year-olds a handful. The first night they had climbed over her, each trying to sit on her lap, and so she had pushed them laughingly to the floor, refusing until they had agreed to take it in turns.

'All right,' Maud had said to her twin. 'You go first.'

'No, it's all right,' her sister Beryl had replied. 'You go first!'

'No! You go first!' And so the argument had turned into a fight which Mrs Morris had had to separate.

'Now stop it, we've had enough fighting. Look at our countries. You wouldn't be squabbling if you could see where it leads.'

The twins had looked at their mother for a second and then restarted their tiff. 'Ow Mum! She's pulling my hair!' Maud had said, slapping her sister in retaliation.

'Stop that!' Mrs Morris had said in despair.

'It's only what our dad used to do to you, mam.'

Mrs Morris had flushed a deep red. Jessie had decided to take control.

'Come on, girls. Let's help your mother get the coal in.' She had glanced across at Mrs Morris. She pitied the poor woman, who had clearly once lived in fear of her husband. She had stood up and grabbed the hands of the two little girls. 'Let's go outside and if you're good I'll take you to the park tomorrow.'

After she had watched the two girls coaxing a stray cat she began a letter to her husband. It was strange to be putting down a different address.

My dear Bill, I just wanted to let you know I'm fine. I hope you are too. I'm sorry but I had to leave. This war has changed me, it's changed all of us really. I'm sorry I wasn't a better wife to you. I tried for a long time, I really did. I think when the babies died something at the core of me died as well, made me less able to love you the way you deserve.

She made no mention of Thomas Walker. She would write to Mary next and send her a parcel.

Camilla came into the bedroom with a box. 'There's a box for you, you lucky devil.'

Mary sat down and turned it over in her hands; who was it from? With her nurse's scissors she cut the string, peeled away the brown paper and tipped the contents onto the bed. Various items were wrapped up in more brown paper. She looked for a note or letter and found an envelope stuck inside the box.

'It's from Jessie. Of course!'

Hello dear friend, how are you? You will want to know how your mother is. She is very well, so are the twins (little terrors). I have some news that will surprise you. I am staying with your mother for the time being. She took me in when Bill and I parted.

Mary put the letter down, 'What? I don't believe it!' Darn it, she'd just written to Jessie and sent it to her home address. Hopefully Bill would have the decency to pass it on.

My neighbour is looking after Bill. She spends most of the evenings there, cooking on my stove for him. I don't like it but what can I do?'

'Blimey!' Mary said.

'What is it?' Camilla asked.

'Never you mind, nosy!'

I can't tell you how much we miss you at the Works – even Miss Lime! She's decided you're a patriotic heroine these days, a shining example to us all.

She suddenly felt a fraud. She hadn't come out here for noble reasons or in a spirit of self-sacrifice like all these volunteers, but to save her dear beloved Daniel. Mary could tell Camilla was impatient to have a look at the contents of the parcel.

'Go on then,' Mary said, 'open them.' The look of childish glee on Camilla's face made Mary smile.

'Look at this!' she squealed. 'A box of Cadbury's chocolates, Bournville *and* milk, you lucky old thing having a secret supply. And a book, how delicious! It's *Jane Eyre*. I've been longing to read it. It was banned in my school.'

'Oh yes, mine too,' Mary said drily.

'And soap!' She held the bar to her nose and inhaled. 'Pine forests! We could do with carbolic though. My head's been itching like mad lately.'

'Funny you should say that.' Mary's hand went to her scalp instinctively. She looked under her fingernails. 'You've given me bloody lice!'

That night they cropped their hair short. One less thing to worry about.

Two weeks later there was a knock on Mrs Morris's door. She sent the twins to answer it, and they came back with a letter for Jessie.

c/o British Field Post Office, Dunkirk

Dear Jessie,

First of all, please don't share this letter with Ma or the twins. Keep it safe or burn it, I don't mind. If for any reason I don't see you again I wanted you to know the truth about Daniel. I let everyone think he was my sweetheart because it was easier that way. But he's not. He's more special than that. He's my dear beloved little brother.

When I was sixteen my mother told me Daniel was conceived of rape. I thought that must be why my father always hated him – a reminder of another man's seed inside her. I didn't realise until later that my father was the animal that raped her. Why do I call him an animal when that's too good for him?

I was seven when Daniel was born. My father wouldn't go near my ma while she was screaming, 'Help me, help me, for God's sake,' so I went in the bedroom to help her bring Daniel into the world. When she was pushing him out I saw the bruise on her thigh – later I realised that the funny shape was the imprint of the b____'s boot stamping on her leg. When the baby came I wiped him and wrapped him up in one of my blankets and clutched him to me and sang to him all the songs I knew. When I finished I started all over again.

Eventually the woman next door came in to see to my mother. Ma was in a bad way and I got shushed off the bed, so I took Daniel to the window. It was the middle of the night and the moon came out from behind the clouds lighting up his tiny, screwed-up face and I felt such a rush of love that he became a part of me. I felt he was mine.

It was clear my father couldn't bear to be near him.

Daniel grew up, but he didn't thrive like we expected. He was sickly, caught every cold going, his chest wheezed like an old man's. His weakness seemed to inflame my father's rage. To see Ma holding Daniel over a bowl of steaming water to clear his chest set him off on one of his rants.

The first time my father hit Daniel he was only five. My brother was running towards my father's chair. I saw my father's arm pull back but before I could understand why he swung his arm into Daniel's path and walloped him so hard he went flying across the room, landing on one of our wooden chairs. I rushed to pick him up and my ma's eyes seemed to be pleading with me, 'Just leave it'. That night I checked him all over. There were old bruises as well as the fresh red and blue weal from where his ribs had landed on the back of the chair. I held him and sang him to sleep. Jessie, that was the hardest song I ever sang. My voice kept cracking but I carried on singing that soft lullaby for Daniel's sake.

My father wanted a son to play football but Daniel would shy away from the ball. It was as if the world was too much for him. He liked reading – he was good at the books like me – or sitting at Ma's feet while she talked to her friends in the yard.

As I got older and ready to start work, Ma said, 'Your father will want most of your wages but keep a bit back for yourself. Then you'll be your own woman.' Don't be like me, she was saying. I was a good saver when I got the job at Cadbury. Only five shillings a week to start with but going up a little each year the more experienced I got.

Meanwhile, Daniel started at school. It was a haven to start with until he got picked on worse than at home. He was like a magnet for the tormentors. Coming home without his shoes. One time I had to climb up the lamppost to get them back. He wrote a composition in lovely handwriting, just like yours, Jessie. He didn't even get to show it to his teacher. It was stolen from him and trodden into a puddle.

When Daniel was ten the twins were born.

Dad was free with his fists in the pub, always spoiling for a fight, so it was no surprise when he got arrested and put in prison for punching a man who turned out to be a policeman. Life improved no end. Do I sound hard? I was glad, Jessie. By then I was earning enough to support Ma, Daniel and the twins. People used to say, 'I'm sorry your dad's in prison.' I had to remember to look sad and bite my lip to stop myself from saying what I really wanted to: 'Isn't it great? I hope the b___ gets beaten to a pulp.' No-one at Cadbury knew apart from Miss Barratt and she was sympathetic and kept an eye out for me.

The strange thing was, Jessie, he never laid a single finger on me. I wanted him to. I'd have taken any bashing from him to save Daniel. I wanted to say, hit me, not him! He respected me for some insane reason. I couldn't fathom it. I still can't.

When my father came out of prison in August 1914 I knew I had to get Daniel away from the house. I'd tried to get him a job at Cadbury but he didn't pass the tests. I had a plan, you see. With us both working there we'd move out and lodge in someone else's house. I had it all worked out but it failed. Then I saw a recruitment poster when the war started and I thought let Daniel apply – get him away from home and Dad, and see the world, and (I'm ashamed to say it) a little bit of me thought, it'll toughen him up. How stupid was I? Daniel needed softness not violence. I had let my father's brutality and attitude begin to infect me.

He went to the recruitment station in Temple Street and got turned away. He was only sixteen and you had to be nineteen. So the next day – do you remember when I asked you to cover for me? – I took him myself and I told the officer that Daniel was nineteen. It was remarkably easy. Daniel swore afterwards it was the same officer but I'd told him to stand up straight and look him in the eye. Five days later he had to report for training camp and then three months after that I met him to see him off at New Street Station. In that time he'd filled out quite a bit.

'Feel my muscles,' he said proudly.

My instincts told me he could stand up to my father now and I wanted him at home but Daniel was excited the men had accepted him, so I had to let him go.

Meanwhile, my father had made enemies in prison. After he came out he was walking along the canal one night, drunk, and someone must have pushed him in the water because we had a policeman at the door to say his body had been found.

He was dead.

We all cried. I sobbed my heart out with my mother and the twins. God knows why. He was a monster, but maybe I thought he'd change one day, or get some understanding as to why he was so cruel like that to Daniel.

And then that night I woke up, sitting bolt upright in bed, realising that now Daniel would be safe. He could come back home and it would be safe place to be.

Jessie put the letter down. My goodness. She'd had no idea of the life Mary had led. Always singing and ready for a laugh or a leg-pull at work. She shuddered suddenly and, bracing herself, picked up the final page.

How stupid was I? I thought I could write to Daniel or someone in authority and have him sent home. I went to the recruitment office and asked who I needed to write to. This time it was a different officer. He laughed in my face and turned to the others and said, 'You won't believe what this one's just said. "My boy can come home now."' He slapped his knee, while I stood there, my face burning and heart about to explode. I went to the ambulance train at Snow Hill to see if I could find out more about where he was. Then a plan began to form in my mind – a beautiful idea, Jessie, so simple and yet so right. If Daniel wasn't going to come home I was going to find him and bring him back myself.

Jessie looked across to Mrs Morris, who was next to the fire plaiting one of the twin's hair. She couldn't reconcile this warm scene in front of her with the horrors they must've gone through. To think this house had seen such evil.

Thoughts of Bill came into her head. He would never have hit her – it was inconceivable. She had a sudden longing for comfort and sanity. She was in awe of Mary's determination; to love someone so much that she'd risk her life to rescue him. Jessie hoped for a safe return for them both.

Mary begged Camilla to let her go on ambulance duty with her.

'I know you mean well, but you have to understand the men don't lie there obediently while you tend their wounds like a modern-day Florence Nightingale and then smile up at you gratefully. Could you face a man begging you to put a bullet in his head because he can't stand the agony a second longer? Can you listen to his screams when you go bumping over the potholes in the road? What about when the screaming suddenly stops?'

The girl's words chilled Mary as she thought of Daniel.

'Here's the deal. You clean out the back of my ambulance the next five times I go out, and then I'll take you. When you've seen the blood and worse on the floor you might feel differently.'

Mary said, 'Do you wish you'd never signed up?'

'I don't know. Most days I loathe it and absolutely long for my bed at home, and Betty bringing me breakfast. That's my maid.'

'Mine's called Anna.'

'I haven't been truly warm for the last three months. But even so, do I regret it? No, but I'm convinced more than ever we must never have a war on this scale ever again.'

CHAPTER 18

Mary decided that although Camilla was different from the Cadbury girls – more refined, better-educated – she was just as willing to get stuck in, in a no-nonsense way, as the girls from the Comforts room had been. She was also passionately against the war.

One night while having a late bread-and-butter supper Camilla sighed and said: 'I wonder what the point of it all is sometimes. You know people call us the tidy-uppers? The governments create this mess and then we go round and pick up the pieces. And for what? So we can send the men back out there and start the whole cycle all over again. I sometimes wonder if this relief work is doing more harm than good.'

Camilla was clearly in a sombre mood. She gazed down at her uneaten bread, and Mary watched her absently pick crumbs off it.

'I've made that fatal mistake. I care. You know those three men I brought in last night? I went to check how they were getting on.'

She paused and looked away to try to hide her glistening eyes.

'The missing hand and the wound to the chest, both dead. The first bled to death earlier and the second, he died in the back of my ambulance and I didn't even know. I thought he was just unconscious. Can you imagine his last moments? It must have been hell.'

Mary put her arm around her but she moved away. Camilla

still hadn't trusted her enough to take her in the ambulance. If only she could get closer to the battlefield, she thought, she might stand a chance of finding Daniel. She had gone around the wards asking the men if they'd seen Private Daniel Morris. No luck so far.

'You've got another letter, it's not fair,' Camilla said, the next day. 'And a parcel.'

The handwriting was different from Jessie's and Mary opened it quickly to see who it could be from.

'*Goodness me,* [Miss Lime wrote] *you caused something of a stir when you left. I was asked to explain to Mr Edward Cadbury what I knew about one of my charges fleeing to France with the FAU convoy. I will admit I was tempted to wash my hands of you. What on earth were you thinking, you silly girl? I suppose you must have felt compelled to do your duty for your country, so your patriotism is to be commended. Out on the front line, treating the men when they are injured. We have the easier job back home.* Praise indeed from Miss Lime, thought Mary, in wonder. *Life continues much the same; we had a concert last week. I understand Jessie Paignton is writing to you separately so I won't spoil all her news. We have an influx of new girls to the Comforts room, all young and rather silly. If I was harsh with you, I apologise. I may have been misplaced in my views and let myself be ruled by prejudice, for which I am sorry.*

Mary put the letter down and shook her head, as if she had swimming water in her ears. Miss Lime's words had the effect of suddenly transporting her back to Bournville and making her homesick. Had she made the most awful mistake coming out to France?

'Why the glum face?' Camilla asked. 'Not bad news I hope.'

'No,' Mary said, snapping on a smile. 'Quite the opposite. A miracle really. Someone who made my life a misery now wants to sing my praises.'

'Hurrah,' Camilla said. 'That's worth celebrating. Do I spy some drinking chocolate in that parcel?'

Mary picked up the tin and threw it to her. 'It's a deal, as long as you make it.'

'Touché.'

Fifteen minutes later they were sipping at the scalding liquid.

'Just the smell is heavenly,' Camilla said. 'You're so lucky being friends with the Cadbury family. We don't have any useful friends that way. All Daddy's friends are in banking.'

Mary was about to explain by saying, 'I only work at the factory, you idiot,' but she stopped herself. She had a vague sense it might be useful for her to keep up the pretence a little longer. Mary drained her cup, 'You finished?'

'If you're washing up? You're top hole, Mary Morris. Are you coming to the Quaker meeting tonight? There's a meeting in one of the huts.'

'I don't think so. I wouldn't know what to do.'

'You don't have to do anything. Just stay silent until you feel moved to speak.'

Mary came out of the meeting strangely calm and ready for what life may throw at her. Camilla looked pleased she'd come.

'How come you're not a Friend?'

'I am your friend.'

'I mean a member of the Society of Friends? With your family connections I thought you'd be a birth right Quaker.'

Mary took a deep breath. 'I came out to try to find someone. In fact the longer I stay here the more hopeless I feel about knowing where to start. If I'd stayed at Cadbury I'd know for sure if he'd been killed from the news dispatches. By the time I left over one hundred and twenty of our men had been lost.'

'Do you mean you're a worker from the *factory*?' Camilla said incredulously. 'But I thought–'

'I was a friend of the Cadbury family? I just let everyone think that because it made life easier. You assumed and, well, I just didn't correct you. Sorry.'

'I'll have to report it.'

'Report what and why?'

'That you're here under false pretences. You're not one of ours.'

'Go on then, report me. It's not my fault you're too dim to have realised I'm not one of yours. Christ, just listen to yourself. I've just as much right to be here as you have. More, in fact.'

Camilla laughed with an air of contempt. 'How do you work that one out?'

'At least I've always known what a hard day's work is. Unlike some people round here with their pampered little lives–'

Their row was interrupted by an FAU officer. 'You're needed. There's been a gas attack. Come on the pair of you.'

Camilla glared at Mary as if to say, *you're not coming with me*.

The officer said, 'Can you drive?'

Mary shook her head. 'But I can go with her. Take gas masks and anything else we need.'

'Good girl.'

Mary and Camilla clambered into the ambulance. Camilla drove in silence, not the serene silence Mary had felt just an hour before in the Quaker meeting, but a brooding silence. The ambulance bumped over the road.

'I can't see a bloody thing!' Camilla said under her breath. The sky was cloudless and the moon illuminated the bare tree branches stark against the sky, but straight ahead the road was barely visible.

Mary wanted her friend to speak or laugh, just to dispel the silence. Miraculously, they reached the tented CCS only about a mile from the main battlefield. She climbed out of the car and made her way over to the army doctor.

'How many ambulances do you have?' he said, peering into the dark.

'Just the one, sir. We came together.'

'Can you fit five men in the back? All gassed. One very serious.'

Camilla took command. 'If they can sit upright then yes we can take four.'

Mary said, 'You can take five if one goes in the front with you.'

'What about you, Mary?'

'I'll stay here.'

'You can't do that, it isn't safe. There could be a shell attack at any time.'

'How many others are injured?'

'Another half-dozen but none so badly as these five.'

Mary said, 'Just get them in the ambulance and I'll stay here with the others.'

'All right,' Camilla said, reluctantly. 'But I'll get another ambulance out right away.' She turned to the officer and said, 'Show me the men.'

He looked her up and down. 'Where's your gas mask?'

'In the ambulance.' Mary ran off to get them and she fitted hers over her face. When she arrived back she could see how shaken the officer was. He looked as though he might vomit on the ground. Mary felt the mud oozing into her boots as she stepped forward into the tent, all but sliding to the ground.

The men were in a sorry state. Two were on their backs, coughing up a yellow liquid that dribbled out of their mouths and into their hair; neither having the strength to lean forward or twist sideways. The rest were sitting, bent forward, concentrating on breathing. Two stretcher bearers carried the five men into the ambulance and Camilla drove off.

Mary wasn't sure what to do first. She'd comforted a man at the Queen Alexandra who'd been gassed and she knew the poison caused long-term breathing problems due to the corrosion of their delicate lungs. The full horror of the scene suddenly overwhelmed her and she began to weep.

'Come on,' she hissed at herself, 'you can do this.'

She scanned each of the men and sat down next to the nearest one. 'Are you all right?'

He nodded. 'What's your name?' he said hoarsely.

'It's Mary,' she said. He smiled and shut his eyes and she saw the life go out of him.

No, no, no. She pressed the side of his neck. No pulse. Behind her she heard a faint voice. 'Is that you, Mary?'

She turned to the figure slumped on the ground. She pulled off her gas mask and looked at him more closely. It couldn't be. Hardly daring to breathe she wiped the layer of mud and grime off the left side of his face and saw the mole on the side of his nose. She took his right hand and turned the palm over. The scar on his inside wrist confirmed it.

Daniel. She had found her brother.

She pressed her head into his chest. He was still alive, still breathing. She could do nothing for him but wait here until the ambulance came back. Reluctant to leave his side but aware of having other men to check, she went round each one in turn, glancing fervently at Daniel every few seconds. There wasn't much room inside the tent, and she had to clamber around, but she checked each man's pulse and the worst one was right in the corner; she could hear a bubbling noise in his chest.

After seeing all the men she went back to sit with her brother. His hand found hers and she was amazed at the ferocity of his squeeze. *But look at the state of him.* One eye was bruised and had swollen so much in the last few minutes she knew he couldn't see out of it.

'Are you in pain?' she said. The question was pointless because they had run out of all drugs. No morphine or other medication. *Where's that ambulance?*

'I knew you'd come in the end,' he croaked. 'I had a feeling.'

She had to keep him talking, keep him conscious. No, she would sing to him to keep him awake.

'Do you remember this one, Daniel?' and she began to

sing his favourite song. *Sleep my child and peace attend thee, All through the night.* Come on, keep listening while I sing the next bit.'

'You sang this when he hurt me, didn't you?' He squeezed her hand in time to the words.

Suddenly there was a sound like the earth cracking open. Mary felt the ground shudder. And a noise like a thousand fireworks cut though her brain. Instinctively, she covered her ears.

When it was over Daniel seemed to be delirious, utterly calm, not screaming to be taken away like the other men were doing. Did he know he was going to die and had he accepted that fact? Were they supposed to die together in this hellhole? Love had brought her to him; maybe this was how it was to end.

She held him, closed her eyes and whispered. 'I love you, Daniel.'

The bombing stopped suddenly. 'Mary,' he said, 'I want to go home. Take me home.'

'I am. I'm taking you home right now.'

When the next explosion came, it was as if an almighty hand had shaken the core of the earth. They rose in the air and crashed back down. Mud and earth rained down on them and Mary heard someone cry out, 'Mother!' She tasted mud. She spat it out and wiped her tongue with her sleeve. Her eyes felt rubbed with gravel. Daniel was next to her, eyes closed with a smile on his face, as though he felt no pain at all.

They were floating free. Nothing mattered to Mary now apart from lying next to him with her arm on his chest. She closed her eyes. Perhaps they would both die here, but she felt ready to surrender. An exhaustion like no other cloaked her, yet at the same time she was exhilarated. The lines of the song came to her. *Though sad fate our lives may sever, Parting will not last forever.* Was this what death felt like; was she about to take the final step?

CHAPTER 19

Leonora arrived early at the June meeting of the Women's Works sub-committee. She slipped through the door and saw Miss Gabriel already seated at the table, upright and brimming with enthusiasm.

'Good day, Leonora. How are you?'

She nodded at the woman and noted the hefty collection of papers on the table. An awkward silence ensued while the two women waited for the other committee members to arrive. Her own career seemed to have stalled. Eliza Barratt had mentioned a two-year Industrial Administration course which she recommended Leonora and Miss Gabriel enrol for. It required evening classes on a Tuesday and Thursday, which would mean sacrificing her supper with the Baileys. Leonora had read through the course topics: general factory management, industrial law, the wages system. Just thinking of those dry subjects left her mind feeling parched. When she heard Miss Gabriel had quietly been attending for the last few months she felt outmanoeuvred once again.

However, Leonora was cheered to learn Miss Gabriel had recently become engaged and was worrying herself to death since her fiancé had been conscripted. Hopefully, Leonora thought, she'll be off to get married at some point in the future.

'What a year it's been so far,' Eliza Barratt said on opening the meeting. The committee murmured their agreement. 'Miss Carter has been struck down by influenza, which is why I'm in the chair today. First, an update on production.' Food shortages were affecting the Works badly, she reported. Mr George had announced that the ban on production of Dairy Milk chocolate would continue. The firm's milk processing plant at Frampton was having to divert all its milk to serve the citizens of Birmingham. Murmurs of dismay and sympathy rippled around the room.

Other changes were afoot, Eliza said, including plans to replace the current Works Committee with a brand new Works Council, one for the men and one for the women.

'What will the difference be?' Leonora asked, somewhat startled by the idea of change.

Eliza explained: 'The present system of selecting committee members will be dissolved. The new men's and women's councils will be democratically elected instead. Mr Edward Cadbury is keen to have representatives from all the departments, and we, if elected, will become the voice of the workers in every day matters.'

Leonora wondered how this new proposal for a Works Council affected her chances of becoming forewoman. *Haven't I been doing the job in everything but title for the past three years?*

'One of the key concerns for the new council,' Eliza continued, 'will be managing the labour force when the war ends.'

Leonora heard Miss Gabriel's intake of breath. 'Has there been news?'

'No, nothing specific,' Eliza answered. 'But the war can't go on forever. It will end eventually and when the Bournville men come home safely,' she nodded at Miss Gabriel, 'we're going to have a surplus of women workers.'

Leonora digested this news. She had not considered this question and immediately felt protective towards the girls under her care. Helen Daw had been the biggest transformation. She thought about the scrap of a girl Helen had been when she first arrived and how she'd blossomed into a young lady under her tutelage. She was a shining example of what could be achieved with the right care and instruction. Hard and purposeful work, nutritious meals, fresh air and gym classes had brought a healthy glow to her cheeks, making her unrecognisable from the timid creature she had once been.

'So,' Leonora asked, 'how will it be decided which women have to go, when the time comes?'

'I think the forewomen's jobs will be safe. It's the part-timers and the married women we shall have to shed first. The company can't expect to keep on those women who effectively took their husband's job, especially when their spouses will be returning.'

'You make it sound so calculated!' Leonora said. 'They didn't steal work from their husbands. They stepped in and served when they were needed. They answered the call, as was only right.' Her cheeks had heated up during her speech.

'That's as maybe,' Eliza answered. 'However, it doesn't alter the fact one jot. When the men come back we will have too many women in the workforce. I should think many of the married ladies, if not all, will be glad to return to the home.'

Leonora pressed the point. 'I'm not so sure. Take Mrs Paignton, as one example. Her husband was sick when–'

'This is not the time to go into specific examples, or we'll never get through the agenda. Now, the next item is the parlous state of the girls' lavatory near B block. Miss Fitzroy has reported missing nail brushes, empty paper boxes...'

Leonora's mind raced. A place on the Works Council was a tantalising prospect – a chance to have a real say in matters! – but she felt strangely deflated by the thought of having to select women to be sacked.

When the meeting closed the committee members stayed in the room chatting.

'We're fortunate that some girls have left already,' Miss Fitzroy said. 'Sarah in B block has left us to start her nurses' training course. And, of course, there's your Mary Morris.' She shot Leonora a sly look. 'Running off to find her fancy man,

I heard. I did feel for you, Miss Lime. What a dreadful embarrassment it must've been.'

Leonora summoned up all her dignity. 'Miss Morris is serving at the Queen Alexandra hospital near Dunkirk. She has far more to contend with than missing nailbrushes in the girls' lavatory.' To her satisfaction, Miss Fitzroy pursed her lips in annoyance and the room fell silent. 'I shall look forward, Miss Fitzroy, to hearing what other urgent matters you bring to the next meeting. I hope the suspense won't kill me.'

The woman opened her mouth to speak then closed it again. She bowed her head in acknowledgement, as if conceding to a worthy victor.

'It's been a rotten year and no mistake,' Mr Bailey said to Leonora that night at supper. He read aloud the news of injuries and deaths of Bournville men from the July issue of the *Bournville Works* magazine. 'Lance Corporal W. Fenner, Worcestershire Regiment, died of wounds. Gunner T. Sprang, Royal Garrison Artillery, killed in action. Private S. Eastwood, Royal Warwickshire Regiment, died of enteric fever – that's typhoid, isn't it?'

Leonora interrupted, her voice shaky. 'What did you say? Read that last one again.'

Mr Bailey repeated the name. Her stomach felt heavy, and she was cold around her neck, as though a draught had blown through the cottage window.

'Did you know him, little Nora?' he asked.

She nodded, unable to speak for fear of crying. Samuel Eastwood, the gardener's assistant. After the fireworks debacle the previous November she had been glad to see him conscripted, but – oh, she would never have wished his life cut short.

That night she slept badly and woke up remembering the day three years ago when the delegation had visited and Samuel Eastwood had tormented her by smoking his cigarette.

She had been obsessed with the forewoman's job back then, she reflected: bitter and slighted by other women's successes. Now the job was in her sights. Eliza Barratt had told her that Miss Dorothy Cadbury had put her name on the list of serious candidates for promotion. 'Well done, Leonora, you've earned it!'

She should be delighted, she *was* delighted, but the news of Sam Eastwood's death had upset her.

The rain lashed down on the way to work the next morning. Leonora had a lump in her throat still. She wondered if Herr Otto had been forced to sign up for his country? Was he at this moment wielding a gun or hurling a shell against us, his enemy?

She arrived at work to a memo from Mr Edward Cadbury asking her to go and see him. She knocked on the door of his office and went in, wondering why he had summoned her.

'Ah, Miss Lime. I'm writing another book on women's work,' he explained, 'and I'd like some photographs to illustrate it. Could you possibly organise a group of girls to have their picture taken outside the lodge entrance at eleven o'clock this morning?'

'Yes, of course, sir.' Her mood was transformed from earlier that morning. She had begun to sense a new mood of respect towards her work and achievements: first, from Eliza Barratt and Miss Dorothy, and now even Mr Edward.

She selected the girls herself, knowing that if she asked for volunteers to model there would be a hundred girls all clamouring for attention. When she had the list she tugged at her sleeves. *Not long until I'm wearing the green blouse!*

She sent a message to Jessie Paignton's department: *Can you be released from work at 11 a.m. to meet outside the girls' lodge?*

Leonora arrived at the lodge by 10.45 a.m. When Jessie appeared she nodded to her. The woman didn't look herself, Leonora thought; she was pale and frowning, her complexion almost as grey as the cloud currently in the sky. The wind was getting up a little, shaking the hedges that lined the path to the lodge building.

Helen Daw appeared just before eleven with the group of girls from Q block, all in their white overalls and caps on their heads. They all looked the picture of health; Helen, in particular, Leonora noted. She had shot up in height. Her face was pink-cheeked, almost plump and the hay-coloured hair shone with vitality. Quite the young lady. *Now, where's that photographer?*

'We may as well get you lined up ready.' Leonora pulled and pushed the girls into a suitable formation. Tallest at the back. Shortest at the front. 'Phyllis, yes, you. Go and stand in front of Helen. Mabel, move next to her. Mrs Paignton, come here.'

The photographer turned out to be one of the convalescent patients from The Beeches hospital. He was dressed in full military uniform, rather than hospital 'blues', and there was the slightest tremor in his hands as he reached into his jacket and pulled out his pocket Kodak camera.

'I see you little ducks are nicely lined up,' he said. At his words, the sun came out and bathed them all in bright light.

'Shall I stand in the middle?' Leonora asked.

'Not for the first lot. Let's just get these angels to begin with, shall we? You can pose for the indoor shots.' He motioned to her to stand aside.

Leonora's cheeks flamed. She took two steps back and felt the hedge prickling into her shoulders. Jessie stepped out of the line in solidarity, saying, 'It's just for the young ones really.' The breeze picked up again and Leonora was grateful for the coolness it provided to her cheeks.

The photographer held the camera in front of him. 'Steady now, ladies,' he said. 'On the count of three, give me your brightest and best smiles.'

At that moment an almighty gust of wind blew down the pathway. The girls shrieked, hands flew to heads to stop the breeze blowing their caps away and ruining their pinned hairstyles. They gulped as the air took away their breath and glued their skirts taut around their bodies – all young, slim, lithe specimens – save for Helen Daw, who laughed alongside them, as the smooth ripe curve of her belly, in a perfect half-circle, made itself visible to Leonora. She closed her eyes, her body swaying slightly, praying when she opened them again she would realise her imagination had played a trick on her.

She heard the photographer ask the girls to rearrange themselves. When she finally looked the scene appeared normal. She turned sideways then and saw Jessie staring at Helen's body with a look of horror on her face; her hand was clapped to her mouth as if afraid of what she might utter.

'Oh, sweet lord,' Leonora said.

'Do you two ladies want a photo now?' the photographer asked her and Jessie. 'For posterity. To mark the occasion.' It was all she could do not to strike him, with his banal chatter.

Leonora shook her head.

Afterwards, when she had sent the girls back to their block, Jessie lingered behind. 'Did you see –?'

'Yes, I did.' Leonora said. 'She's–'

'In the family way!' Jessie's voice sounded high-pitched, strangled.

'But how?' Leonora sat down on the bench nearby. 'I don't understand.'

Jessie said, 'Does she have a sweetheart?'

'A sweetheart? Of course not. I'd know!' But would I? Leonora thought. She seized upon a thought. 'Maybe we've jumped to the wrong conclusion. The girl's been eating well lately. Perhaps she's just put on weight, no?'

Jessie shook her head. 'I don't think so. It's pretty obvious she's having a baby. But I wonder if she realises. She had no knowledge of menstruation. She thought the bleeding meant she was dying.'

'You're wrong. She must have learned about it in her adult

classes.' Leonora remembered her own classes at Helen's age: they had done the basics of homemaking, including sex hygiene lessons.

'But she missed some of those classes to learn first aid so she could help out at Fircroft.'

Leonora slumped on the bench. She was partly culpable for that.

As if reading her mind, Jessie touched her arm. 'It's not your fault.'

'What are we going to do?' She stared ahead, unseeing. Her stomach felt tight with unease. A new feeling emerged out of the shock of this discovery: Of all the girls for this to happen to – she might have expected Mary Morris to get herself into such a predicament, but Helen! How could she let me down me like that?

Jessie was calmly practical. 'We don't know the facts. We must talk to Helen. What about letting the forewoman deal with it? She'll know what to do.'

'No!' Leonora said. She wasn't going to have Eliza Barratt crowing over her, offering fake sympathy. 'Let me think and decide what to do next. Do not, I repeat do not, talk to anyone about this.'

'If you need my help–'

'No, the best thing you can do is get back to work while I think about it.'

This was beyond her realm. Sex, men, the making of babies. All of that belonged in a dark and murky passageway she had never needed to enter. She had once gone to an evening lecture on 'The Modern Woman', expecting useful advice on gaining promotion at work. The speaker, a lady doctor with a supercilious manner, had begun to talk about sex and devices for the prevention of pregnancy. Leonora had walked out in disgust. She didn't need to know all that, she had reasoned. Now she cursed her ignorance.

Who could she go to for help? She thought of all the ladies she knew: Eliza Barratt, no. Miss Dorothy Cadbury, definitely no. Mrs Bailey was a possibility, but she needed someone with experience, expertise. What about Dr Russell-Morgan? He was a medical officer, and a man of the world. After all, he was from London. She would go and seek his advice.

At lunchtime the next day she took the unusual step of feigning illness and securing the rest of the afternoon off from Eliza Barratt.

'I hope you're not sickening for influenza, too,' she said, signing Leonora's pass and giving it to her with her arm outstretched.

Tracking the doctor down was not that easy. The Fircroft matron said he was overseeing a number of auxiliary hospitals now and flitting between them all. She suggested Moseley Hall, where she finally found him.

'Miss Lime!' He greeted her with his usual bonhomie and then saw her flushed face. 'Oh dear, what's wrong? Nothing too dreadful I hope.'

She squirmed as she began to explain.

'One of my girls is in a spot of bother and I... Well, I find myself quite at a loss.'

'Let me guess. Got herself in trouble, has she? Silly girl.'

Leonora sighed with relief. His blithe tone lightened her burden instantly.

'You know her. It pains me to say it, but the girl in question is Helen Daw.

He raised an eyebrow in surprise and then frowned. 'That's rather unfortunate. She has the makings of a good little nurse. How advanced is it?'

'I'm sorry?'

'The pregnancy. If it's at an early stage we can do something about it.'

'I don't know.' It was like trying to give directions to a place she'd never been to. She put her hands in the air, mimed a semi-circle and then quickly put them back in her lap.

The doctor bit the inside of his cheek before speaking. 'I see. Quite far gone. Never mind, we might be able to fix it. Tell her to come and see me at Fircroft tomorrow and we'll have a chat.'

She looked at him gratefully. 'There's just one thing. I haven't told the Works' doctor. Should I?'

'No need unless you want to. Is it general knowledge?'

Leonora shook her head. 'Oh no, there's been no whisper of rumour. Her pinafore must have kept it well hidden. I can't see how I missed it. Oh, and one other thing.' She held her hand to her throat. 'We don't think she realises the situation.'

'Who's we? You said you'd told no-one.'

'Only Mrs Paignton. She was with me the moment I realised.'

'All right. Leave it with me, Miss Lime.'

Mary woke up and looked around her. The ceiling with its peeling paintwork appeared familiar, as did the wardrobe and the jug of water on the bedside table. This was her room, but where exactly was she? Light came from outside, the sun making a square patch on the bedspread. She felt its warmth on her hand. Despite being deliciously cosy, she told herself she ought to get up. She made to sit and then screamed as a pain shot though her stomach, like her flesh was being torn apart.

'Camilla? Are you there?'

A woman dressed as a nurse came in, 'There you are, you naughty girl. Trying to get out of bed. I don't know.' Mary thought, who on earth is this woman?

'Do you remember what happened? Anything about last night?'

Last night? She tried to think. Her brain felt emptied.

Bright lights flashed in front of her and a roar stormed through her ears. She winced and put her hands to her head.

'It's all right,' the nurse said, soothingly. 'Don't worry if you can't remember.'

'Please tell me,' Mary said, 'I don't know what I'm doing here. Am I ill?'

'Let me go and get a doctor.' The nurse slipped out of the room. Mary had wanted to call out, don't leave me. She touched her hands to her head again, this time feeling bandages she hadn't noticed before.

The doctor came in, a calm-looking man with a reassuring, no-nonsense voice. 'Now, Mary, may I call you that? It seems you sustained the impact of a shell. It landed next to you. At the time you were in the clearing station tent.'

'Tent? What tent? None of this is making sense!'

'Tell me your full name and something about yourself.'

'I'm Mary Morris, I'm twenty-six. I live in Birmingham.'

The nurse glanced at the doctor. 'Do you know where you are now?'

'In France. I signed up for the FAU.' She smiled with relief as that bit of information came back to her.

'We can't find any work records for you.'

'I know. I lost my papers before I arrived.'

She looked across the room. 'What about Camilla? She knows me. Where is she?'

Something was odd about Camilla's bed. It had been stripped bare. On top of the blue and white mattress was her folded silk bedspread. Her photographs had been removed from the wall and placed on top.

'Are they moving her? Why?'

The nurse and the doctor glanced at each other again, and Mary felt a horrible premonition of what the doctor was going to say.

'I'm very sorry–' he began. He took her hand but she

snatched it away. She turned on her side away from him, her stomach twisting in agony; she began to howl.

Some time later – minutes or hours – the nurse came in with a bowl of soup and a hunk of stale-looking bread. She helped Mary sit up, plumped her pillows, reassuring her when a wave of nausea passed over her.

'Don't worry if you feel unsteady. You had a nasty bump to the head and you've been injured in your stomach.'

'Tell me what happened to Camilla.'

'Truthfully?'

Mary nodded, although her mind was screaming, *No!*

The nurse's tone was stark and unemotional. 'There was a shell attack last night. She was driving the ambulance back from the CSS to the hospital with four wounded men in the back and one in the front. There had been a chlorine gas attack.'

Plumes of yellow-green smoke danced, tantalising her memory. 'Go on,' she said to the nurse.

'It was dark. Pure bloody bad luck the shell landed on top of the ambulance. It burst into flames. I imagine they were all killed instantly,' the nurse said, 'although I don't suppose that's much comfort to you. We've telegraphed her mother and she'll have a visit in due course.'

Mary found it easier to imagine a swift death for Camilla rather than her enduring some burning agony; she didn't know if the nurse was telling the truth, but she would choose to believe her version. What else could she do? Something else to do with gas niggled at the back of her mind. Its acrid scent...

'So what happened to me?'

'You still don't remember? What do you last recall?'

'Oh, my God, we had an argument... I don't remember what it was about but she wasn't talking to me. I was in the ambulance with her and we drove near to where the casualties were. I kept wishing she'd smile, but she was angry with me about something.' She screwed her eyes up in concentration.

'I remember arriving, there had been a gas attack, we helped the men and… No, it's a blank after that.' Another flash came to her. Her brother? Her mind was a roaming searchlight, illuminating parts of her memory while others stayed hidden in the gloomy darkness.

'Don't be in any rush to remember; it'll come back in the next few days. Now open your mouth.' The soup spoon came towards her.

'I'm not a five-year-old,' she complained. But she tried to suppress the flash of temper. The soup was filled with vegetables, barely thicker than a broth but tasty nevertheless.

The nurse offered bread that she'd dipped in the soup to soften, although it was still stale. 'Sorry about the bread, it's a week old and all we've got until tomorrow.'

After eating, Mary slumped back on her pillow, exhausted. She would try to piece together the memories that still eluded her. But sleep called her and she felt her eyes closing.

The nurse stood up and got ready to leave. 'By the way, there's a young man in A ward who keeps asking for you. A Private Daniel Morris. No relation, I suppose?'

CHAPTER 20

On Saturday afternoon, Jessie was doing an hour's volunteering at Fircroft sitting with a patient, helping him to write a letter. She heard a kerfuffle of voices and a female calling, 'Mrs Paignton!' Jessie apologised to the man, who gave her a weary smile.

Miss Lime came over to the bed. She was in a state of extreme agitation judging by the way she almost danced on the spot. 'I need you now,' she said. 'Please, you must come quickly.'

Jessie hastily pulled off her apron and put her coat on as she walked out of the hospital with Miss Lime. She was led through a shortcut of fields and a wooded area. Miss Lime ignored her questions about where they were heading.

'Just hurry,' Miss Lime urged her. 'This way.'

Once they came out on Woodbrooke Road Jessie automatically headed towards Linden Road. Grabbing her arm, Miss Lime pulled her into a side road.

'Please, can't you tell me where we're going?'

'To my home. Please, be as quick as you can.'

'What's wrong?'

'Wait until we get there.'

Miss Lime had left the door slightly ajar and they entered the bungalow. Jessie noticed a scent that was a more intense version of the soap Miss Lime used. The woman called out to say, 'It's all right, I've got more help. Don't worry.' Her voice was high with tension.

Jessie followed her into the front room and surveyed the scene. Dr Russell-Morgan was sitting on one end of Miss Lime's couch, his medical bag open at his feet. Helen Daw lay flat on the couch, her head at the opposite end. Her face was damp and clammy. Not the flu? Jessie looked around at Miss Lime, who stood wringing her hands, then at the doctor who busied himself with his medical bag. Helen's eyes were closed, her fringe stuck to her perspiring forehead. Jessie felt the back of Helen's neck – her temperature was normal.

Then came a sound – a quiet murmur that didn't come from any of them. She followed the sound to a bundle wedged between Helen and the back of the couch. *My god!* Swaddled in some sage green fabric was her baby, with a screwed up face and tiny fingers that clutched at the air. Jessie couldn't believe it. The baby had come.

As if sensing her presence the baby began to whimper then built to a scream. Instinctively, Jessie stepped forward and carefully picked up the baby, resting it in the crook of her left arm. The baby turned its mouth to her, rooting for milk. Jessie closed her eyes and inhaled. She felt a tingling sensation in her breasts. She became aware of voices around her, making arrangements. With a supreme effort, but determined to keep the baby close to her, Jessie said, 'What can I do to help?'

'Her parents need to know,' the doctor said. 'Her mother, at least.'

This brought cries from Helen, 'Oh, please don't tell them. I'll do whatever you want but please don't tell them.'

Jessie remembered her feelings towards Helen's mother before and she felt the same lump in her throat.

'I can look after the baby,' Jessie said, knowing it wasn't her place to offer, at least not until she'd asked Mrs Morris's permission.

'No,' the doctor said, firmly. 'I'll arrange it.'

Afterwards, when it was all over, Miss Lime said, 'Oh Jessie, I didn't know what to do.'

The doctor had taken Helen and the baby away in a motor car.

Before he left he had given them a tight, tense smile and said, 'We'll sort things out. Try not to worry. Not a word to anyone else, yet, for the girl's sake.'

Jessie took a sip of the tea Miss Lime had made. She'd offered to make it herself but the woman clearly needed to occupy her mind and burn up some of her nervous energy.

Miss Lime sat down and began to speak, staring at the rug the whole time. 'I found Helen stumbling outside not far from work. She was in great agony and it was clear the baby was coming. I brought her here and ran to Fircroft to get help. The doctor and I got here just before it came. I had to wrap it in something.'

'It?'

'Her. All I could find was my... oh, never mind that.'

'So it's a girl,' Jessie said.

'The doctor sent me out to find you. He told me he'd seen you at Fircroft so I hurried all the way back again. In my mind, I raved at the girl.' She bowed her head. 'I called her all sorts of names, a common slut, a whore, words I didn't even know that I knew. I can't believe it of myself.' She looked up, as if waiting for Jessie's judgement.

'Where's the doctor taking Helen?'

'To a home for unmarried mothers, I think. We had already planned to get her into a place of confinement. The doctor asked me if I knew who was responsible. But I don't. Do you?'

Jessie shook her head.

Miss Lime said, 'I'd thought of Samuel Eastwood perhaps.'

'No, he's still a boy.'

'*Was* a boy. He's dead, you know. Anyway, the doctor had some of idea of making the father take responsibility for his action. But the girl wouldn't say anything other than begging us not to tell her parents. Lord knows how, but she managed to hide it from them.'

'But Helen,' Jessie said. 'Of all people. She must be completely bewildered by it all. I just can't imagine that she'd do that sort–'

'I know! That someone in my charge should get herself into such a situation. It beggars belief.'

Jessie kept her hands pressed to her side for fear of what she might do to Miss Lime.

'Let me know where she is. I want to see her. She needs our help, not our judgement.'

With a heavy heart Jessie walked home to Mrs Morris. If only she'd kept a closer eye on Helen. How could she not have noticed? Poor, poor child.

On Friday lunchtime Jessie stood outside her old house; no longer would she call it home. She was there to collect the final bits and pieces that belonged to her. The step was scrubbed clean and traces of water ran down the path. She rapped loudly on the door, refusing to be cowed. Florrie Tops opened it and Jessie's heart clenched at the sight of her former neighbour in her house. The woman had been expecting someone else, judging by the way her smile suddenly contracted at the sight of Jessie.

'Well, look what the cat's dragged in. I wondered when you'd turn up.'

'I'm not stopping. I just wanted to collect some things.'

She opened the door wider.

'You can come in, but mind the floor. I've just mopped it.'

The younger of the two boys stared at her. The older one must be at school now, Jessie thought. They were sweet boys with their mother's wide dark eyes.

'If you've come to see Bill, you can forget it. He's not in.'

'Do you love him?' Jessie asked. Tell me you do, she

thought, and I might just be able to bear it. But if you're using him it'll break my heart.

'I like him. No-one can replace my Frank, but the boys need a father and we get on well enough. We have a laugh and that's a good sign.'

Then it must be serious. 'Good,' Jessie found herself saying.

Florrie Tops narrowed her eyes. 'You're a cold-hearted one and no mistake.'

She followed Jessie upstairs into the bedroom, but then left her.

She looked around the room and saw the bed had been moved to a different position. She went over to the cupboard and pulled out all her remaining clothes, her best coat and the hat she'd worn at her wedding. It felt like she was clearing out the possessions of a dead person.

She opened a box at the bottom of the cupboard and saw the dried petals from the red rose she'd been given along with her Bible when she'd first left Cadbury. She'd forgotten she'd preserved the flower. The petal crumbled to powder when she picked one up. Sighing, she fastened her bag and looked around the room for the last time. She tried to commit it to memory, but what was the point? It was time to move on. Suddenly an overwhelming sadness washed over her; she sat on the edge of the bed and clutched her hand to her chest. The pain was real, a sharp, stabbing ache so intense that it frightened her. Crying would be the only release. She sobbed, not even trying to stop the tears, but whimpered, conscious of Florrie downstairs.

She lay down on the bed staying close to the edge, inhaling Bill's scent on the bed cover. What a mess she'd made of her life. If she'd stayed at home like a good wife she'd have got up today, seen Bill off to work, before getting stuck in with the washing, scrubbing the front step. But she knew there was more to life than that.

She had made a decision: once she left Cadbury she would find a way to do proper nurse's training.

She must have drifted off to sleep because she was suddenly aware of cool delicate fingers on her face. She opened her swollen eyes to see Florrie's little boy looking at her with concern. He must be about six now; he clearly didn't remember her.

'Are you all right? Don't cry,' he said. His own eyes were filled with tears and he looked afraid. He had come in to find a strange lady in his mother's bedroom.

'Come here,' she said, and he allowed Jessie to embrace him. He was so tiny and so precious. *All those men who've been killed were once little boys like you.* She stroked his hair and held him close.

'You're a good boy, aren't you? Such a good boy.' He nodded solemnly. *Just stay as sweet as you are. May your life always be as simple and uncomplicated as this. May you never be called up to fight. May your mummy never know the pain of losing you before your time.*

She made an effort to stop weeping and took a deep breath.

'Go and find your mummy and tell her the funny lady's leaving. Fancy doing all that crying on a lovely sunny day like this.'

She found Florrie sitting anxiously at the table.

'I'm not going to stand in your way. I'm glad Bill's happy. He is happy, isn't he?'

'What's happy? I look after him if that's what you mean.'

Jessie nodded and walked away without looking back. *Just keep walking, keep your head up, you can do it. Just one step and then another.* The road in front of her blurred with tears. *Just ten more steps before you turn that corner into a new street.*

News had got out from somewhere that Jessie was no longer living with Bill.

There were a few curious looks from the men and women in her new department, but no gossip-mongers of Rose Entwistle's calibre. She was grateful for that. Her new job was as monotonous as the card-cutting had been. Hands washed, she took her place at the chopping board with a heartfelt sigh.

'See this block of fruit pulp here? I want you to chop it into smaller pieces, about this size.' The foreman, Jonathan, indicated the first digit of his finger. 'It's quite tough and the knife is sharp, so be careful you don't chop your finger off. It wouldn't do for Mrs Wilson to find it in her fruit biscuits now, would it?'

Apart from the fact of speaking to her like she was an idiot, Jessie quite liked Jonathan. He was in his early fifties so had managed to escape conscription.

Jessie sat down and picked up the knife to open the sack of fruit pulp.

'Not with that, girl,' he said crossly. 'Let me.' He took a cutting tool from his pocket and slashed open the top of the bag in one efficient step. He tipped out most of the contents onto the tray on her left. 'Reckon you can get this lot done by home-time?'

She looked at the mountain of food. 'I'll try,' she said, without caring. She picked up the dark brown slab of compressed apricots and sliced her way through, working methodically to ensure all the pieces were approximately the same size.

She was unaware the man was watching her until she heard a pleased, 'Good,' over her shoulder.

The mechanical motion was soothing and repetitive and as she concentrated she was less likely to think of her own troubles and the mess she had made of her life. As the afternoon wore on and home-time came, the men started to tidy their machines. She removed her apron and put on her coat back in the girls' dressing room. Crowds of other girls hurried in and swept her along. Jessie wondered what would happen if she just surrendered, let herself lose balance. She thought she would be carried along by the girls – it was a comforting thought.

'Are you all right?' Miss Lime was at her shoulder with a look of concern on her face.

'I'm fine, thank you,' she replied, unable to keep the weariness out of her voice. She sat on the bench and pulled on her outdoor boots. Because she had missed lunch that day her head swayed when she sat up again and for a horrible moment she feared she would black out.

The room was emptying, with cheerful cries of, 'Night all. See you in the morning! If we're still alive then!'

'Shall we walk together?' Miss Lime appeared at her side again.

Not quick enough to find an excuse Jessie was forced to say, 'Yes, all right then.'

'Don't worry. I can see what you're thinking. It's written all over your face. You think I'm going to stand in judgement on you.'

Jessie spoke bitterly. 'There's nothing left for you to moralise over. My marriage is over – my husband no longer loves me! What have I got left? Nothing. And it's all I deserve.'

CHAPTER 21

Richard Ockwell, the FAU officer, came to visit her, bringing hot chocolate. Mary had demanded to be moved from her sleeping quarters down to A ward in a bed next to Daniel.

'I hear you made a right hullabaloo.' He pulled up a chair and sat down. 'You're a grade A nuisance. We'll be glad to see the back of you.'

Mary smiled. The wound to her stomach was getting better but she was in no rush to get up. She was terrified they would send her back home and Daniel back to fight. While the two of them lay in beds next to each other she was perfectly happy.

Richard sipped his drink. 'One day this war will be over and you won't be able to believe it.'

Mary said, 'Can you remember what life was like before? I can't.' Weariness was in everyone's bones. She hated what had become the sheer normality of the hospital. Bodies painted with blood, limbs blown away, tender skin rubbed off like new potatoes. It was inconceivable that things would ever be normal again.

'When I was a boy,' Richard said, 'we had this teacher at school. Old fella by the name of Rixon. A cruel sod he was.'

Mary flinched. 'Don't tell me anything horrible. I can't stand it.'

'I was only going to say he'd give out random punishments whenever he felt like it. He'd make you stand in the corner holding a great big wooden box. Lord knows what was in it – concrete lumps, for all we knew. Anyway, you'd have to hold this box with your arms outstretched until he gave you permission to put it down. As the minutes ticked by your muscles were screaming, your arms trembling and he'd say in a deep voice, like he was giving commands to a dog, "Hold it!" and then finally he'd say, "Down!" and you almost dropped it on the floor. At first it was blissful to let go, you'd been holding it that long. Then you'd suddenly get a pain in your arms, the sinews, that was ten, twenty times worse than when you were holding the darned box. It took your breath away. I'm worried that's what it'll be like when the war ends.'

'Won't you be celebrating with the men, drinking wine and stuff, parading through the streets?' Mary had heard some of the soldiers discussing their plans.

'No,' he said. 'Quakers don't drink. I've never even tried alcohol.'

'I hate alcohol, too,' she said, thinking of her drunken father. To change the subject she asked, 'Have you got a sweetheart waiting at home for you?'

He shook his head. 'There was a girl. Amy. But I'm all done in with people now. No-one back home will ever understand what it's like.'

'You've seen some horrors–'

'Enough to last a lifetime.'

'How can people say you've got a cushy number?'

He smiled wryly. 'Shall I tell you something, Mary? I look at my elder brother. He signed up for the war–'

'Did he? Weren't your parents worried to death?'

'Of course, really bloody worried but I wonder if deep down they wished I'd done the same. In the circles they mix in, you see, there's a lot of bragging about children. It's very artfully done but it's there.' He put on what Mary called a frightfully frightfully voice. 'Um, "Had a letter from the boy today. Gained honours at Ypres, you know?"'

Mary put out her hand and rested it on his sleeve. 'What you've done is really brave. You deserve a medal.'

'I don't know; sometimes I wish I'd got stuck in properly.'

'Not to all the killing? It's against everything you believe in.'

'I don't know,' he said wearily. 'I've no desire to kill anyone, ever. It's repellent. It's just that–'

'You're envious. I understand.'

'What?'

'You heard. I said envious. You've been upstaged by your brother and you can't stand it. Good old sibling rivalry.'

She waited for the explosion of temper. He looked shocked for a moment and then burst out laughing, a musical laugh as sweet as a song. On and on he laughed until she joined in, neither of them able to stop. She held her stomach, groaning.

'Shhh, we'll wake everyone,' Mary said, before collapsing into giggles again.

'My dear Mary,' he said, eventually. 'You're a tonic and no mistake.'

The superintendent came along and said, 'Miss Morris. Good to see you so much better. I've got a space on the ambulance train for you tomorrow night. You're going home.'

She looked at Richard for confirmation. 'What, really? What about my brother?' she whispered, glancing at Daniel in his bed to make sure he was still asleep.

'He'll be staying,' the superintendent said. 'When he's patched up we'll send him back to his regiment where he belongs. Now don't look like that.'

'You can't. He needs to come home with me. Have you heard his lungs? He needs fresh air and sunshine and proper care. I can do that for him.'

Richard stood up. 'I'm sorry. If I could make it any different, I would.'

She brought her knees up to her chest and felt the wound in her stomach pull. She lay on her side and wept.

Then she crept into Daniel's bed and lay there for most of the night, stroking his hair while he slept, until one of the new nurses bounded over and hauled her out.

'This is a hospital, not a whore house.'

'He's my brother!' Mary shouted.

'Oh, I thought you were one of the...'

She climbed into her own bed and shuddered beneath the cold sheets. Her memory was still not fully recovered. Fragments emerged as if she were walking through a dense forest with flashes of sunlight. She suddenly pictured being at the Birmingham recruitment office on Temple Street with Daniel. Without her there, she realised, he'd have lacked the confidence to lie successfully about his age. She lay there thinking for the rest of the night.

When dawn came, she begged one of the other nurses to go and find Richard. 'You know, Richard Ockwell. From the FAU.' The nurse refused and tucked Mary's bed sheet back in. *To hell with you*, she said to herself. Mary waited until the nurse was occupied and then sneaked out of the ward. With a blanket round her for protection but no shoes, she stumbled down the street in the direction of the town square. People were staring at her. At the Hotel Pyl she collapsed on the front step in pain. The concierge hurried over to her.

'Richard. Please-get-Richard.'

'Quoi?'

'The doctor man.' She mimed wrapping a bandage around her arm.

'Ah!' he said. He disappeared and came back with Richard. He helped her stand and walked her to a seat in the hotel lobby. 'My goodness, where are your shoes?' He went away for a few minutes and returned with some thick woollen socks. Kneeling and with gentle movements he rolled them over her frozen feet. He went to examine her stomach but she swatted away his hands. 'It's bleeding,' he said. 'Look, your wound's opened up. It needs a new dressing.'

Mary clutched his arm. 'He was underage when he signed

up. He was only sixteen! We could get him arrested!' she cried. 'Would he be sent home if he's found guilty?'

Richard took a while to piece together what she was talking about. 'Daniel? Not a chance, I'm afraid. The government's short of men and they simply don't care anymore. He's nearly twenty now.'

'I know, but he still broke the law.' Mary saw from Richard's expression that it was hopeless. Outside a man walked by on crutches. Another thought came to her. 'I heard something once about men deliberately injuring themselves to get home.'

Richard's face clouded over and he gave an involuntary shiver. 'There was a case I saw of a man who... but no. I'll spare you the details of the state he put himself in. The worst thing when we found him half-dead was the duty to preserve life. I wouldn't have kept a dog in that state.'

Mary's eyes lit up. 'But if someone else did it to him. Someone who no-one would suspect. Someone with enough medical knowledge...'

Richard said, 'Wait a minute, Mary, I don't know what insane idea you've got this time but I don't much like the drift of this conversation. I'm taking you back to the hospital before you freeze to death. Or bleed to death.' He went to carry her.

'Please,' Mary begged, pushing his arms away, 'just listen. If someone were to get hold of a gun or knife and injure Daniel – something quick, serious, but not life-threatening–'

'You're asking me to take up arms against another human being? I thought you understood what I believed. You wouldn't ask me to do that if you knew me.' His voice was high with panic.

'Not even if it's an act of mercy? Then get me a gun and I'll do it.' Tears of frustration were building behind her eyes. 'I just need him home with me where he's safe.'

'So do all the other sisters and mothers and daughters. You're not special. None of us is special, don't you understand?

Do you think we can go around injuring and maiming our men just so they can be shipped back?' His voice became heavy with sarcasm. 'What'll it be today, sir? A shattered kneecap or perhaps your eye removed. It's insane. You have no medical knowledge yet you're acting as if you can control the human body. Who do you think you are? God? Daniel might never recover.'

Mary slumped. He knelt down in front of her again. 'You're tired. Exhausted. Not thinking reasonably.' He put his hand on her shoulder. She shook it off, as if it burned her.

'Look at you. You swan around with your Red Cross armband and your Friends Ambulance Unit badge sewn on. Well, be a friend. A friend to me.'

'I'm sorry. I can't do it. I won't do it.'

She stood up and he scrambled to his feet. 'You mean you don't have the guts. FAU? F_ All Use! That's what you stand for. You haven't got the balls to do it.'

Without speaking he scooped her up and carried her outside to a waiting ambulance. He put her in the passenger seat and drove her the short distance back to the hospital. The anger radiated off him like heat. She was feeling faint with pain now as they bumped along the road. He dropped her at the entrance to the hut and said to a nurse, 'Dress that wound again and see she gets to England safely.'

Mary's breath came in pants, like she'd run a race. Despite her best efforts she knew she had lost. Protocol, 'doing the right thing', had bloody won. Had defeated her in the end.

Richard will never forgive me, she thought, as she lay in bed. Yes, he probably would. She would never forgive herself though. She despised herself for what she had said to Richard, poking him in his most vulnerable area, cruelly, deliberately wounding him with her words. With a dread creeping over her, she thought, what if I've inherited my father's cruel streak; suppose his evil was in her blood, too.

Forcing Daniel to sign up had been a huge mistake. She almost laughed out loud at her own naiveté. Thinking he'd be safe, protected. If only she could take his place. If only she could stay here and nurse and he could go home on the ambulance train tonight. But they were such sticklers for the rules. She sat up in bed and looked across at Daniel, still asleep, his face almost white against the pillow, his mouth pinched in pain.

Another flashback came into her mind: her father holding Daniel's head under water in the bath tub to 'teach him a lesson' for some trumped-up crime of his insane invention. She felt herself choking and tasting the scummy bathwater, felt it in her lungs, her own legs kicking against the mattress. Daniel would never be rid of the damage, even if he did get sent home. Could she let him live with the continuous nightmare, she asked herself. No.

She smiled, her heartbeat slowed, her limbs relaxed. The answer had come to her out of nowhere – the perfect solution. Simple, beautiful, with the clarity of a sharp wind on a sunny day. Mary swung her legs down to the floor, hardly noticing the iciness of the ground on her feet. She reached for her pillow and held it to her face. In her bedside cupboard she found the bath soap sent from the girls at Cadbury. Fresh, woody, antiseptic, pine. She removed the paper wrapper and rubbed the soap softly against her pillow, imbuing the cotton with the scent. Let Daniel's last moments be filled with the aroma of pine forests.

He was fast asleep now – the sort of sleep that brought rosy pink flares to his cheeks. The frown between his eyebrows was still there. She took his hand – it was warm – and began to sing a low lullaby, her voice holding, despite the tears rolling down her cheeks. The pillow was light in her hand. She placed it over his face and lay down next to him on the bed. Do it gently, she said to herself, and in a minute it will all be over. She increased the pressure.

Something was pulling her away. A strong grip around her waist crushed into her wound – she kicked out as best she could.

'What the hell are you doing?' Richard's voice hissed in her ear. She would fight him.

'If I don't do this, he'll be haunted forever.'

'No, he won't. We'll get him help.'

'He's not strong enough to keep carrying the load any more. This way he'll never have to carry it again.'

'It's over.' He let her go and handed her an official paper. 'Daniel's being discharged.'

Her heart leapt. 'Does that mean–?'

'It means he's going home. You both are.'

Bill had asked if he could see her, suggesting Kings Heath Park. 'Meet me outside the bird house,' his note had said. He was already there as Jessie crunched along the gravel path towards him. She had made an effort with her appearance and she was pleased to see he had too. He wore his best suit, his hair was neatly combed, and she felt a sharp tug of desire that mingled with her feelings of nervousness. Under his arm he carried a bulky brown bag. He explained his clothes, saying he'd come straight from Hugh's funeral.

'Hugh? Oh no,' she said, remembering his friend from Tressler's. 'When? How?'

'They recruited him as a fitter in the Royal Garrison Artillery. He got sent home on leave with pneumonia. I went to visit him two weeks ago at Uffculme hospital. I could see he was in a bad way. The next day he was dead.'

She looked at his face, saw the struggle to keep his composure. 'I'm really sorry, Bill.'

He rubbed his face. 'Let's walk, why don't we?'

They wandered in silence down the path. Suddenly, Bill stopped and turned to face her.

'I can't fathom it, Jessie. How can something as good as we had... How could it crumble so fast?'

At his words Jessie felt a tide of sadness. 'I don't know. Sometimes you can search for reasons and never find them.' Or sometimes the truth is too complex to unravel.

He sat down on a bench and she joined him, her legs weak. 'I wish you'd packed up work when I got the job at BSA. But I could see you liked it. Some nights you'd come in after your district nursing and you'd be shining. Oh, I could see you were exhausted but there was a light in your eyes, and I was jealous. Maybe you liked being out more than staying at home? And who could blame you?' She had the sensation they were in a boat, navigating a small island of truth. They were circling closer and closer to that island, which was small, bleak, filled with thorn bushes and deadly plants. No resources on it to save them. She had to steer the boat away before they touched land. *Too much truth will destroy us both.*

'What about you and Florrie? What are your plans?' She wrapped her arms around herself for protection; her throat felt full.

Bill's next words were spoken softly. 'I like her. She's a good woman. The boys – they miss their dad something rotten. I try to give them a bit of fun.' He smiled, as if recalling some escapade with the children. 'I'm teaching Michael to carve with my penknife, although I have to do it when Florrie's back's turned. And the little one – he's a bright kid and no mistake! Sits on my lap when I'm trying to read the paper and points to words for me to say.'

He doesn't mean to wound you, Jessie told herself, forcing the smile to remain on her face. She pictured Bill and Florrie sitting in the facing armchairs with her children at their feet. What a perfect family portrait it would make, Jessie thought. The image caused such pain that she almost doubled over.

He continued, 'If anything serious ever happened between us we'd have to move. Maybe Wolverhampton. Fresh start and all that. Florrie says there's a new furniture manufacturers just opened.'

'You're taking up upholstery again. Good.'

Bill stared at her as if not believing she could be so calm. He stood and began to walk again; she caught him up and they went past the glasshouse and towards the putting green. A bicyclist sped past and Bill grabbed her elbow to pull her out of its path.

'The last straw was that night you told me to go round and see Florrie. Do you remember?'

Jessie thought back to Helen, poor little Helen, knocking at her door, with the news that Thomas Walker wanted to see her. She remembered how badly she had wanted to see him too. She nodded slowly at Bill.

He looked at the ground. 'You said it so casually. I felt like a dog being tossed a bone—'

'It wasn't like that,' Jessie cried out. But she knew she had been careless of his feelings, too caught up in her own world to take sufficient care of their love.

'Well, I'd better go. Be happy, Jessie. Whatever you do.'

She swallowed. *So this is how it ends.* He took the package from under his arm and held it out to her.

'What's this?' she asked.

'Just a few of Hugh's books. You can send them to the soldiers.'

He bent down to kiss her goodbye. At the feel of his cheek against hers and his breath on her neck she closed her eyes. He spoke some words into her ear but his voice was so soft it took a few moments to discern what he had said. By then he had already turned and begun the process of walking away from her, out of her life. She watched his slight limp, the straight line of his shoulders, his neatly-pressed trousers, the shine on the backs of his shoes.

In a whisper she repeated the words he had said to her: 'You know I'll always love you.'

Jessie arrived back at Mrs Morris's house to two pieces of news: Mary had telegraphed to say she was on her way home with Daniel and Helen Daw was dead, probably by suicide.

CHAPTER 22

There was to be a full investigation into the cause of Helen Daw's death, Eliza Barratt told her. 'As someone who supervised her and her work, you'll be required to make a statement, Leonora. Just tell the facts clearly and frankly.' Leonora was certain she detected a hint of blame in the forewoman's words.

On the morning of the inquest she got ready at the usual time, as if she were going to the Works, but sat at the table, leaving her breakfast untouched. She forced herself to take a sip of the tea she had made, but she recoiled from the taste like it was brandy.

She arrived at the Victoria Courts in Birmingham town centre. As she entered the room, she saw a crowd of people already seated and her nerve almost failed her.

The coroner was a small kindly man in his fifties. 'Hold nothing back, Miss Lime. If we are to get to the bottom of this awful tragedy, we must have a full disclosure of all that has happened.

'When did you become aware that Miss Daw was in a state of pregnancy?'

'Only a few months ago. I had no idea she had got herself into that condition.' Her voice trailed off and she kept her head bowed low.

'How did you discover the fact?'

'I suddenly noticed that she had gained weight.' Her face flushed with embarrassment as she thought back to the day with the photographer and the sudden gust of wind that had revealed Helen's plight. 'At first I couldn't make sense of it but I spoke to Mrs Paignton – she is one of the ladies under my supervision – and she had exactly the same suspicions.'

'What was your next course of action?'

'I decided to contact Dr Russell-Morgan for advice.'

The coroner looked at his notes. 'He's the medical officer in charge of the auxiliary hospitals? I see. Not the official Works' doctor? Wouldn't that have been the normal procedure? To encourage the girl to seek help from her workplace.'

It was the question she had dreaded – the one she couldn't hide from. She hesitated. She became aware of two pairs of eyes boring into her. Helen Daw's parents. She saw the girl in the man's snub nose, and the woman's pale freckled complexion. But nothing in their faces of the lively young woman Helen had blossomed into.

The coroner's voice brought her back. 'May I remind you, Miss Lime, you are not on trial? We simply want to establish the series of events that led to this unfortunate death.'

She almost squirmed against the back of her chair, wishing she could be anywhere apart from here in this public space. Her armpits prickled. She felt as exposed as if she were taking a bath in public.

'I don't know why I didn't go to the Works' doctor,' she replied. 'I was in a panic, and not sure what to do. I thought of Dr Russell-Morgan as someone who would genuinely be able to help. After all, Helen had been working at one of his local hospitals as a volunteer, and he knew of her through her work.'

How could she admit she had felt tarnished by Helen's pregnancy, as if it were her own dereliction of duty? She had wanted the matter to be dealt with discreetly and not spread around the factory as gossip and titillation.

'So when the doctor said he would sort it out, what did you think he meant?'

'That he would recommend a suitable place of

confinement, a nursing home, while she gave birth. That is what had happened previously when girls –' she stopped, not wanting to impugn her company's name. 'I mean, it's a very rare occurrence. It's only happened once in my time at the Works. I'm at a loss to understand how it could have–'

'Thank you, Miss Lime. Can you tell us about the birth of the child? I understand that this did not take place in the nursing home but at your house.'

She held herself straight. 'I make every effort to ensure girls in my charge are strictly segregated from the man. Any liaisons must have taken place outside work time.'

'If you could keep to the question...'

Leonora took a deep breath to steel herself. 'I discovered Helen in the road not far from the Works. She was distressed. I managed to get her to my house. Then I fetched Dr Russell-Morgan and the baby arrived. Shortly afterwards he sent me to find help from Mrs Paignton. When we both got back the doctor was getting ready to leave with Helen and the child. They went away in a motor car, I presumed to the nursing home. That was the last time I saw her.' Her voice had become shrill.

The coroner's expression was sombre. 'That will be all. Thank you.'

His tone made it clear that her ordeal was now over. With trembling limbs she stood up from the chair. She recalled her words. Any liaisons must have taken place outside work time. She was struck as if by a flash of lightning. Fircroft. The other hospitals. She had pestered Helen to do the first aid course and to volunteer at the hospital with all those men. Mary Morris had even tried to warn her. *It ain't right. All those men.* But she had refused to listen. She had sent Helen to her fate.

Outside in the lobby, Helen's parents came towards her. She forced herself to look the mother in the eye.

'Are you Miss Lime?' she said. Leonora nodded.

'We heard all about you from Helen. She idolised you,

worshipped the ground you stood on.' Mrs Daw looked her up and down, as if evaluating her worth. Like cattle in the market.

'I'm so very sorry, Mrs Daw. Helen was an excellent worker, someone who–'

'Shut up. Don't you dare sing my daughter's praises to me. You're not fit to utter her name!' She stepped forward and slapped Leonora on the cheek. Then she shrank into herself and her husband led her tiny form to a bench a few yards away.

Leonora held her hand up to her flaming flesh and looked around her to see if anyone had noticed. She approached the couple and Mrs Daw looked up. Her face was wet.

'Oh, it was great to start with and I won't deny her wages came in useful. Then she tried to tell me something was wrong and I didn't listen! She said she didn't want to go to the hospital any more but you kept sending her back. I didn't like you. I was jealous. What mother wouldn't be, the way she kept going on about you, Miss Lime this, Miss Lime that, but I overcame my feelings? I said, "Come on, you don't want to let Miss Lime down." Why can't I take back those words? I want to snatch them out of the air and swallow them.

'Then one night she didn't come home. I was sick with worry, wasn't I?' She looked at Mr Daw for corroboration. 'Then we got a letter saying she had been transferred to another hospital far away and wouldn't see us for a few months. If only we'd known! You should have told us. You can't keep things like that from us!'

Leonora closed her eyes momentarily. To know she had been held in such esteem by Helen was news to her. It brought a lump to her throat. This woman was right.

'I'm sorry,' she said. 'I'm truly and deeply sorry.'

In her pocket as she walked away she felt her application form to stand for election to the Works Council. She took it out, glanced at what she'd written so far and then dropped the form down the drain.

Two days later, Leonora bought a copy of *The Birmingham*

Daily Post. She had been on tenterhooks at the thought of being named in the press report on Helen's death. She flicked though the pages and at the bottom of page seven she read:

BIRMINGHAM INQUESTS

SAD CASE OF POISONING

An inquest was held today at Victoria Courts by Mr Percy Bradford, City Coroner, upon the body of Miss Helen Daw (18), a machine operator, who was in temporary residence at Mannerley Nursing Home in Herefordshire. The young woman had recently given birth to a baby, father unknown. Her parents believed she was working away from home. On Monday evening she reported a stomach ache which she had self-medicated before going to lie on her bed. On going into the girl's room the following morning the nurse found Miss Daw unconscious. There was a bottle of liniment and a spoon on the bed table. Miss Daw was taken to the General Hospital where she died shortly after admission. A post-mortem examination showed traces of a toxic substance identical in nature to liniment. A verdict of "Accidental Death By Poisoning" was recorded. Miss Daw's baby will be put up for adoption.

Leonora's heart thundered. Thank God! So it wasn't suicide, after all, but a dreadful accident. She took a moment of comfort from thinking Helen had accidentally mixed up the bottles. But the fact remained the same. She was responsible for the predicament that had led to her death. She lay her head down on the table and closed her eyes.

'Mary! Where's all your hair gone?'

'Did you bring us back a present?'

'Give me a piggy back, Daniel!

'No, me first!'

Jessie watched the twins' delight at the return of their brother and sister. Mrs Morris clutched her hand to her chest, utterly overcome. Jessie slipped out to make a cup of tea for the home-comers. Let them have their celebration first – she would take her turn later.

She heard neighbours knock at the door and come in offering congratulations. She put biscuits on a plate. They tasted like sawdust these days but with the sugar shortages that was the best they could get. It sounded like a joyful riot was going on in the next room.

Jessie glanced up to see Mary standing in the doorway. She looked terrible, almost emaciated, her shining eyes huge in their sockets.

'Come here,' Jessie said. Silently, the girl went into her arms and they embraced for what felt like minutes. Mary's shoulder blades jutted out through her dress. She was all skin and bone. Mrs Morris would enjoy feeding her up.

'I can't believe I did it. I brought him home, Jessie.'

Jessie swallowed down the pain in her throat so she could speak. 'I know, you clever, dear girl. Look what your love did. Your love made things right.' Perhaps, Jessie thought, she should follow Mary's example. She knew she had to make her own plans. She couldn't stay here forever. There simply wasn't room in the house and she would feel like an intruder.

'Thank you for everything you did. Coming here and looking after Ma. You've been such a good friend, Jessie.'

Mary failed her medical at the Works. 'The doc says my stomach's still too weak to operate the cutting machine.' Two weeks later Eliza Barratt sent a letter from the Cadbury directors; they wanted to offer her and Daniel jobs tending the allotments at the Works. 'She's as good as gold that woman. She's always looked out for me!'

'I'm delighted, Jessie,' Mary said. 'I want to be outdoors all the time.' She was dressed in overalls with a scarf tied around her head.

Jessie broke the news about Helen Daw to Mary and showed her the newspaper report on the inquest.

'My God, I never expected that. I told Miss Lime she was too bloody young to do the volunteering!'

'I know,' Jessie said quietly. 'I remember and so does Miss Lime. She's eaten up with guilt about the whole thing. She's not applying for a seat on the Works Council.'

'Blimey.'

'Yesterday I went up to her in the dining room and I swear she hadn't washed properly. She's stopped taking care of herself. I said to her, "Why don't you take some time off work?" and do you know what she said? "I'll wait until they sack me. It won't be long, I'm sure." She's convinced they'll be getting rid of her.'

Mary was thoughtful. 'This business over Helen and the baby is really bothering her. Did anyone ever find out who the father was?'

Jessie shook her head. 'There was plenty of speculation. Poor Sam Eastwood was mentioned. I know, that's ridiculous,' Jessie said, seeing Mary's expression.

'It must have been one of the men at the hospital. One of the soldiers. Or that doctor.'

'Not the doctor!'

'Why not? Whoever it was, someone took advantage of that girl. They ought to pay for it.'

A silence came between them, which Mary broke, saying: 'Look after Miss Lime. It isn't really her fault from what you've told me. Blame the bastard that did it to Helen. Go and see that doctor bloke. I bet he knows more than he's letting on.'

So Jessie went to Fircroft to investigate.

A fresh contingent of convalescents had come in and the nurses bustled around with barely any time to glance at Jessie. Callum, the soldier who was a long-term resident, called over to her.

'Hey, it's Jessie.' The nurse tried to guide him back to bed. 'Where's your little friend? Ain't seen her since July. Tell her I'm missing my treatments.'

The nurse had gone off and it was just the two of them.

'Tell me about this treatment,' she whispered. The nurse was on her way back.

'I can show you if you like. Come in the treatment room, we'll lock the door and me and you can have a happy ending.' He reached out and grabbed her arms in a vice like grip, pulling her onto his lap, and pressed himself into her.

Vomit rushed up from deep inside her stomach. She swallowed it down as she broke away and ran to Dr Russell-Morgan's office. The door was ajar. She knocked, and hearing no reply, slipped inside, shutting the door behind her.

She was shaking after her encounter. Anything to get away from that awful man and the understanding that was dawning on her.

She heard a man's voice outside. It was the male orderly. 'If you're looking for the doctor you're wasting your time. He hasn't been here for weeks. They called him back to London.' *Damn!*

Jessie sat down on the chair behind the doctor's desk, her legs still trembling with shock. All his belongings were piled in a small heap: the swimming trophy, a scarf, a small heap of books. She picked up one of them – it was on treatments for the effects of shell shock. She rifled through the jumble of papers in the drawers, not knowing what she was looking for. She steadied herself while her pulse slowed down, and her gaze landed on the picture of the two little girls, now on the floor resting against the wall. An outline of where it had been was visible on the wall. She saw a glass nub in the wall; she moved closer and felt its smooth rounded surface. She pressed her eye to it and it gave her a view of the whole of the room next door. A spyhole. Jessie saw the wash basin, the cabinet with instruments, an examination table, the armchair where Callum sat, Jessie imagined, for his special treatment with Helen while the doctor watched. It was insane. She could never prove it.

She heard a sound behind her. The orderly had come into the room.

'I'm not sure you should be in here,' he said, smiling at her and staring. His look was unpleasant and she felt the first prickles of anxiety.

'Yes, you're right,' she said, and made to walk past him.

He stepped sideways into her path, blocking her way. She tried to move around him; he blocked her again.

'What are you doing? I'm going to leave now.'

His smile dropped and she saw the look in his eyes; there was no emotion or feeling at all. They stood opposite each other; she knew she was trapped. He began to loom over her and she galvanised herself, trying to dart around him and into the corridor to safety. He grabbed her, bustled her into the treatment room and locked the door behind them. Her mouth went dry. She couldn't scream. As he fell on top of her, she blanked her mind, and had one single thought: *I don't even know your name.*

'I did the girl in this room and now I'm going to do you.'

His words, and their import, caused images to tumble through her mind. This monster had attacked Helen in this room. He poked his tongue out at her in contempt, his mouth stank, and Jessie shoved him under the chin as hard as she could. His mouth was a bloodied mess where his teeth had cut his tongue like her cutting machine. She broke free of him and ran to the door, unlocking it with trembling fingers. All eyes stared at her as she ran into the ward and collapsed on a bed. 'Help me, it was him.'

'So it was nothing to do with the doctor in the end?'

'No, I don't think so. I hope that monster gets put in prison for a long time. I hope they do to him what he did to Helen.'

Mary nodded. She understood.

Helen's baby couldn't stay at the nursing home indefinitely so she was put in the Works' day nursery and in the evenings Evelyn Jackson took her home. The girls had gone mad, fussing over baby Helena, going to visit her at lunchtime. Evelyn showed Jessie the outfit she had knitted. 'Have you seen her, Jessie? She's just like her mother!'

Mr and Mrs Daws didn't want the child. With Helen's wage gone and another mouth to feed – it wouldn't have been possible for them. Jessie, of all people, understood what it was like to be short of money. She didn't judge them.

On the day of the adoption panel Jessie went over to the nursery to say a final goodbye. Jessie approached the crib and peered inside. The baby was thriving, now seven months old, just like a little doll. She had been swaddled in a knitted blanket and her mouth worked as though seeking milk. Her face contorted momentarily, as though in pain, then she smiled and went back to sleep.

'I knitted her a hat.' Jessie made a show of rummaging in her bag to find it, while she blinked back tears. 'Can I put it on her?'

The nursemaid nodded. 'I'll leave you to it.'

Now she was alone in the room with Helen's baby. Her sadness for Helen and the waste of a good life full of potential was underlined by hope for this child.

She was part of the future generation. Helena would grow up in peacetime and hopefully never experience a war on such a terrible scale as this. Jessie lifted the baby up and held her to her breast. Helena was so slight. Later today she would be going to a loving couple without children of their own.

The baby stirred and moved its head towards Jessie; she felt a powerful surge of love. 'Oh Helena,' she sighed, 'I wish I'd looked after your mother better. She was so young and innocent. How were we so blind that none of us could see what had gone on?' She kissed her forehead and inhaled the baby smell. Proud of herself for not weeping, she placed Helena back in her crib gently.

'Bye bye, my darling, be happy. If I could I'd adopt you myself. There's a lovely couple who are going to have you and they love you so much already and will love you even more once they get to know you. You'll make their family so complete. You'll grow up in a nice house and they'll give you so much love.'

Her voice fractured and she gulped in air, willing herself to carry on. 'Oh yes, Helena, they will care for you and love you so much.' She stroked the baby's cheek for the last time.

A couple came into the room, and Jessie looked at them.

The woman spoke to Jessie, 'Are you on the adoption panel?' She was anxious looking but with a cheerful face. 'Oh, I hope it goes in our favour. I know I'm speaking out of turn. I always do that when I'm nervous.'

'Fanny,' her husband said with a rebuke in his voice. 'Don't be trying to influence the decision makers. What will be will be.' He folded his arms.

'I'm sorry,' the woman said to Jessie. 'It's just that I want her so much. We can give her a lovely home and I can't bear to think about what would happen if we were turned down. What would happen to her? I mean, we've got a lovely home and her room is all nice and ready–'

'Fanny!'

'I know I'm rambling, it's just we've been on tenterhooks knowing the panel makes their decision today. Will you have decided by today?'

She thinks I'm on the panel! Jessie thought. This woman really wants Helena. She sat with them while the panel met. An hour later the news came through. They had been successful. Jessie hugged the woman. 'I'm so pleased for you.'

Jessie went down the corridor to see Helena off, with her new parents. She was all dressed up in woollens and there was a case at her side. She lay chuckling in a blue pram while the crèche nurse blew bubbles on her hand.

'Isn't that pram a beauty? It was donated by one of the trustees of the adoption panel,' the nurse said.

Jessie said, 'You'll be travelling in style, little one.'

This evening, Jessie reminded herself, she had to complete the forms to do her nurses' training at the Queen Elizabeth. She had decided.

CHAPTER 23

Leonora passed through the weeks in a daze. At work she heard whispers behind her back: Is she all right? I think she's gone doolally. Jessie had approached her, rambling about the man who had been responsible for Helen's pregnancy. It made no difference. Helen was still dead. That fact would never change.

Then one Monday in April she hadn't been able to face going in to work. By lunchtime Eliza Barratt was knocking on her door. Leonora opened it, still wearing her dressing gown and her hair loose around her back.

'May I come in, Leonora?' She carried with her a bunch of daffodils, a packet of biscuits and a card from the girls. Without asking, Eliza took the items through to the kitchen and, after a few minutes, came into the room with the flowers in a jug.

'Beautiful, aren't they? Freshly picked from my garden this morning,' she said cheerfully. 'Would you like me to bring some food in? Your cupboard is bare.'

Leonora shook her head. She was drowning under a tremendous wave of tiredness. Her head was foggy and she would quite happily have crawled back to bed if only sleep would come.

'Leonora, I shan't pussyfoot around. Simply to say all the girls are worried about you. They're coming to me in droves, asking if you're all right and if you're going to stand for the

Works Council. I had to tell them you missed the deadline for applying.'

'Is that all?' she said wearily. 'Perhaps you wanted a look at the scene of all the drama so you can broadcast it to all the others?'

'I beg your pardon?'

'There it is. That couch you're sitting on is where the girl gave birth.'

Eliza stood up instinctively, as though the couch were electrified. She quickly recovered her composure and said, 'If this is about the Helen Daw situation, believe me, we all feel responsible in some way. It was months ago, however, and you can't keep blaming yourself. Everyone knows you had nothing to do with her death.'

'Not until the coroner said so! They made me stand there and answer all those questions!'

'Now come on and get a grip of yourself.'

'It was a punishment, from God. I can see that now.'

'What is? You're not making the slightest bit of sense!'

Leonora hugged herself as she spoke softly, almost to herself. 'You see, the week before the baby came I'd gone into Underwood's again and bought three yards of green holland.'

'And?'

'Don't you see? It was to make a forewoman's blouse. I'd waited and waited for you, or one of the directors to tell me I'd definitely got the job, but nothing. I'd waited weeks, months, kept hanging on your promises! I gave the best I could, trying to show you all what I was made of, that I was worthy. I waited for someone – anyone – to notice and say, "Well done, good and faithful servant." But I was impatient and the good Lord saw fit to punish me for my presumption.'

She waved her finger as though admonishing herself.

'Oh Leonora.' Eliza Barratt came to sit next to her. 'You've got your promotion. You're going to be made forewoman. That's what I came to tell you. We need you, Leonora. The war's not over yet but we need to start planning for when it does end.'

Leonora spoke to herself. 'She came and lay down on that couch, in agony. I used all the towels I had to put underneath her and by the time the baby came out I had nothing left but the green material I'd bought, so I wrapped the baby up in that.'

By the time Leonora returned to work fit and well, with a tonic prescribed by the Works' doctor it had become clear that many of the Bournville women would have to lose their jobs.

The directors had surveyed the serving men, asking them what their intentions were when the war ended. Ninety-five per cent of them intended to come back to Cadbury and they wanted their old jobs.

Leonora explained these facts to an impromptu meeting of girls at the local tea room, a gathering to discuss the demobilisation problem.

'Well, it ain't fair,' said a blonde woman Leonora knew only by sight from the Print Room. 'We've got three married women in our section and they all stand to lose their jobs to make way for the men.'

'But if their husbands are coming back here, that's only fair.'

'Not in all cases though,' Ruth said. 'What about Jessie Paignton? She's on her own now, so shouldn't she get to keep her job?'

'Yeah, no-one works harder than Jessie,' Evelyn said loyally.

'It's all right,' Jessie said. 'I'm going for nurses' training. What about you, Mary, though? You can't stay on the allotments forever.'

Ruth said, 'Mary would've been okay if she hadn't gone flitting off to France.'

'Don't you dare,' Jessie spoke for the second time. 'Mary was there saving lives, isn't that right? It was just as important, more important, than the nursing and other things we've been doing.'

Mary was silent; she kept her head low and appeared to be gathering her thoughts. 'I saw things out there that no-one should ever have seen. Sometimes I wish I could just scrub it clean from my mind.'

She looked up and around the room at every one of them. Leonora felt the hush descend on the cafe. 'Those men. Our men.' Mary faltered. 'You don't have the imagination to see what I've seen. Those precious scarves you knitted – saturated with blood. Those socks you knitted with such love to go on the feet of a man who stood in a muddy trench for days on end, so that by the time you had to cut them off his dead body they were baked on solid.'

Someone inhaled sharply. Leonora put a hand on Mary's arm.

'I'm sorry,' Mary cried. 'I don't know why I said all that. It's this bloody war. Is there anyone who it hasn't turned into a selfish bugger?'

Evelyn said, 'To get back to the point, one of us should blooming well go in and see the Cadburys about getting our work recognised, so all our jobs will be safe.'

'What do you think, Miss Lime, do you reckon it'll become illegal to sack us?'

'If the vote for women does come, and with it subsequent legislation,' Leonora spoke, with her back rigid against the chair, 'I'm afraid it will be too late to help you.'

'Notice she doesn't say help *us*,' the blonde-haired woman said. 'She'll be all right. She's been sucking up to the bosses for years.'

'I shall go in tomorrow and appeal to Miss Dorothy Cadbury personally; she is the only woman on the board and she will be sympathetic to our cause. I'm sure once I've explained the situation to them, they will be understand that jobs will need to be found. When everything's back to normal and we're making chocolate again. Of course we must understand it's a difficult time for the firm.'

'I hope you're right. I don't know what I'm going to do if I get the sack.'

'There's going to be trouble from all quarters, you mark my words, the men will take to the streets if they don't get their jobs back, not after giving four years of service–'

'Not all. Some only joined up when they had no choice.'

'All right,' the woman replied irritably, 'but you take my point. They're going to come demanding their jobs back.'

'Why should we just move aside? What about our contribution to the war effort? We've worked our guts out in the factory in the daytime and then in our breaks we've been doing volunteer work all over the place. Betty, you raised twenty pounds, didn't you, with those concerts of yours? Did you keep any of it yourself? Of course not. You gave it to help the poor men and their families, didn't you?'

'But,' Jessie interrupted, 'it wasn't just about the hours we put in or the money we raised. I don't know about you but I found friendship.'

Murmurs of agreement went around the room. Leonora saw Mary smiling at Jessie.

'Let's face it – if you're married, what kind of life is it?' Evelyn said. 'One day you're working with all your mates, the next you're at home and keeping busy cleaning the house all day long.'

Leonora drew the meeting to a close. 'As I've said, I'll have a word with the directors and do my very best, ladies.'

Miss Lime came out of the meeting, a shocked expression on her face.

'What is it? Can I help?' Jessie said, rushing towards her. She looked unsteady on her feet. 'Let me help you into a chair.' A group of women waiting for news crowded round, so Jessie was forced to say, 'Give her some air for heaven's sake!'

Miss Lime's face was deathly white but for two pink spots in the centre of her cheeks. She looked up at Jessie and clutched her hand in a firm grip.

'I'm sorry, I can't believe it,' she said softly. 'They're sacking you. Three quarters of the war women have to go. All the married women – whatever their circumstances – and many of the temporary single girls. Jessie, I'm sorry, they're not keeping you on.' She sat up straighter in her chair. 'Oh, I fought for you, Jessie. I fought for all of you all right and nearly talked myself out of my own job.'

'Does she want a medal?' one of the print women said. 'Her job's safe and never mind the rest of us.'

'Shut up!' Jessie said. 'Be quiet.'

'I'm going in there myself,' the woman said. 'I'll tell them Cadburys what I think of their stinking agreement.'

Miss Lime stood up. 'You will not! You will write down your concerns and you will take them through the proper channels. Through the Works Council.'

'All right, but I want it on record that we think this whole lousy situation stinks. After everything we've done for them. We've put in the hours, done overtime, changed jobs, supported our men fighting.'

Miss Lime said, 'We did it because it was the right thing to do. Do you wish you'd never done any of it? Do you wish you'd turned your back on the firm when it needed help? On our men that needed help? On our country that needed help? Do you wish you hadn't sacrificed your own need in the service of others?' She looked round at them all. 'If so, then you don't belong in the factory anyway.'

Jessie clapped softly; others joined in and soon there was applause for her speech.

The news that she was losing her job had forced the decision for Jessie, but she felt sorry for the others. Going back to their married lives as they were before the war and yet not. The war had changed and scarred them all.

She went to find Miss Lime later to thank her for her support. She found the woman sitting in the old Comforts room with tears quietly rolling down her face and onto the collar of her green blouse.

Jessie tried to hug her but her body would not yield, so she let go awkwardly.

'I have failed,' she said. 'I've failed you all. Believe me, I tried. You do believe I tried my best, don't you?'

'It doesn't matter,' Jessie said. 'To the other women, yes, but not to me. I wasn't going to stay on anyway.'

'You're just saying that. Credit me with more intelligence than that.' After a pause, Miss Lime said, 'They've offered me a seat on their new committee to oversee the transition of the women out of the workforce and the men back in.'

'I hope you said yes.'

'No, I told them no.'

'You must accept! Go and tell them you've changed your mind. Just think what you can contribute. Please go and fight for those women. So you lost the battle with me, but think of the others.'

Jessie saw Miss Lime considering her words. 'Go on,' she urged.

Miss Lime stood up. Jessie took out a handkerchief and wiped the woman's cheeks. She did it tenderly, like she would a child.

'Thank you, Jessie.'

Jessie went to the gathering of women out on the terrace of the dining room. They were clearly disappointed when Jessie came instead of Miss Lime. She told them the news from the meeting.

'I knew she wouldn't have the guts to face us.'

Jessie said, 'It's as much a slap in the face for her, remember.'

'How do you work that one out?'

'She helped to get you here and now, when she's doing her best, you're turning your back on her.'

'You bloody hypocrite. Worming your way in so you don't get the sack. You're even beginning to sound like her. She's pulling your strings like a bloody puppet.' The others laughed bitterly.

'You're wrong,' she said, walking off.

The committee was set up to oversee the demobilisation and to integrate the men back into the workplace. Miss Lime was at the very heart of it and she had fought for the women, securing a small victory by ensuring the redundancies were staggered and a small allowance was given to the war widows.

Jessie's last week came round quickly. She had successfully applied for a place to study nursing. She showed the letter to Miss Lime.

'It says my experience district nursing tipped the balance in my favour.'

'Good girl, Jessie. You will be a very good nurse.'

'How are you getting on? Has all the tension died down?'

'It's rather hard being stuck in the middle of it all between the workers and directors. Still, that's my cross to bear.'

'You don't have to put up a front with me, Miss Lime. I'll be leaving tomorrow.'

Miss Lime stared hard at her and said, 'I shall miss you a great deal, Jessie Paignton. When you first arrived I admit I felt threatened and I apologise if my manner was a little–'

'Hostile?' Jessie said, smiling.

'I wasn't going to go that far, but yes, let's not sugar-coat it. You see, you represented a threat. To have a married woman under my command was disconcerting. I revelled in my single status and every time a woman looked like matching me, I cheered if she announced her engagement. One less competitor! Of course this must never go any further.'

'It won't. One thing though, there are loads of widows of men who worked here. It doesn't have to mean the end for the Comforts programme. The need will be greater than ever.'

Miss Lime's eyes sparkled. 'Yes, a new programme. What a good idea, Jessie. I'll call a meeting this lunchtime. No, wait, better do it tomorrow. I'll see if one of the girls can get a poster done. We can do knitting and fund-raising for a children's Christmas party.'

Jessie watched her: she gets her energy from situations like this. Give her a problem and she relished it; solve the problem and she didn't know what to do. As long as Miss Lime had a good cause in her life she would be fine.

Jessie walked away from the Works. She had decided. She would be fine too.

On the day she moved into her nurses quarters Mary helped her with her things.

'What's in this bag, Jessie?'

'Oh, that. It's some books I meant to put in the Comforts room. Could you take them in for me? Miss Lime can sell them for the Widows' fund.'

Mary peered inside the bag and took out the pile. Jessie was excited about her training course. With a testimonial from Dr Russell-Morgan and Miss Lime she had secured the place. With a pang she thought of Bill and wondered how he was getting on and whether he'd moved to Wolverhampton.

'Oh,' Mary said, 'this one's no good. It's got pages missing. Who's Jessie Fairfax?'

'Let me see,' Jessie said. She took the blue book from Mary and turned it over. It was her Cadbury Bible. The last time she had seen this was when she picked up the two halves of it and put them in the grate for burning. Bill had tried to repair it. She pictured him stitching the two halves back together with his upholsterer's needle. The cover was in perfect condition; he had used a soft blue leather. Just visible on the inside cover was her maiden name, Fairfax. He'd been unable to do anything with the torn pages but there was a note in the middle. She opened it up and read the two words. *I'm sorry.*

She stared at Mary. 'Bill.' It was all she could say.

Mary intuited her feelings. 'Go and see him. Do it now, Jessie. He loves you and you love him. It's as clear as daylight.'

'He's at work now. How do I get to Small Heath? What bus do I catch?'

Mary laughed. 'Come on, Jessie. If I can get to France to bring Daniel back, I'm sure you can get to Small Heath.'

Realising this was her final chance, and she could be too late, she began to run. She would do it for love.

CHAPTER 24

21 MAY 1919

Jessie had secured the day off from her nurse's training at the Queen Elizabeth Hospital to attend the royal visit to Bournville. In her pocket was the embossed invitation from Miss Lime.

She had arrived early at the Girls' recreation ground. This afternoon the area would be heaving with crowds of Bournville girls in readiness to welcome the king and queen. For now, though, she enjoyed its tranquil calm and the stillness of the lily pond. The flowers had been restored to the beds – yet one more sign that order was returning.

Miss Lime and the girls had organised and planted a tree as a memorial for Helen, and the dead girl had also received a Mention for Services to Nursing for her volunteer work. The tree had grown steadily over the months since the war had ended. Jessie often visited it, where she found peace and reflection; a calm and soothing contrast to her busy hospital days.

Inside the Works the girls in Q block swarmed around the trolley when it was brought in from the design department. Leonora caught the wave of excitement and, for once, stood back to let the girls go first although she was eager to see the boxes herself.

Then one of them said, 'Let Miss Lime have a look,' and the crowd of girls parted respectfully for their forewoman.

The king's box was already completed. Rectangular-shaped and covered with stone coloured silk, it featured two gold clasps with the initials G and R inlaid in each one. The box had been filled with four trays of the finest handmade chocolates and then tied up in a sumptuous chocolate brown bow.

There was just Queen Mary's souvenir box to finish off. Leonora stepped forward to check the components: the box, the lid, two trays of chocolates, a doily, a pair of silver tongs, the hand-written card and a length of ribbon in vivid heliotrope. She picked up the round box lid and examined it carefully – the silver brocade top was centred perfectly on the sliver-clothed flange.

'Good.'

'Why has it got MR on it?' one of the new juniors asked, standing on tiptoe to look over Leonora's shoulder at the monogrammed initials on the lid. 'The queen's not a mister!'

Evelyn answered, 'It stands for Mary Regina, you idiot.'

Leonora put the silk-lined trays of fancy chocolates in individual silver cups into the box. She picked a cup out and said, 'Look at these bands – miniature Bournville scenes.'

Leonora cleared the lump in her throat and read the message on the card out loud. *To her most gracious Majesty the Queen, with the best wishes and loving affection of the women and girls at Bournville.*

The girls cheered.

She went to put the lid on and hesitated. 'Here, you do it,' she said to young Lizzie. The girl looked at her hands, turning them over to make sure they were clean. 'Go on,' she said. The lid fitted perfectly.

'Are you up to doing the bow as well?' The girl looked at the ribbon and shook her head.

'Can I do the bow?' her friend said. 'I've been practising in my arts and craft classes.'

Leonora nodded. She watched the girl thread the wide ribbon underneath the box just slightly off centre so that the

MR monogram was visible. The girl deftly looped the ribbon, her lips pursed in concentration, and then it slipped off.

Leonora sensed the other girls turn their heads to look at her. Her own heart beat fast and she pressed her lips together and kept her arms at her side, in the effort not to interfere. She had to let the girls learn. She looked back to see Lizzie's friend give a smile of satisfaction at the perfect double bow she had achieved.

'Excellent. Good work and well done to everyone.'

They put the king's and queen's boxes with the others on the trolley: one for the princess, and souvenir boxes for all the members of the royal suite including the Lord Mayor and Lady Mayoress.

Leonora went outside, stood at the top of the wooden steps and looked down onto the men's recreation ground and across Bournville Lane. The entrance to the village was marked with white pylons covered with blue and green chevron silks. Modest, but effective. The majesties had asked to see Bournville in its normal state. This is how they'll find us, she thought, rushing back to the girls waiting in Q block.

The crowds had assembled already on the girls' grounds. Hundreds of girls in white uniforms formed the front rows and, at the back, older women in coats and hats, including those who'd once been employed at the Works. All had pennants that they waved wildly.

Jessie turned to Bill when she saw the sight. 'I'd better stand with the girls. I'll see you later.' He nodded and gave her a squeeze around her shoulders.

'You go and enjoy being part of it again, my love. I'll be here when you get back.'

And that, she thought, is the great joy of my life. In the crowds she spotted Rose Entwistle. Widowed Rose, her children now six and eight, having to make the best of it like so many married and engaged women who'd lost their men. Jessie remembered their encounter in the store room. She lifted her hand to wave but Rose had not seen her.

The stretching movement must have stirred the baby, because she felt a lurch inside her stomach and then a definite kick. She smiled down at her stomach and said, 'Hello Buster.'

'Jessie! Look, it's Jessie!' There was a cry behind her and she turned to see Mary with a gentleman on her arm.

'You came as well.' Mary said. 'Come on, we can all walk together.'

The man stood still, with a wry expression on his face. Jessie looked equally quizzically at Mary.

'Oh,' Mary said. 'This is Richard Ockwell. Sorry I forgot to introduce you. Jessie, meet Richard, he's my, well, he's my sort-of fiancé. How do you like that? You've got to feel sorry for the guy, marrying a nuisance like me. We're moving to London.' She whispered to Jessie. 'I've no idea if it'll work. We've got such different temperaments. He's opening a new school, doing music therapy for the ex-servicemen and he wants me to help him run it, and I can sing in my spare time. Daniel's coming with us.'

'That's wonderful, Mary. How's your mother?'

'She's fine. Says she misses you though. I'll send money home for her and the twins when I've gone.'

She glanced down at Jessie's blossoming stomach. 'You're not?'

Jessie nodded. Mary squealed and squeezed her hand tightly. 'You made the right choice going back with Bill. I knew it would work out.'

She had a good feeling about this pregnancy. 'After the baby's born, I'm going to finish my nurses training.'

'You're not staying home to be a good little housewife? You're a trail-blazer for married women, Mrs P. '

'You know something?' Jessie said. 'I like working. I liked it here. It was a rotten job in many ways but the fun we had–'

'Remember when Miss Lime burned the sausages and let off the fireworks?'

'She got her promotion in the end though. Forewoman and a place on the Works Council,' Jessie said.

'We did a lot, didn't we?'

'All those greetings cards we wrote.'

'You wrote!'

'All those socks and vests.'

'Don't forget your hospital work,' Mary said.

'Nor yours.'

They fell silent for a moment, each lost in thought. Jessie felt a clutch of the heart every time she remembered Thomas Walker. She would put him in a box and seal it the way his injured body had been put in a coffin and buried in France along with all the other men.

Then her thoughts turned to Helen. Jessie wondered how the baby was. Helena would be be almost two by now. She'd tried to keep in touch with her new parents but her last few letters had gone unanswered.

Leonora led the group of girls and inspected their overalls and fingernails while they waited at the lodge for their turn to go out. Everything spotless. She brushed down the sleeves of her own green blouse, fresh on that morning.

She had a number of new girls under her wing. Good girls, most of them, but not much gumption about them. Not like Mary Morris, who at least had had a bit of sparkle about her. It was a pity they'd had to let the girl go from the Works.

'Come on girls. Don't droop like lilies in a vase. Stand up straight!' She smiled nevertheless. With a final check of her cuffs, she said, 'Are you ready, girls?' She stepped out into glorious sunshine, glad that just this once the weather was on her side.

Today she was going to enjoy the king and queen's visit. Afterwards, when the day was over, and the decorations and flower baskets were taken down from lampposts, and the dais dismantled and put away for another occasion, she knew there was still work to be done within these walls of living stone. She had a list of recommendations to take to the next Works Council meeting. At the top of the list was a proposal to formally recognise the women's contribution to the war effort.

The women had been asked to stand aside and make way for the returning men and they had done so without much protest. They'd had no choice. But the door would not, *could not*, be slammed fully shut again, Leonora resolved. She would see that it was wedged open permanently.

Eventually the world would catch up and women would have a say in how the country was run.

Her thoughts turned to Herr Otto of Germany and all the other city garden delegates she had met that day. She wondered what they were doing right at this moment. Repairing and rebuilding the same dreams, she hoped.

Through the speaker she heard George Cadbury's voice loud and clear. 'I hope that one day countries will emulate each other in acts of peace and not in devising the most efficient manner in which to kill each other. From now on we must meet to discuss how we can best save life.'

The girls surged behind her and the applause that broke out almost split her ears. The king stepped onto the dais to begin his speech and when it was over, Leonora moved among the crowd, her sisters and brothers, in a sea of smiling faces.

There was work to be done, but they would do it together.

ACKNOWLEDGEMENTS

My heartfelt thanks to the archivists, researchers and information managers who made their collections available to me: Sarah Foden and Jackie Jones at the Bournville Archives, Mondelez International; Jenny Childs and Martin Killeen from the Cadbury Research Library; Nicola Gauld of Voices of War and Peace First World War Engagement Centre; Sian Roberts of Library of Birmingham Collections; Colin Pitt; Bob Booth and The Bournville Society.

All errors remain my own responsibility.

I'm grateful to the people I've had the pleasure of meeting on the speaking circuit, and who have shared their Cadbury stories with me.

Thanks also to Jim Whiskens for the impromptu tour of the 'other' Fircroft, and Andy Vail, whose knowledge of non-conformist church history is second to none.

I am indebted once again to the property stewards of Acocks Green Methodist Church for allowing me the use of The Guild Room to write in peace and quiet. Thanks also to Michael Albutt, Bob Moseley and Enid Smitten, who furnished me with Cadbury-related books, articles and stories.

My writing chums, Kathleen Dixon Donnelly and Robert Ronsson, are unfailingly supportive, as are my Room 204 writing colleagues. Thanks, guys. Thanks also to David Viner, formerly of Solihull Libraries, whose help with my previous book led to many interesting speaking opportunities.

Thank you to Jonathan Davidson, Sara Beadle, Joanne

Penn and Abigail Campbell for the mentoring, support and opportunities provided through Writing West Midlands. I'm also grateful for support from the Birmingham Literature Festival and West Midlands Readers Network. Thanks also to Bella Hamblin for the audio recording.

Enormous thanks to Stuart Bache for a beautiful cover design and to Caroline Smailes of Bubblecow, whose editing was incisive, instructive and always encouraging.

Finally, thanks and best love to Peter, and our girls, Anna and Stella. I couldn't do any of this without you – nor would I want to.

SUGGESTED READING

Useful background material for *Comforts for the Troops*.

BOOKS

Birmingham: Remembering 1914-18, Sian Roberts

A Bournville Assortment, Margaret A. Broomfield

Bournville Through Time, The Bournville Society

Bournville Works and the War: A record of the form and workers' activities, 1914-1919, Cadbury Brothers Ltd.

Cadbury's Angels, Memories of working with George Cadbury from Bridge Street to Bournville, Iris Carrington

My Small Share: A Quaker Diary from WWI, Ernest W Pettifer

Not So Quiet: A novel by Helen Zenna Smith, Helen Zenna Smith

The Firm of Cadbury: 1831-1931, Iolo A. Williams

ARCHIVES and RESOURCES

Bournville Archives, Mondelez International

Cadbury Research Library, University of Birmingham

The Library, Woodbrooke Quaker Study Centre

First World War Engagement Centre, 'Voices of War and Peace: The Great War and its Legacy,' Library of Birmingham

ABOUT THE AUTHOR

Fiona Joseph was born in Birmingham, UK, and has lived most of her life in the city.

She is an author of fiction and non-fiction. Her best-known book is a biography of Beatrice Cadbury. *BEATRICE The Cadbury Heiress Who Gave Away Her Fortune* was long-listed in the 2012 International Rubery Book Award. Her short stories have appeared in many anthologies, including *The Sea in Birmingham: 30 Years of the Tindal Street Fiction Group.*

During her postgraduate diploma in Writing at Birmingham City University, she won the National Academy of Writing 'Prize for Fiction'. Her ELT graded reader *Oscar's Journey* was a Finalist in the 2014 Language Learner Literature Award.

Fiona is a member of the Alliance of Independent Authors (ALLi), the Society of Authors and an associate member of Tindal Street Fiction Group.

She enjoys speaking at clubs and societies, literary festivals, and in libraries.

Contact Fiona by email: fiona@fionajoseph.com or through her website: fionajoseph.com